GETTING I

Gary Wilson's *Getting Right* got right to me. It's smart and funny but, more than anything, it's achingly honest about family – the hurts that persist no matter how many apologies or how much forgiveness, the unreliability of shared memories, and the constancy of love, imperfect and annoying as it may be. This is a beautiful read.

Achy Obejas, author of the novel *Ruins* and editor of Immigrant Voices. Winner of the Lambda Literary Award for Lesbian Fiction

Aptly titled, Gary D. Wilson's compelling novel *Getting Right* indeed gets it right through a colorful, conversational narrative about the lives and deaths of a man's all-too-human brother and sister. Like a conversation with a good friend over a beer, the book is full of stories both comic and sad. This is an honest, memorable work about family and its demands, honorably told, a book full of grace, grit, and gentle humor.

Anthony V. (Tony) Ardizzone, author most recently of *The Whale Chaser*. Recipient of two National Endowment for the Arts Fellowship Awards, the Flannery O'Connor Award for Short Fiction, and the Pushcart Prize

Gary Wilson has written here a poignant tale of imperfection and frailty and the bloody root of living mortality: the madness of family and illness and regret and the muddle of life claiming victory, even over implacable death. His story traces the profound force of individual origin, how the conditions from which we hail transcend time and memory and linger beyond their own limits within us, authoring fate, making a mess of well-laid lives, and proving the willful a feckless lot. For all the morbidity usually bound up with such themes, Wilson tells his story from a deep reserve of caustic humor and endows this narrative with an insight that cuts to the quick. It is a deeply personal tale of the price of survival that manages to get at something relevant to the mad ways of humanity and being.

Bayo Ojikutu, author of *Free Burning* and *47th Street Black*. Winner of the Washington Prize for Fiction and the Great American Book Award

Here's a ticket to the end of life's guilt trips. Flying always back home to Kansas, burying first his hopeless brother and later his hyper-resentful sister, Gary Wilson's narrator whips up what seems a lifetime's worth of bad jokes, great stories, and mislaid joys – and in the eye of the storm somehow strikes a note of mordant gutsiness and clear-eyed love. A book about death that is rippling with vigor and comedy, *Getting Right* embraces all that is wrong with life in a bear hug that won't let go.

Benjamin Lytal, author of *A Map of Tulsa*

Getting Right

Getting Right

Gary D. Wilson

Winchester, UK
Washington, USA

First published by Roundfire Books, 2016
Roundfire Books is an imprint of John Hunt Publishing Ltd., Laurel House, Station Approach,
Alresford, Hants, SO24 9JH, UK
office1@jhpbooks.net
www.johnhuntpublishing.com
www.roundfire-books.com

For distributor details and how to order please visit the 'Ordering' section on our website.

Text copyright: Gary D. Wilson 2015

ISBN: 978 1 78535 189 1
Library of Congress Control Number: 2015943106

A CIP catalogue record for this book is available from the British Library.

Design: Stuart Davies

Printed in the USA by Edwards Brothers Malloy

We operate a distinctive and ethical publishing philosophy in all
areas of our business, from our global network of authors to
production and worldwide distribution.

For Modena and my brother, my sister, my mother and my father

Oh, how I hate my mind,
all those memories
that have invented their own memories.

from "Peaches or Plums"
Alan Michael Parker

Act One

Connie

To Begin

The hole in the crook of Connie's arm resembled a miniature red mouth going OOO! A Betty Boop mouth puckering for a kiss, a greedy little baby mouth sucking through a plastic tube injection after injection of clear liquids and antibiotics, none of which assuaged her real hunger as she asked everyone who entered her room when and what the next meal would be. Barring that, couldn't they at least bring her a snack?

The tube was, in medical terms, a line, specifically a peripherally inserted central catheter—a PICC Line, for short—that was put in under local anesthesia by a doctor who threaded it through the complex branching of deep arm and chest veins, via an x-ray monitor, like a spelunker in night-vision goggles exploring the darkly intricate path of a subterranean river system, until it entered finally the superior vena cava. There was little, if any, discomfort during the procedure, since veins, unlike arteries, have no nerve endings. Other than some itching around the tape holding the tube in place, she hardly seemed to notice it was there.

Nurses said the reason they had to install the line was because she kept blowing her IV. No matter what they did, they said her veins collapsed, making the drips ineffective, and she was so damned hard to stick in the first place. They just couldn't keep doing that—to her or themselves. They said the only way she could lose this line was if she deliberately pulled it out.

What they didn't say was that the line was ordered as soon as she came back from surgery, her lung still largely intact because removing it had proved to be impossible due to the cell type of the tumor and the extent of the disease in the lung cavity. Consequently, Plan B was initiated, for which a PICC Line is a standard interim measure, according to medical literature, ideal as it is "for multiple infusions or continuous infusions given in a hospital or at home with a portable pump." But it would stay in only until after she left the hospital and a Porta Cath was implanted under the skin just below her clavicle, with a short tube that went directly through the chest wall into the superior vena cava. A Porta Cath was clean and efficient, making therapy more convenient for caregivers and less immediately painful for her. And it could remain in place indefinitely, although, again, no one seemed willing or able to say how long that might be.

She phoned one night before she knew she was going to have surgery and said hi in her usual hangdog voice that always irritated me and for some reason that night irritated me even more, and I said hi, what was up and she said nothing much, how about with you guys, and so on — the usual litany we'd been going through every week or two since we'd given her the 800 number my wife and I had set up for our sons to call home on while they were at college. She rarely talked about anything beyond weather and her and Sammo's need for more money, which was where most of our conversations ended up, and I was dreading the inevitable she hated to bother us again, but. . .with her all the while resenting the fact that she was my sister and had gotten into such straits that she had to ask for money in the first place and was angry at me because of it, as though it were somehow my fault that she was having to call me — and not only that but was doing it for free on our 800 number to boot. Except that night she didn't ask. That night she said she was afraid she had some bad news, and I said what was that, and she said that a couple of days ago she'd gone in for a checkup and when her doctor had looked at her chest x-ray he'd found a shadowy area in her left lung. And I said shit I was sorry, and she said yeah, we both pretty well knew what it meant, didn't we? and I asked if her doctor had said anything else, and she told me he wanted to do this and that test and that maybe she'd have to have surgery, depending; and we started talking about might-bes and what-ifs and she stopped at one point and sighed and said with everything that'd happened in her life, she should just sit down and write a book about it because otherwise nobody would ever believe it. I asked why she didn't, and she said she'd sure like to but doubted now that she would get around to it, so she guessed that I was going to have to write it for her. I asked what she meant by that and she said what did it sound like, and I asked if she was serious and she said damn right she was, and I said I would think about it but she had to know that, if I did decide to do it, the story would have to be more than just a testimony to her suffering. After a long pause, she said with tears in her voice that, silly her, here she'd been thinking things were different between us, if I knew what she meant; but that was okay, it might even be better this way, knowing in the end how little I'd changed.

Who's Who

I sat on a metal folding chair beside her bed as she slept, benefit of a morphine drip, her most recent husband, Sammo, opposite me, hunched over the electronic solitaire game he'd been playing all morning. He'd rarely looked up and hadn't said a word about winning or losing or anything else, for that matter; but since he did the same thing when she was awake, I wasn't offended. She seemed to like him, and so far I had no reason not to. He was her rock, she said. Strong, steady, always there.

And just as silent, I thought, wondering what might be going through his mind other than autonomic responses to which virtual card he should play where. Was he worried about Connie? What was happening to her, them, what was going to happen? Or the weather or how soon he could have another smoke? Food, sex, sleep? Was he curious about the book I was reading in which a demented pseudo-doctor killed and picked clean the bones of innocent young women lured by the promise of work and excitement at Chicago's famed Columbian Exposition? Was he concerned about the effect of embedding reporters among U.S. troops in Iraq or irritated by the incessant blare of the game show—COME ON DOWN!—from the other TV in the room, the one Connie's roommate left on while she moaned and groaned in her sleep or talked in a too-loud voice on the phone, ignoring the fact that she had windows when no one else did and could see the vast flat roof beyond, the red brick walls—rain? sun? clouds? daylight? dark? Did he notice the new names and phone extension numbers nurses wrote every shift change on dry erase boards above the foot of each bed in handwriting that was sometimes perky and light, sometimes more minimalist, reminding me of the waitresses at a restaurant near Chicago my wife and I enjoyed going to who were trained to write their names upside down on a white paper table covering at the same time they said them—Hi, I'm Lisa/Lillie/Loren (with a looping L)— what would we like to drink?

Did he have any idea how I longed to be out of that room, to be away from them and back in Chicago with my wife, sitting in my own chair, sleeping in my own bed, living my own life? I had arrived at the hospital three days earlier, after Connie had called again to tell me she'd been scheduled for almost immediate surgery and asked if I would come. I said what about Sammo and she said he would be there, but she would feel better if I could come, too, and I said I didn't know, maybe, I might be able to for a couple of days, already dreading the reason for the trip, not to mention the seven-hundred-fifty-mile drive made necessary by the short notice. She told me not to be ridiculous, of course I was coming and I should plan to stay as long as she needed me.

A nurse named Kim, according to the board—extension 5765—tall and blonde and so lean as to be almost skinny came in to send another shot of something into the PICC Line, which woke Connie enough that she rolled her head in my direction, blinked and told me again how much I looked like our father. I was about to ask what that had to do with anything other than an apparent need that she and other people seemed to have for everybody to look like somebody else, even if in hardly

5

noticeable ways. And I would have gone on to say it was a concept born of a primal instinct we have to group with similar life forms that eventually manifested itself in our family as a way to legitimize offspring, to make certain that we all did, in fact, belong, because if enough people said I looked like Great Uncle Harold or my father, then I must for sure have been one of them. And for good measure I was also going to tell her how much she looked like our mother—the greying hair, the roundish face and baggy eyes—but had no chance to say any of that as she rolled her head away from me and toward Sammo and said, don't he? and Sammo, not missing a key punch said, what? and she said look like my dad, and Sammo, of course, didn't say anything because he'd never laid eyes on the man and never would.

Sammo looked nothing like his mother or his father, Sally and Jim, who came in and out, alternating their time between my sister's room and the waiting area down the hall near the central nurses' station. They had arrived originally right before Connie's surgery and stayed until she was given the all-clear from intensive care, then returned to visit once she'd been transferred back to a ward room. They were regular folks, plain folks, nothing fancy. They would come in and say hello and I would get up so Sally could sit down, Jim standing to one side and slightly behind her, hands stuck in his jeans pockets because he didn't know what else to do with them. A more corpulent American Gothic, minus the pitchfork. Sometimes Sammo would look up and maybe say something, sometimes not. If Connie was awake enough, she would make him put the game down and sit up so we could see his face and the lovely eyes she said she depended on. But even when you had full view of him—the thinning brown hair pulled back in a loose ponytail, the perpetual three-day beard, the slack jaw, the eyes my sister loved—you didn't find any Sally or Jim there. Sammo was just Sammo.

He worked in a steel mill, which you might also think odd, and rightly so. I never personally paired Kansas and steel mills, and I grew up there. Which is not to say he didn't work in one. If he said he did, he did, although I didn't ever understand the exact nature of what he did. I heard him say once it required heavy lifting, and it must have been dirty from the appearance of his clothes when he came home. As far as I know, he made good money for the location and type of work and seemed to be well thought of at the mill. But he had precious little to show for his labor, seeing as how the vast majority of his pay was taken for back child support from two earlier marriages.

Most of his kids were still in Texas, but one daughter, Janice, lived close enough that she saw her dad and Connie fairly often. She had grown quite attached to Connie, whom she called Mom when her real mother wasn't around, and she had decided that she wanted to be at the hospital the day of Connie's surgery, a desire that seemed a bit strange to me, but I said nothing, as I had learned to say nothing about a good many things. She was a nice enough kid, with a budding sardonic wit, wire-rimmed glasses, long brown hair and a body so lithe that when she crossed her legs, she could wrap her foot on around the back of the opposite calf, like a vine. So she wasn't difficult to be around. It was more that I didn't understand why she would want to be there that day. And Sammo? He was married to Connie. Me? We've been through that. Sally and Jim? To support Sammo, I suppose, and probably Connie, too. But Janice, who was so normal in every other way you wouldn't have been able to pick her out of a crowd, why was she so anxious to learn this fine art of waiting, a far more complex and subtle exercise than most people ever realize?

Killing Time, or Rules of Occupation

You would think that by the time we have to do it we would be better prepared than we are for serious waiting, since we practice for it from the beginning of our lives. We wait for food, the water in the tap to turn cold enough to drink, someone to take us off hold, someone to answer a question or a prayer. We wait for a word, an idea, a train/bus/plane. We wait for Godot, traffic to move, quitting time, spring. We wait in or on line, depending on where we're from. We can't wait to get to where we're going. We are wait-listed and if we're rich enough might have a man or woman in-waiting. We wait to hear a baby's first cry and sometimes a person's last gasp. But we rarely wait patiently, since the process is inextricably bound to a heightened awareness of time passing and our lives passing with it. Except for serious waiting, of course. Then time itself seems to wait, hands on clocks and watches freeze, the world shifts into slow motion and we take a momentary leave of our senses.

Early the morning of Connie's surgery, we stood at the entrance to the waiting room, books, bags, pillows and drinks in hand, like a band of nomads trying to decide where to set up camp. Two other groups had gotten there before us and settled in at opposite ends of the area, leaving free a small sofa and four chairs grouped around a coffee table in the center. It seemed a perfect location, since it allowed us to see not only what was going on in the room but also the double doors to the surgical suites, through which Dr. James J. Jameson III would eventually appear with news of Connie. The area was clean and close enough to the television that we could check out what was on without feeling obligated to watch anything. What hesitation we had about taking over the area was born purely of inertia—it was early and we had stopped our forward motion and needed a boot to get us going again, which soon appeared in the form of another family rounding the corner at the end of the hallway and heading in our direction. While there are other ways to ward off challenges to waiting room territory—you may scowl and frown at the interlopers; you may feign pain, confusion, fatigue, old age, injury, illness or even pregnancy—it is best in the end to avoid conflict altogether and move as quickly as possible, without making eye contact with the oncoming party, to the spot you have chosen and lay claim to it. Which we did.

It should be noted here that, as any veteran waiter knows, occupation of an area involves compliance with unspoken but generally accepted rules of conduct. These include, but are not necessarily limited to, the following:

—After you have inhabited a given territory, you should mark it as yours. Urine and/or fecal material are not acceptable for this purpose, except in the case of infants; books, jackets, sweaters, games and other spreadable, non-marking materials are. It is also up to you to maintain the territory by purging it regularly of used food and drink containers, as well as spent reading materials, such as daily newspapers. Cleanliness and order promote not only your happiness but also that of your neighbors.

—Under all circumstances, you should speak solely when spoken to—and to strangers no more than necessary to maintain good relations—preferably in a low, well-modulated voice. You should avoid profanity and other expressions that might discomfort those around you. You should smile when appropriate and laugh quietly, if at all. You should not argue.

—You should turn cell phones to vibrate and use them only when speaking about the current crisis. To call or receive a call from anyone else, you should remove yourself from the common area. Audio devices should be used only with proper headphones.

—You should spend as much time as tolerable pretending to read.

—You should wear appropriate clothing. Interpretation of this rule seems to vary widely, but you should keep in mind that your bare midriff probably looks better to you than anyone else. The same holds true for exposed boxers. In addition, you should keep body jewelry to a minimum.

—You should limit displays of affection to brief hugs, kisses on cheeks or foreheads, pats on the back or holding of hands in a supportive way. Prolonged, full-body convergence is prohibited, but such contact as using another's shoulder or—in the case of younger children—lap as a pillow is allowable. You should not, for any reason, cast lingering looks at another person of the same or opposite sex.

—Weep if you need to, but keep in mind that wailing, excessive blubbering and other theatrical displays are discouraged.

—You should not drink alcoholic beverages anywhere in the hospital or on its grounds—your car, however, is not considered hospital property. You should not smoke inside the hospital, except near exhaust vents. You should partake of recreational drugs only in the privacy of a lavatory stall.

—You should leave the room to spit or relieve yourself of intestinal discomfort.

—You should never, ever, change the television channel.

Jim and Sally sat in the two armchairs by the wall at the far end of our area, under a painting of a rolling rural landscape done in such muted autumnal colors that you had to stand directly in front of it to make out individual shapes. Janice lay on the sofa, her feet toward Sammo, who was slouched in a recliner that no longer reclined. I was opposite him in a straight-backed, grey upholstered chair with smooth, rounded wooden arms and legs that looked more inviting than it proved to be. Everyone was passing the time as best they could—Janice napping, Sally knitting, Jim alternately peeking at the TV and nodding off in his chair, feet out, hands in his pockets, Sammo solitairing. We'd been told the operation could take anywhere from two to four hours and that the earlier someone came to talk to us, the worse we could expect the report to be. So we settled in hoping for a long wait, with people naturally reluctant to leave regardless their level of physical discomfort, since what news of Connie we finally got, we wanted straight from Dr. Jameson, not some rehash from one of us after he'd gone. But eventually people began to squirm and sigh and clear their throats more than necessary, and since it would be a minimum of two and a half hours before we heard anything, I suggested that it might be a good time for people to go do whatever they wanted or needed to—to smoke or eat or go to the lavatory—I'd stay around until they got back, then I would go. No one moved at first, but Sammo finally stirred and said he wouldn't mind a bit having a little time away from that goddamn room, then Janice said she wanted to take a walk, meaning to the vending machines for snacks, then Sally said she had to go you know, and I said great, see you soon. Jim eventually blinked his eyes and rubbed his face and said what the hell, he guessed he'd just get along, too, then, if everybody else was, although he didn't seem clear about where he was going or why.

After everyone left, I sat back and tried to relax, read a couple of pages in my book but couldn't remember any of it, closed my eyes, only to see jagged monster mouths floating before me, got up, walked to the painting and pretended to study it, except there was nothing to study, no center to engage me, so to speak. I walked back to my chair, picked up my book, laid it back down in almost the same motion and began, as I often did when I was bored, to trace bullet trajectories around the room.

It was a habit I'd acquired years earlier, at a party, as I recall, that I didn't want to go to in the first place and was determined not to enjoy. I was sulking by myself in a corner when an imaginary bullet entered the room from some unseen source and began ricocheting here and there with seemingly endless energy. Everyone else appeared to be carrying on as usual, chatting, smiling, drinking, glancing over each other's shoulders to see who else was there, so I tried to locate the projectile again, and there it was, cutting clean, clear angles all about the room. It never hit anyone, nor even came close, for that matter, always seeming to find an empty space, regardless how narrow, to strike and rebound from. It wasn't long before I realized that I was the one directing it, determining its flight by where I looked. I could send it between someone's feet, under an upraised arm or a tucked in elbow. I could pass it between a person's palm and the stem of a wine glass, or directly under a nose. The only rule was, it had to go in a straight line and never through anything or anyone. When I got tired of the game, the bullet disappeared, but I found that I could call it up again at will. It materialized, for example, when I was at dinner with people who could talk about nothing but their cats, or was trying to stay awake at a classical concert, or was simply sitting somewhere trying to move time that seemed as inert as a slab of concrete. Like that day in the waiting room.

The bullet flew from where I sat to the ceiling about two inches from the wall, ricocheted down and off it, traveling to the floor about two inches short of the opposite wall, ricocheted up to it and back nearly to its original point of impact. Except that I altered it slightly for the next pass, creating a parallel line to the first, over and over, until I finally angled the ricochet enough that a new line crossed all the others, constantly working the pattern toward a corner, since from there I could be the most creative, sending lines all over the room, in time incorporating yet another corner, and another, eventually filling the whole space in a huge, intricate web I sat at the center of, puffed up like some cartoonish spider on steroids.

I was relieved when Janice came back, carrying a can of soda in one hand and small bags of chips, nuts and candy in the other. She sat primly on the edge of the sofa, knees squeezed together to hold all her treasures. She opened the chips first, took one herself, then offered the bag to me. No thanks, I told her, I needed to watch my weight, and she laughed and said I was being silly because I wasn't fat, and I said maybe not, but if I ate chips all the time I would be. She said look at her, she wasn't fat and she ate at least a bag of chips a day and drank pop all the time and ate candy. And hamburgers, I supposed, and hot dogs and god only knew what else. She ate another chip and said yeah and shakes and ice cream and macaroni and cheese, too, and I asked if she ever had fruit and vegetables, and she wrinkled her nose and said ewwww, but then cocked her head in my direction and smiled and said, yeah, she did, she had vegetables, all right. Fries were a vegetable, weren't they? I said I thought she was right, they were sure enough and tapped my finger to the side of my head and said kidneys. She looked at me a moment, not quite able to decide whether I was serious or crazy, then got a sudden impish glint in her eye, grinned and said, yeah, that was right, kidneys. And I was thinking jesus, what a bright kid—they always are when they get your jokes, right?—what a gem, what a great—I was going to say future—she had but couldn't. Couldn't even think it. Not considering Sammo and Connie's condition and the kid's mother, who designed and hand-sewed costumes for certain ladies no one named specifically, and even Jim and Sally, decent as they were. What could they do? Everywhere Janice went she was drowned out by noise and confusion, and it made me heartsick to think of her growing up in the midst of that, because the only way to survive was to succumb to it. I wanted to pick her up and take her away from that, take her home to my wife, like a stray kitten, and raise her with at least some comfort, some security, choices that allowed for more than leaving home, moving in with her boyfriend, getting pregnant and being abandoned with another child Grandma Connie—if she were still alive—could welcome with open, uncritical arms, while stare-daring me to say a thing about it.

Was something wrong? Janice asked, I looked sad. No, I was just thinking, I told her. About Connie? she wanted to know, and I smiled and silently thanked her for the escape and said yes, about Connie, and she said she knew, she was, too. I patted her on the shoulder and told her then that I might have a chip after all, maybe even two, if she had any to spare. She laughed and said sure she did, what did I take her for? and handed me the bag just as Sally's stocky frame wobbled through the doorway, her round face smiling as it always did, as though she'd had the corners of her eyes and mouth permanently tucked up, or had been born that way, or something.

She stopped, maybe even smiling a bit more, so that there was a slight mean tinge to it, and said she was glad to see Janice and I were having such a good time, what with everything that was going on and all, and I said without hesitation, before the ill humor of her remark could sink in completely, that she could bet her sweet bippy we were. Janice nearly choked on a chip and said sweet bippy? and I said yeah, bippy, and held the bag toward Sally, who all but made the sign of the cross to ward us off and said no, no, she could never have anything like that because of her sugar, and I said how sorry I was, I didn't know. She said that was all right, we shouldn't worry about her, she'd be fine. And Janice said bippy again as a question, and Sally looked at her a moment and asked if she hadn't ever heard that word, and Janice said, no, what did it mean? Sally, as though relieved to be off the subject of chips and off the hook in general, tried to explain bippy as a thing, like, you know, you bet your something, and Janice asked then why it was a sweet something and not just a something by itself? Sally said that was a way of calling more attention to the word, and I said, yeah, it gave bippy more emphasis, which sent Janice into squeals of thirteen-year-old laughter—a clear violation of the clause in Rule #2 governing outbursts of humor—that obviously annoyed the family at the end of the room who seemed to be seriously watching television. I tried to get her to settle down and she said she would, but only if I told her what bippy meant. I began by asking if she knew what a euphemism was, and she said yeah, she thought she did— like shoot for shit and—which was exactly right, I said, so she should think of bippy as a euphemism for, pointing to my rear end. Janice's face flushed red and Sally told her I didn't mean ass in that way but ass as in donkey, and Janice looked at me and I shrugged and she said, yeah, that was it, people always said they bet their sweet donkey, didn't they? and Sally put her hand to her face to cover a real smile and Janice glanced at me and grinned and I tapped kidneys on the side of my head. She nodded and Sammo, appearing with a monstrous drink, straw sticking out of the plastic top, asked what the hell was going on in here, without really wanting to know, and Jim, who'd come in with him, went over and settled back into his chair, and we all got quiet again.

I tried to read but after going over the first paragraph of a new chapter a half-dozen times still without comprehending what had been written, I gave up and went to the restroom, which I would need to do sooner or later and thought that the longer I waited, the greater chance I took of not being there when I needed to. Of course, Dr. Jameson was there when I got back. Like he'd planned it, a stupid little game where he stood on the other side of the double doors until I left, then burst through and took up a place on the far end of the sofa, surgical mask untied only from the top, so that, pulled loose, it dangled down against his throat. When I entered, I swear not two minutes later, he snapped his head in my direction, eyes clear and dark as coffee beans, hair still impeccable, face as smooth as if he had stopped to shave on his way to see us. He cast me a careful, annoyed smile and I told him I was sorry and slunk into my chair and he picked up where he had left off, saying that they had opened Connie's chest, only to find that the primary tumor at the top of her lung—the one near the aorta—was much bigger than they had anticipated, much more involved with "the surrounding tissue"—meaning, I assumed, that if they had tried to remove it, they could have caused massive arterial bleeding—and that the cancer in general had spread farther into the lung cavity than any of the tests had shown. Therefore, they were not able to remove the lung as planned, since they would not have been able to "clean her out" to the extent necessary to have even a remote chance for a surgical cure. It was an unfortunate but not completely unexpected situation, one he had tried to present as a real possibility when he had talked with us at the pre-op meeting in her room. He cleared his throat, more as a signal that he was changing subjects than from any real need, and said that he was going to recommend her case be turned over to an oncologist who could then propose whatever treatment regimen he. . .or she. . .thought might be most helpful. Not successful, mind you. Not curative. Just helpful. Were there any questions?

In the stunned silence that followed, tears welled in everyone's eyes but for Dr. James J. Jameson III, grandson of James J. Jameson the elder and son of his son—all sons of the first son of James, whose birth was recorded in 1574 in Hereford, England, and whose great-grandson, William, sailed on the *Destiny* for Pennsylvania in 1668, thus becoming the first Jameson to set foot in and propagate sons of James, both male and female, across the New World. I wondered, despite his DAR lineage, his descent from preachers, teachers, merchants, farmers, doctors, lawyers, miners, pioneers and all their amassed knowledge and wisdom, if he ever cried, and if so, what about. I couldn't even look at Sammo. There was something too raw and unexpected, too utterly broken in his countenance for me to watch. Dr. Jameson rose to his feet after a moment, said, all right then, gave us what he must have considered his kindly smile and started from the room; but Janice, in a voice just above a whisper, said no, he should wait, please, there was something she— He turned, slowly, hands clasped behind his back, and said yes, and she hesitated a moment, as if to be sure she had it right, then asked if what he'd said just now, about the new treatment and everything, did that mean that Connie was going to die? He cleared his throat—in earnest this time—and spoke to the ceiling: He didn't honestly know. He'd done everything he could and now it was up to the other doctors. Maybe she would want to wait and ask them what they thought, and she said yeah, sure, she might just do that, thanks for the tip.

A Favor, Please

She, Connie, got it honestly—her predilection to distill the events of her life into strands of an ongoing soap opera plot. It was a trait she inherited from our mother, who indiscriminately collected tales of affliction and despair and repeated them in weekly phone calls to me, like someone reciting the rosary: Yeah, Raymond's ulcer's acting up again; Clara, Joyce and Betty have colds and fever, the highest around a hundred and two; Jack's coming down with another cyst, and Lawrence fell and busted his arm at school; Grandma's got pain again, but god-almighty-jesus who don't; Shirley's sugar was back up to two-fifty; Ima Jean's contact cut her eye; Mikey's eardrum broke and pus run all over the pillow; the doctor said my lungs was no worse, but no better, either; your Uncle Fred, he died last night about eight, yeah. And this wasn't because she was perverse or particularly morbid. It was simply what she saw going on around her, what she chose to tell about, unadulterated by modulation.

I wish she could have had something better, a better marriage, better kids, a better way to die, someone who could have been with her, as I was the last time I saw her alive, and said more than so. So what's up, at least, what's happening, how's the weather, read any good books, seen any good movies, TV, heard the one about. . . ? Anything but the silence I offered, her cold, bony hand in mine, skin drooping and wrinkled like the bags under her eyes as she watched me, waiting for something more than so? To which she replied mawright, her emphysema so bad that each breath sounded like a weak, wet cough, as though the very water she had feared her whole life was rising up inside, soon to overwhelm her. She had survived one flood in Kansas, which destroyed her house and all family belongings, and two hurricanes in Louisiana, which caused far less devastation because she had learned to pare her life down to what would fit into the trunk and back seat of a car. She never learned to swim— refusing to any time she was offered the opportunity—and distrusted anything associated with water, such as boats and floats, although she did like fish, especially pan-fried crappie or bass, except for the bones, which she worried would stick in her throat and choke her. Bridges of any design or length paralyzed her. If she were driving, she would white-knuckle the steering wheel with both hands and fix her gaze straight ahead, never looking to the side or down. If she were a passenger, she would close her eyes and lower her head, as if in prayer, although I never knew her to be a particularly religious person. God was rarely mentioned, except for an occasional oh my god or you'd better by god get yourself down here or goddamnit, Cecil, to my father when she got so frustrated with him she didn't know what else to say, which was more often than I like to remember. Otherwise, god was the man upstairs or my maker or you know, with a skyward glance, not so much from a lack of anything more sophisticated to say as, I imagine, a concern that if she used some other term she might be assuming too much intimacy.

She was born January 10, 1916, in Ocheltree, Kansas, to Axel Doolan and Martha Frantz, the third of six surviving children. Axel, a section chief for the Frisco Railroad, was a caring person, although he already had a reputation as a heavy drinker. Martha was a homemaker of stern Germanic stock who believed rules were not to be broken. The children played and fought (outside the house) and went to school like everybody else, until, during their teenage years, they one by one left home for money or matrimony.

My mother's first attempt at marriage was with a man I know only as the bastard. There were no children between them, and it remains unclear whether there was any love.

My father soon roared in on his Harley, and from her first ride, she was sure he was the man for her. He soon quit work at a nearby dairy farm and took her off to Kansas City where he'd gotten a job at a company that would become part of what was later called the aerospace industry. Before long (exactly how long isn't clear) she became pregnant with my brother Len, who would have been her one and only child if she'd had anything to do with it. Labor apparently exceeded her tolerance for pain, and she dipped into severe depression after he was born. It would be nice to think that our father was there beside her during her distress or was pacing back and forth in the waiting room, fraught with worry about her and the baby—whether they would make it through the birth itself and how they would make it later, financially, emotionally, every other way. But of course he wasn't. He was gone. Somewhere. Which is what I remember most about him.

At the beginning of World War II, my mother and father moved to Southern California, where everyone was going at the time to strike it rich. She didn't care for the climate or the people or the constant threat of earthquakes, and by the middle of the war they returned for an even better paying job to Kansas City, where I was born. After the war, they moved into Central Kansas and started a filling station/restaurant business located at the intersection of Highway 50 and the Cottonwood River, which flooded in 1951, destroying the business and our house across the highway from it. We witnessed the whole scene from a neighbor's hillside farm—the uprooted tree floating downstream into a parked semi-trailer beside the filling station, the two of them forming a wide V, like the blade of a snow plow that slowly but with undeniable force struck our house, lifted it from its foundation and shoved it down the river, a trail of debris—all of my mother's keepsakes included—fanning out behind it. It seems fair to say that she never completely recovered from the flood, but life did go on in Carter, another small town (where Connie was born) that was not near water but was close enough to Wichita for our father to commute to work at Boeing Aircraft where he stayed until Boeing moved him, along with our mother and sister, to New Orleans. There, he worked on the Saturn V rocket engines used on the manned Apollo mission to the moon, our mother survived two hurricanes and Connie, between storms, got married directly out of high school and was divorced five years and one son later. By then our parents had already moved back to Kansas because of our father's ill health. He died less than ten years after their return, and our mother wrote in his obituary that he was a man totally devoted to his work. She mentioned nothing about his relation to family or her.

The truth was, he was an obsessively jealous man who never let her work outside the home, except in businesses they owned jointly where he could keep an eye on her. But there was never provocation. She was blindly loyal to him—foolishly so, considering how bitterly they argued over money and his drinking; and there was some suspicion (largely from stories Connie told me) that he might have stepped out on her once or twice when they lived in New Orleans. On one occasion, Connie said, our mother had the car packed to leave when there wasn't even the hint of a hurricane, and all she would say by way of explanation was that he'd by god better not try to stop her.

She was a good-looking woman—five-three or -four, raven hair, thin, nice figure, quiet, but with an easy smile—although I never thought of her as such until Len showed me some pictures from her high school days that her sister Eva had saved for her. The last one was probably taken her sophomore year, since that was when she dropped out of school. Sweet sixteen and. . .what? Never been kissed? Or had she? And by whom? The bastard? Was that how it all fit together? He came along and off they went, but he turned out not to be Prince Charming after all? By then, though, it was too late to go back to school and catch up, so she drifted around for a year or so until the old man appeared, and as attractive as she was, she could have had anybody she wanted, and maybe did, and maybe that was why the old man was so jealous.

I imagine all that because, as I said, I always wanted something better for her. Something more exciting than I thought

I remembered her having. She and my father were rarely affectionate. An occasional peck on the cheek, maybe, or a touch; but in all my years with them I never once saw a full embrace, standoffish or body-smashing either one. And I could never imagine them having sex, but it obviously had to have happened at least three times. A sex life, though? Sex in life? I wanted her to have known passion. I wanted her to have been consumed by desire. I wanted her to have lived with a man who satisfied her, who made her feel alive and loved and was rich enough to have given her a few nice things, soft cuddly things—angora sweaters and velvet skirts, a real fur coat if she wanted it—and a house that had heat upstairs and was filled with furniture she wasn't ashamed of and had an in-law apartment where his mother could live, and a car with cloth seats, and shoes that made her feet feel good, a man who could be loved in return and appreciate it, a man who could fill her with hope and dreams and give her children who didn't cause her pain, a man who couldn't imagine life without her.

I suppose you could say like mother like daughter, but that wouldn't be entirely true. There was no doubt Connie got a full dose of her, our mother Ruby Caulkins—the attitude, the anxiety, the perceived lot in life—but some things turned out differently. Until she got sick, for instance, Connie worked—most recently at Walmart—because she had to, because there was no way she and Sammo could make a go of it without her income. And she was married more often than our mother, to three separate men in four ceremonies—the middle husband twice.

She met her first husband, Baxter Billingsly—Bax for short—in high school. According to my parents, he was a dyed-in-the-wool coon ass, a term of endearment they said everyone used to describe natives of New Orleans, and it seemed perfect for Bax, since they never really took a liking to him. He was too loose. Too laid back. Too lazy. Too Southern. In their eyes, the best thing he had going for him was that he wasn't black. But the more critical my parents were, the more Connie claimed she loved him. And maybe she did. He was handsome enough—well-built, with a boyish smile and caramel-colored hair that gave him a certain exotic cast—and he was charming in the way he held doors for Connie and my mother and always said yes sir and yes ma'am. And, oh, was he full of plans. He was going to go to Tulane and when he graduated get a good job with a good company or a bank or some such, and he was going to buy a big car and get himself a place in the French Quarter—you know, one of those with a wrought iron balcony and fancy shutters?—so he could listen to jazz all night every night and live among other beautiful, sophisticated people. He was going to give his wife the best of everything, too (a glance at Connie, a wink). The best clothes, dinner at the best restaurants. His kids (another wink) would be the smartest ever and the nicest looking and would go to the best schools. Connie could listen to him forever, it seemed, which made my mother and father crazy. They actually made fun of him, saying yeah, yeah, we'll just wait and see; we'll just wait and see about that. But even such open ridicule didn't bother Bax. Not in the least. In fact, he appeared to thrive on the attention and began to spend even more time at the house; and when he wasn't there, Connie was at his place and it got to the point that our father the old man, as Len came to call him, finally said that they might just as damn well live together, and they said okay, they would and he said he'd meant that as a figure of speech because there was no way in hell any daughter of his was going to go off and live like that. Like what? they wanted to know. Without being married, he told them, and they said fine, they would get married then, and that's what they did.

But they didn't end up in a funky place in the French Quarter. They spent the first six months of their marriage instead holed up in the spare bedroom of Bax's parents' bungalow on the west side of the city. Bax's father, Buford—Bu for short—was a night-duty guard at a huge Winn-Dixie warehouse and Mrs. Billingsly (what she preferred to be called when Connie asked her) was a stay-at-home mom with no more kids to tend to who spent her days watching TV with the sound off so her husband could sleep and doing what few chores she still had around the house. After Bu left for work, she tried to sleep but most nights tossed and turned and swore that she wasn't going to keep living like this forever, they'd see.

Connie and Bax crept around the house talking in whispers all day, gliding from room to room like ghosts. At night they could hear Mrs. Billingsly muttering to herself an uninsulated wall away and assumed she could hear them equally well, so they had sex only once during the time they were there and that was one evening when Mrs. Billingsly went out with friends. They told her how great they thought that was and how she might want to consider doing it on a regular basis—you know, like a supper club or canasta club, but she said no, no she couldn't do that, leaving them here at home alone and all. That just wouldn't be right.

It wasn't too long before a guard who worked with Bu Billingsly retired, and Bu suggested that Bax might want to apply for the job. Bax may not have been as ambitious as our father the old man might have liked, but he wasn't stupid and told his father that, sure, he'd be happy to. Anything to get the hell out of that house, which, of course, he didn't say. But that left Connie with Mrs. Billingsly, a mute TV and a new husband she saw in the morning when he came home and in the evening before he left for work. She said she felt like a widow forced to live in the mausoleum where her husband was buried and soon reached her wits' end. I have no idea what that meant exactly. She could have been horribly depressed or homicidal or suicidal, or she and Bax might have had a single hushed-but-bitter argument during which she threatened to leave him if things didn't change. For the sake of the story let's say that was what happened and that during the argument she hissed something like your own mother would leave if she could, for god's sake, and when he didn't disagree she went on to tell him she'd die before she let herself turn into that woman. So what was he going to do to keep that from happening? she wanted to know. She had to know, had to hear directly from him. But what if he just shrugged his shoulders and she clenched her fist like she was going to hit him and he smiled his boyish smile and said maybe she should look for a job, it was all right with him, and maybe she said that wasn't the issue, that wasn't going to solve the problem of being where they were—in that place, that house, with those people. The only thing that was going to help with that was for them to move somewhere else. To which he might have said but and she might have said that's what she thought he'd say, and he might have said but again which most likely made her angry enough to say okay, forget it then, fucking forget it and stomp out of the room.

I don't know for certain that she said fucking. I can only imagine she did, since I wasn't actually there. In fact, I wasn't present most of the time all of this was going on with Connie and Bax. I was out of the country. I left before they got married and came back after they were divorced. My only source of family news was aerograms from my mother that carried the same flat-line emotional pitch as her telephone calls had before. There were a couple of letters from Connie that covered much the same ground, and despite the positive slant she tried to put on things, her life sounded utterly meaningless and futile. Which it may well have been, who was I to say? Or maybe that was just the way I heard it. Wanted to hear it? Maybe, but if so, it wasn't conscious. My honest intent is and has always been to record what I've come to understand about things as faithfully as I can. The broad strokes are easy. We all recognize them. They're the general direction of hers and everyone else's lives, part of our shared canvas, so to speak, our more or less common knowledge of each other. Details of individual lives, however, are just that.

Individual. Unique. Fundamentally unlike anyone else's because we have lived them in our own ways. And it's in resurrecting those details that I have to rely on my imagination. But I exercise it as honestly as I can. That is my guiding principle. Not egotism nor narcissism. Not even love in its usual blind sense. I have no other aim than to tell this story as accurately as is humanly possible.

So let's return to the facts. Fact: Connie and Bax did eventually move out of his parents' house into a rented bungalow of their own a few blocks away. Fact: within a month of their moving, Connie became pregnant with a son who would grow up to break her heart. In the beginning, though, she and Bax and Baby Bo—not short for anything—were happy. Deliriously happy, as they say in the movies. She told me once (in fact) that that might have been the most contented she'd ever been. You could see it in pictures from that period. There weren't many, but in the ones she had everybody was smiling. No exceptions. Big, happy smiles. Real smiles. Baby Bo's filled his whole face and squinted his eyes almost shut. Later, that same smile, combined with his father's black hair and garrulous manner and his mother's youthful prettiness, gave the boy a nearly irresistible charm.

And that was what she wanted now—her young Bo, her happy-go-lucky Bo—to replace the one who wrote recently that he couldn't believe what a class-A bitch she had turned into, that she was the worst mother ever and he hated her and he was leaving for Mississippi to find his real father, since he at least wouldn't do the kinds of things to him that that motherfucker she was married to now had done.

Which was why, lying on her hospital bed, she held a small slip of paper out to me and tried to explain through tubes and an oxygen line her hurt and disappointment, how she accepted some responsibility for what had happened to Bo, but that she really didn't know what was going on at the time, and how she couldn't stand not being able to talk to him, to let him know her condition and ask if he couldn't in this one instance, if not in general, forgive her enough to at least phone and say hello. There were three numbers on the paper—two in Mississippi and one in Louisiana—could I please call them and if I talked to Bo try to convince him to contact her? Could I? For her? For Bo? For all of them, so when she died, she could at least do it with a little more peace of mind?

A Change in the Weather

A pall of clouds draped the city in a drizzle that didn't so much fall as hang like near rain on the still air, so dank and chilly it soon made everyone as listless and irritable as a bad head cold. Connie said she couldn't stand it much longer, and I told her she was lucky she didn't live in a place like Rhode Island or Seattle then, where it was overcast and misty all the time. She said it couldn't be like this all the time, and I said okay, almost all the time. She wanted to know how people stood it and I said they not only stood it but liked it, looked forward to it, thought it was normal. She shook her head and said she was sorry but she'd take good old Kansas weather any day, you know, the quickie front that was in and out in a matter of minutes, hours at most? Whambam-thankyouma'am and it was over. I said maybe so, but that didn't seem to explain this current miasma, did it? She wanted to know what the hell that was supposed to mean. Miasma? I asked, and she said no, why did I use a word like that in the first place? I told her it seemed like the best word to describe the weather, and she said that was bullshit and I knew it. What I was really trying to do was make her look stupid, wasn't I? Wasn't that right? I asked if she honestly felt that way, and she said absolutely, I did it to her all the time. Always had and as far as she could tell always would. I said I was sorry, and she said no I wasn't and I asked how she could be so cock sure of that. She tried to cross her arms as she always used to when she was angry, clamp them, more precisely, over her chest—which wasn't easy with all the lines and wires going in and out of her—and glared at the TV, even though it was me she was pissed off at. I finally said, hey, what was she so worked up about, it was only a word. She rolled her head slowly toward me, as though it were a water balloon in danger of bursting, and told me the problem was that with me a word wasn't just a word it was a club. And I knew what people did with clubs. Her head flowed back to the upright position and the only sound in the room for a while was the clack of keys from Sammo's solitaire game.

I leaned back against the window ledge, my own arms crossed, and looked at her and thought maybe she's right, I can be an asshole. Arrogant, insensitive—plain mean at times, I suppose, although I honestly tried to keep that in check as much as possible. And I especially didn't want to be hurtful then, with her, given that she was probably in the first stages of dying. She was my sister, after all, despite everything, and she deserved a better me than I was giving her. I dropped my arms, slipped one hand into my pocket and laid the other on her left cheek and said I was sorry it was cold. Her head was her head again and she turned it toward me and assured me it was all right, she didn't mind. It felt good, in fact. And with a slight smile and softened eyes, she asked what I thought, a few degrees lower and there'd be a pretty good chance of snow, wouldn't there? She'd like that. Snow was pretty, and she didn't know if she was ever going to see it again—so, no, it wouldn't bother her a bit. Bring it on, in fact. We'd all go out and play in it. Just let them try to stop us.

The Other Brother

She'd already had breakfast, but she was hungry again. Said she was anyway, hungrier than ever, back in the other room, the one without windows and the view of the flat roof and brick walls and grey sky, after surgery. She wanted to know how she could be so hungry and so sick at the same time. Somebody had told her that his girlfriend's uncle's second wife, Marie, had eventually lost her appetite completely when the cancer started eating her. But apparently that hadn't happened yet with Connie. Had it? Otherwise, why couldn't she think of anything but food? Unless—a silly morphine smile crept across her face—unless she was eating for two, like they said you did when you were pregnant. Eating for it so it could eat you? Funny, huh? Kind of like cannibalism, self-cannibalism. Or was that the right term? Could you eat yourself? And, no, she wasn't trying to be gross, so I should just shut up! She was trying to figure this out, goddamnit. To be a cannibal, you had to eat somebody else, right? Another person and not yourself. So, no, it wasn't the same. It wasn't cannibalism. And she asked Sammo if that wasn't right and then told him to ask me if I wasn't amazed that she knew all that shit. Sammo sighed and shook his head and said something about the fucking drugs, and she said she knew a lot of things that might surprise me. Go ahead, just ask her. Ask her anything. Where the hell was the nurse? They could at least give her a piece of fruit, couldn't they? Where the hell was Len? He'd always looked after her. He would give her something to eat. She was worried about him. Had I seen him or talked to him? Did I think he was getting enough to eat, or did he still drink all his calories? Beer and chicken fried steaks up at the Carter Inn. Chicken fried steaks and French fries. Did I remember how he could never get through a meal without a cigarette? Could I imagine him having to quit smoking? She wouldn't mind a cigarette herself, now that she thought about it. Sammo? Fucking drugs. Len would give her one. He wouldn't let her just lie there and suffer. God, she was hungry. Where was he anyway? Len. I needed to go get him, bring him to see her. Maybe she would go with me to pick him up and we could stop off on the way for a Big Mac or a Whopper. Maybe—

She fell asleep as quickly as she had started talking. Like dropping into a hole. I told Sammo he should take the opportunity to get himself some breakfast, and he said he'd already eaten but he might, you know, tilting his head vaguely in the direction of the front entrance, where everyone stood around chain-smoking as many cigarettes as they could before having to go back in, shoulders hunched, heads down, not making eye contact, like people roaming the aisles of a porn shop. Before he left, though, while he was still perched on the front edge of the chair, arms cocked to push himself up, he swiveled his head back toward me and said that he supposed I knew what I was going to have to do now, didn't I? and I said well, no, I guessed not, and he scratched at his ear and told me that if I knew what was good for me—glancing toward Connie—I'd damn well better go and get that little sonofabitch brother of ours because, drugs or not, she'd remember; she'd be looking for him when she woke up. And I said, oh, he meant Len, and he gazed at me for a moment, as though trying to figure out how anybody so supposedly smart could be so fucking simple-minded, and got up to leave without further comment, which I was thankful for.

I called Len as soon as Sammo was gone and was shocked that he answered. I told him I was calling on my cell phone and asked if he could hear me okay, and he said yeah, he could, although I sounded like I was a million miles away. I told him to hang on and walked out past the waiting area toward a bank of large windows and asked if that was better. He said yeah, yeah, it was. I asked how he was, and he said okay, he was okay. What was he doing? Just sitting around watching TV. What was he going to do today? Oh, not much, nothing much, he guessed. I asked if he remembered Connie was going to have surgery, and he said sure, sure, how was she? She seemed all right, I told him, but she wanted to see him. There was a long pause. See him? Yeah. Another pause. At the hospital? Yeah. Pause.

And that was the way conversations with Len had gone—the repetitions and pauses—since his spell several months ago, when his good and only friend, Petey, had called Len's daughter

Suz to tell her her dad didn't seem quite right. He was having trouble speaking and was favoring his right arm like he'd hurt it and didn't want to use it, so maybe she'd want to go check on him. Which she did and could tell almost immediately that he'd probably had a stroke. She'd tried to convince him to go to the doctor, but he refused—no, no, not yet, not yet—the same answer I got for two straight hours when she called me and put Len on the phone. I talked to her again then and we decided that, since there was no way to force an adult to see a doctor, we would leave him alone and see what happened. So far he was still alive and hadn't seemed to get any worse, except that he was maybe more stubborn than ever.

No, he continued, no, he didn't think he could do that. What? Hospital, couldn't do hospital. She was his sister, I reminded him, and he said yeah, yeah, he knew. I told him that if I could come seven hundred miles he could come fifty. Pause. Especially if I was the one driving. He still didn't know, he said, didn't know. And I told him I did, should I pick him up at his house? No, no, not— At Petey's, then? Yeah, yeah, Petey's, he'd been on his way there when I'd called—a minute later and he wouldn't have been home. I told him to give me an hour. He said okay, even though he didn't mean it. Okay.

Sammo was back when I returned to the room, the smell of smoke and wet leaves clinging to his clothes, as though he had been walking or sitting in them. I said I'd talked to Len and was about to take off to get him, and he said fine, he wasn't going anywhere and neither was she, talking about Connie in the odd third-person way men in his family seemed to refer to their women. I told him I'd see him later, and he said be careful, but whether to me or the solitaire game wasn't clear.

I followed the highway straight north to Newton, then angled northeast through Walton and finally turned due east again toward Carter, where I found Len exactly as he'd said I would, drinking beer and smoking cigarettes at a table in a rickety little house just past the car wash on the east edge of town. The table was round and he and Petey sat across from each other, filling time with empties and butts, framed perfectly by a window with a view of the old highway that, until the bypass was built, was the sole access to town but now carried only local traffic or people like me who were looking for something or someone in particular.

I shook Len's hand, and he said I knew Petey, didn't I? and I said sure I did but it had been a long time since I'd seen him, and I shook his hand as well. I was the only one standing and no one offered me a chair, and I looked back and forth, from one to the other, and thought it must be true that people who spend a lot of time together eventually start looking alike. Petey was a smaller, younger version of Len, with a long, dark brown beard, brown eyes and brown hair that billowed from under a green John Deere cap. He had on jeans, black and white running shoes, a flannel shirt and a red fleece vest that seemed somehow too colorful for the setting. Then if you greyed everything, thinned the hair, lined the face with an extra quarter century and wild, unruly whiskers that looked like storm clouds ringing a craggy peak, you'd have Len, who was asking me in his stroke stutter how it went, Connie's operation. I told him fine, she was fine, everybody was fine, was he ready to go see her? He told me yeah, yeah, but we didn't have to be in such a goddamn hurry, he wasn't finished yet, holding out a newly lit cigarette and shaking his beer in its cozy. Besides, I remembered how he felt about going to hospitals, didn't I? I asked if that meant he still didn't like them or what and he looked at me as if he couldn't tell if I was joking then flipped an ash curl off his cigarette and said no, no, I always was a card, and told Petey that even when I was a kid he never knew for sure if I was pulling his leg. Petey smiled a wan, uncertain smile and asked which leg, or was that numb, too? and Len shouted no, no, that wasn't what he was—while Petey sucked on his cigarette and floated a stream of smoke between them, free hand stroking the air in a loose fist.

Len told him yeah, yeah he could fly straight to hell and then said that if we were going to that goddamn hospital, we'd damn well better get on the road, yeah. And he went out to pull his car alongside Petey's house under the only tree in the yard, left his keys with Petey and said he expected it to be right where it was when he got back. Petey asked where Len thought he could drive it even if he wanted to with expired license plates, and Len said no, no, he didn't need any smartass remarks as he took out another cigarette, announcing it would be his last for a while, since he wouldn't smoke in my car; he still had some sense. After he lit the cigarette, I asked Petey about the garden behind the house, a huge plowed space that looked like it could support several families, and Petey told me about beans and peas and tomatoes he would eventually plant, until Len abruptly said wh—what the hell, he might as well get used to it and dropped the cigarette to the ground, grinding it under the sole of his shoe.

When we waved goodbye to Petey, he was already on his way back into the house, presumably for more beer, and as I turned onto the old highway I asked Len if he wanted to go by his house and pick up anything, since we'd be staying overnight. He said no, no, he didn't need anything. The dog, I wanted to know, was there enough food for him? and Len said yeah, yeah, there was plenty. He didn't even want a change of clothes or a toothbrush? and he said no, no, what he had on was clean and he could make it a day without brushing, and I said fine, then, we'd get going. He smiled and glanced away, relieved no doubt that he had avoided yet again any chance that I might see the house. The house where all of us had grown up. The one Connie and I gave him after our parents died and he got divorced and had nowhere to live. If the outside of it—the peeling paint and broken upstairs windows, the collapsing wraparound porch—was any indication, I had no more desire to see the inside than he had to show it to me.

He asked me again what had gone on with the surgery and I told him again that it was exploratory to see if they could get the cancer by removing Connie's lung but that they'd found that they couldn't and had closed her back up. But, but she was okay? As okay as anyone in that condition could be, I told him, and he said well sure, sure but was she going to be okay? I said I had no more idea than he about that. There would be treatment of some kind, probably radiation and chemotherapy, which would make her even sicker, but it should help. The problem was, I told him, that nobody knew how long it would help. Sometimes it could seem almost miraculous, the cancer looking like it had disappeared. Which was good, great, and maybe it would stay gone—isn't that what we all wanted?—but it might not, too, because of the kind it was. It might stay gone a while and then come back like a mad bull, I told him. Like a goddamn mad bull, and I started laughing despite myself, and he said wh-what the hell? and I said I couldn't help it and asked if he remembered that bull that chased him that day out east of town? He looked at me like he thought I'd dropped what few marbles I had left, and I told him I couldn't even remember why we were there, but we'd climbed under a barbed wire fence to cut across a field and for some reason hadn't seen that big bastard black bull in the corner. I'd always been able to outrun him and did that day, too, if he remembered, and I made it to the far corner of the field and back under the fence, which left the bull to concentrate on him. He'd never run that fast in his life—come on, he had to remember now—that bull's horns about six inches from his ass all the way across? But he got there, he made it and only had a ripped knee in his jeans to show for it.

He said I was as full of shit as ever and tilted his head in the direction of the quick-shop: Did I mind? He said he wanted to buy something to drink, but I knew it was really because he needed to take a beer piss. I got our drinks and waited beside the car, and when he came out, I asked if he wanted a smoke, too, before we started again, and he said I didn't need to be a smartass like Petey, we could go.

Carter was at the west end of the Flint Hills, and by the time we reached the five-mile curve, heading west, the road had pretty much flattened out across an ancient seabed now called the High Plains that gradually—a foot a mile, I'd heard—rose to the Rockies. As we went, hickory hedgerows bordered ever larger open spaces, until eventually, far out beyond where we were going, there were stretches of only land and sky and the point where they met at the horizon. It was a land that either bored you into a somnolent Zen-like state—I am the emptiness, the emptiness is me—or brought on a desperate desire to fill the void with words—even when it was as hard to do as it was for Len— to raise questions we never would have otherwise, such as my asking what was that all about? as I imitated the loose-fisted stroking gesture Petey had used earlier.

Len said I knew, knew what it meant as well as he did, so why was I asking him, and I said sure, I knew what it usually meant, but what about between them, him and Petey, did it mean anything there? He looked at me with one eye squinted shut, like he'd bitten into something sour or bitter and said jesuschrist, what, what did I take him for anyway? That, that was Mason's thing, not his, remember? Meaning my sister's second husband, whom, if you recall, she married twice, each time refusing to believe what she was hearing about him with other men. And, hell, hell he—Len—didn't even have sex any more, so what difference did it make? Oh, he did once or twice, maybe, after his divorce, with different women, but no, no, not now, not with anybody any more. And Petey, he might take off after some gal if he was out tomcatting around at the Legion or something. But mostly there was nothing for either of them but hanging at Petey's place while his mother was at work down at the grade school, where she'd been secretary for thirty-six years. So no, no, shit no, there was nothing there, nothing between them. And it's not that he had anything against that kind of thing, I shouldn't get him wrong. Whatever Mason did, he did, but it wasn't for him, that was all.

Twenty-five or so miles from the hospital where Connie was waiting to see him, Len said he needed to piss again, and I asked if he had problems or something, and he said what, what kind, and I said shriveled bladder, swollen prostate, I don't know, and he stopped just short, I could tell by the slight silent hesitation, of giving me the finger or saying fuck you and meaning it. I left it at that and stopped at the next filling station and watched the wind blow until he got back—twenty to thirty mile an hour gusts, streaking the road with dirt, bending what trees remained permanently north like lines of old people with humped backs.

I didn't know what had happened to him while he was inside, but he began talking as soon as he got back into the car. Like somebody had flipped a switch while he was in there or he'd been thinking about all this and it finally spilled out. He kept asking did I remember this or did I remember that, and most of it I did, since I'd either heard about it my whole life or had lived through it myself. But he seemed so intent on telling me, seemed so in need of telling me that I couldn't disappoint him and pretended that I didn't remember after all. Hon-honest to god? he'd say, and I'd say that was right and he would wait a second, a wrinkled eye squinted shut, and say I was sh-shitting him, and I would ask if he was going to goddamn tell me or not, and he would shake his head like I was a truly hopeless bastard and start on about the time I fell down the stairs and had to go to the hospital. I couldn't have been more than two or three years old, and Mom got all upset and thought I was dead and it had to have been her fault because she hadn't been watching me like she should have been. I told him nope, nothing, and in this case that was the truth, although if I tried hard enough I could create a child—me, we could say—sailing backwards down a flight of stairs, a shadowy figure running over and kneeling beside him/me. A weeping figure, we could say, and we could call her Mother. Then how, how about the car wreck? he wanted to know. The one in Mississippi on that dirt road when Dad took the curve too fast on our way home from visiting Aunt Louise? Hit the ditch and rolled over and over, all kinds of shit flying through the air? Did I remember that bu-butcher knife floating at eye-level right between us, the whiskey bottle spinning on the ground as we crawled out of the overturned car? By some miracle—his word, not mine—no one was hurt. Scared as hell. Crying. I didn't remember all of us sitting there on the side of the road? God was wa-watching us that day, all right, he said, although I didn't know if he really believed that. I suspected it was just a cliché, an empty phrase that sounded like it gave meaning to why we'd survived. The flood? he wanted to know. Surely— Jesus! I didn't remember him and me taking our bikes out? as much a command as a question. Riding them through the water? Mom telling us to be careful and him saying what difference did it ma-make, we were all gonna die anyway? I didn't remember that? Standing on the bridge with Dad and Grandpa, watching the water come up? Them saying finally that we better get our butts out of there, loading the freezer and refrigerator on Grandpa's pickup and hightailing it to that farm on the hill and sitting there as water poured across the road and eventually washed our house away? God-goddamn, man. Walking through that shi-shit afterward when I fell into a hole and nearly drowned? I had to remember that.

His fingers twitched for a smoke as he sized me up, and we listened to the wind and the clap of tires on asphalt strips until he finally said he, he couldn't blame me, he guessed, my not remembering. I asked why and he said most likely nobody would want to after being treated the way I was, and I asked what he meant— and I really did want to know about that—and he said for one thing Da- the old man had always been on my ass about something, but I probably didn't remember that, either, right? I said right, and he said well he was, and was mean as hell about it sometimes, too. I asked him if it really had been that bad, since—honestly here—I could recall only a couple of things, getting smacked or whipped or yelled at but thinking even while it was happening that I'd deserved it. Yeah, he said, yeah, it was, bad enough he didn't want to be around. But then he guessed part of it could be my fault, since I couldn't or wouldn't keep my mouth shut, and what the old man hated worst was backtalk. From anybody. One of us—me usually, since Len said he learned early on to keep quiet, to go upstairs or outside, anywhere to get away, stay away from it—or Mom, dear god, Mom. He wondered why she put up with all that sh-shit. Why she didn't leave. He sure as hell did—as soon as he'd been able to. Wh-why else did I think he joined the Navy? Not out of any sense of duty, for goddamn sure. It was to get away from all the fighting, him and her, or me and him, but fighting and yelling and slamming around and saying things everybody regretted the next day, the old man especially, hung-over and contrite, begging us to forgive him, but then saying we could do whatever the hell we wanted, because regardless what we thought of him, we would by god respect him. And we'd better listen, too. By god. So Len left. Then I did. And eventually Connie did. But not Mom. She never did.

Len peered for a moment at the low, hazy sky, blinking like someone lost in thought or fighting back tears. I clutched the steering wheel as we passed a semi and were sucked into its wake, only to be spat out into a nasty gust of wind that nearly blew us off the road. Sh-shit man! He glanced at me, the ditch, me again, pale blue eyes reconnecting us, and I asked what, as in what about it? but he said nothing, settling back into the seat and asking me if I had any idea how, how hard it was the day Mom died? He'd never done anything like that and only hoped he'd made the right decision, and I said I had no doubt he had and thought Connie felt the same way, and besides hadn't the doctor agreed? He nodded yeah, yeah, he said it was best because she wouldn't live very long anyway and would be in constant pain. But, jesus, it was so hard to say yes then see her later on that bed, so quiet, all curled up, like she was, was asleep or something. He laid two fingers against his lips, as if holding a cigarette, and gave me a stony, accusatory stare, which I thought was for not being there with him but, as it turned out, didn't involve me at all. Did I fu-fucking know what happened after that? Did, did he ever tell me? The next day, the next goddamn day after Mom died, for chrissake, Josie up and decided she wanted a divorce. How, how was that for timing? and I said it stunk, and he went on to tell about how he'd just gotten home from work and had made himself a sandwich and sat down in his recliner to eat it and watch something on TV when the door opened and in pranced Josie, who he thought had spent the day shopping in Newton. She said there was something she needed to tell him and, fu-fucking christ, she didn't tell him anything but handed him divorce papers drawn up by her brother, the lawyer, which it turned out was where she'd been instead of shopping. And he put his sandwich down without ever getting a bite of it and said you what? and she said he could read, she didn't need to explain anything, it was all right there in black and white. And he told her she couldn't fu-fucking do that, and she said she sure as hell could and while he was at it, he might want to pay particular attention to the restraining order. He had forty-eight hours to pack up and get out and couldn't ever come back without her permission or he would be arrested. He asked if she'd lost her goddamn mind and she said no, she'd finally found it and walked into the kitchen, and he followed her, asking wh-why him, why now? and she didn't say a fu-fucking word and he kicked some cabinet doors until they splintered and told her he hoped the fuck she was happy now. Then he found out a couple of days later that she'd been screwing his best friend for months, getting up in the middle of the night and saying she couldn't sleep, she was going for a walk or a drive or some goddamn thing and all the while was going to Ray Johnson's and fucking him. That was right, he'd said fu-fucking, since that was all he could think to call it. There sure as hell couldn't have been any love in it, could there? so you couldn't say they were making love. No, they were fucking, plain and simple, only in the end he was the one who got fucked, right?

I didn't know what to say. No one had ever told me that version of the story. Not with that kind of blow by blow. But even then, he painted the picture he wanted of himself—the innocent victim who got waylaid. Other people added details that put a slightly different slant on things: yes, there had been an affair, but the fact was that Len and Josie hadn't been sleeping together for months and everyone who had eyes knew what was going on between her and Ray. Even I did when I saw the two of them once at a party where they did everything but get down and dirty in the middle of the dance floor. And what about the constant bickering and attempts not to be in the same place at the same time when possible? What about their putting on a valiant face for Mom in her last months so she wouldn't have to die with their troubles on her mind, too? What about their own children knowing separation, if not divorce, was inevitable, even if he claimed he hadn't seen it coming? What about the fact that his inability to recover from the divorce was his own fucking fault and not hers? So no matter how many times I heard the same story, and regardless the source, there was always an empty, unexplained spot I couldn't fill in—the real causes and consequences of the split-up—either because there were too many conflicting accounts of the truth or, as now, I simply grew weary from the attempt to understand and gave up trying.

Len seemed stuck at that moment himself as he hunched over, scowling at the dash, mumbling fuck now and then like a mantra, hands wringing, fingers fidgeting, wanting in the worst way a cigarette and probably a beer.

The hospital was on the north side of town, not far from an

enormous grain elevator, its string of dirty white tubes stretching into the distance like a remnant of a castle wall. I asked Len if, as I'd heard, it really was the longest elevator in the world, and he said he didn't know and didn't much care either, except that it was pretty damn big now that he'd gotten a good look, as if he had never been here before or, if he had, had paid no attention to it. He didn't get out much; he said so himself. This was the first time he'd been away from Carter for six or eight months and then only to go to the next town to buy a part for his riding lawn mower. He hadn't stayed overnight anywhere but home for years, except maybe at the Rod and Gun Club when he'd go fishing and sometimes sleep in the back of his pickup. Otherwise, it was just him and Petey, he said, and beer and cigarettes, and he shook one out of the pack in his shirt pocket and held it in anticipation of our arrival at the hospital.

He smoked in the parking lot beside the car, crossing and uncrossing his legs and squeezing them together. He had the piss miseries bad he said, but made no move to go inside, throwing his butt to the pavement and lighting a second cigarette. Connie had smoked right up until her surgery, I told him, and Sammo still did, so he'd probably figured out all the ways to do it and not be too far away in case the doctor came by or Connie or one of the nurses asked for him. Had he met Sammo? and he said no, no, not yet, and I asked then when was the last time he'd seen or talked to Connie and he said he couldn't remember, it must have been back when Sonny—his son—and Bo, before he left, had been arguing over something stupid and came to such loggerheads that they drew Len and Connie into the fray to the extent that they stopped speaking to each other, too. And he glanced at me and kind of smiled, as though saying, yeah, yeah, he knew how stupid it was, I didn't have to say anything.

He finished the second cigarette and thought about a third but rejected it with a quick shake of his head, and we started inside. He halted in the middle of the lobby, eyeing the darkish woodwork, the carpet, the welcome staff woman behind her curved counter, then found a restroom sign and skittered off, tight-assed, body thrust forward, as though he might have waited a minute too long.

When he came back, he said the place looked like a god-goddamn funeral home, and I asked him if he meant morgue—you know, where they keep dead people—and he cocked his head at me again, one eye squinted shut, either out of habit or as a way to let me know he didn't get it, didn't get me, and said finally that he guessed maybe that was what he meant, I could call it whatever I wanted, meaning of course that only a dumbass would.

We followed the signs to the surgical unit, and the closer we got, the more slowly Len walked, until he stopped and grabbed my arm and said wh-what was he supposed to say? To her? I asked. Yeah, yeah. Anything he wanted to, I told him, and he said but, and I said come on, she'd be happy to see him even if he didn't say a word, and I led him by the elbow into the room.

Sally and Jim were there, Janice was there, Sammo was clicking away at solitaire. Connie drifted in and out of consciousness, her head floating across the pillow one way, the other as I made introductions around the room. Len shook hands, said, hi-hi, nice to see you, hi, until we got to Sammo, who glanced up from his keyboard, nodded and went back to his game. Connie was awake then and asked if Sammo couldn't at least say hello to her brother and he said he had, and she said like he meant it and he didn't say anything, so she told Len not to pay attention to him, they would just talk, how was he anyway? Fine-fine, he was fine, and she patted the bed and told him to have a seat, it had been too long. No, no, not yet, he'd just gotten out of the car. Well, she'd been lying in bed all day, too, but she still had to, a reference he didn't seem to understand, so she said to come on anyway, he could set down and keep her company. He rested a hip against the bed and she took his hand in hers and asked if they'd brought her lunch yet, wasn't it time for lunch? I tapped the side of my head, but Len didn't notice and she pulled him by the hand closer to her and asked if he'd brought her anything. He'd always taken care of her. He wouldn't let her starve, would he? Len tugged at his chin whiskers with his free hand and Sammo glanced up and said fucking drugs, and Sally said she wished he wouldn't talk that way, and he said all right, he wouldn't and got up and dropped his game into the chair and stalked out of the room. Janice said jeez, what was wrong with him, and Sally smiled and Jim shrugged and Len stared wide-eyed like he'd just witnessed an accident and couldn't tell if anyone had been hurt. Connie said to no one in particular that he was upset was all, and he really was a good person, she didn't know what she would do without him. I thought to myself she might want to give it a try, and Len said yeah, yeah, and Connie, not knowing he did that as a filler when he couldn't find the words for what he really wanted to say, squeezed his hand and told him thanks, she knew he would understand. I tapped my head again and he looked at me and tapped his own, like he thought we were all crazy, and I had to smile and so did he, and Connie asked what was going on, what was so funny? I said nothing was, and she said we always did that. What? Got together and made fun of her, she said. Ganged up on her. I told her that was nonsense, and Sally said she thought it was, too, nobody was trying to make her any more miserable. Why were they being so mean to Sammo, then? she wanted to know, and Sally said they weren't, really. They were all just tired and worried about her and were out of sorts because of that. Sometimes people said things they didn't mean under those circumstances, like he did and she, Sally, did. And with that she'd talked Connie back to sleep, which might have been her intention all along. Len gazed longingly at the door, and I asked Sally and Jim if they minded if he and I stepped out for a few minutes, and they smiled like they truly would be happy if we did, and even though she kept wiggling her eyebrows to get me to ask, I didn't invite Janice to join us.

Getting Right

As soon as I walked into her room the day after her surgery she asked me where I stood. Not hello, how are you, nice to see you, but where I stood. And she wasn't talking about near the window or beside her bed. She wanted to know if I was with god, her god. It was like she'd been waiting all night to ask me. And there I was, and she did. She'd hinted at it before, saying how wonderful it was still to be alive and wanting to know what I thought that meant, what I thought God—there was a capital G in her voice— must have planned for her life. She didn't have money and she didn't know anybody important enough to influence things one way or another. All she could see was He wanted her to tell as many people as possible about Him and the amazing power of His love. And we all needed it, didn't we? We all needed somebody else, somebody to lean on (hear the music?). Somebody bigger than us, because we couldn't possibly do it alone. We needed somebody to trust and surrender our burdens to. Somebody like. . .you know, the man upstairs— spoken with a shy little laugh, as if worried she was being too familiar. We all needed Him—me included. Especially me. Didn't I agree? Except she wasn't looking for a simple yes or no answer. She wanted rousing affirmation. She wanted a chorus saying she was not only right, she was absolutely right. And I wasn't about to tell her that.

Or anything else, for that matter, because if I did, she'd only argue with me, say I was wrong and going to hell if I didn't mend my ways. Or she'd go tisk-tisk and feel sorry for me, think what a miserable, pitiful fuck I was not to believe and have a chance to stand with her at the right hand of her god.

I'd like to say that her attitude toward religion and my damnation in particular was an aberration, a distortion of the loving grace of god found in most mainstream theologies, but it wasn't. I'd like to say she just had a screw loose, although I'm afraid she came by her attitude honestly. Both our mother and our father had undergone similar sickbed conversions and died satisfied that they had also been saved. From what or for what I was never quite sure, since they, unlike Connie, didn't feel the need to talk about it incessantly. And, of course, there was Grandma Caulkins, who came to live with us when I was eight and Connie wasn't even born yet. Grandpa had died two months before one Sunday morning as he was feeding livestock. Grandma was in the kitchen watching him through the window over the sink and she said there he was, standing in the doorway of the shed, and all of a sudden he went straight down, dead in his tracks, like he'd been shot. He was only sixty-one, having just retired with Grandma to a small farm they'd bought in northern Arkansas. She was left with a mortgage bigger than her survivor's benefit and decided there was no way she could stay there even if she'd wanted to, which she didn't, seeing as how she wasn't about to live alone. So she came back to Kansas, Grandpa's casket in tow, buried him in the family plot near Chanute, moved in with us and stayed off and on until I left home for college and my parents for New Orleans.

She was given the middle bedroom upstairs, which she initially refused, saying she didn't want to put anybody out, and my father said she could count as well as he could: Len and me and her—three people, three rooms—she wasn't putting anybody out. What about when the baby came? she wanted to know. Meaning Connie, who was due to be born that summer, and my father said the baby would sleep downstairs in a crib, so Grandma didn't need to worry about it. She said all right, then, she'd do it, if she could take care of her own laundry and maybe pay a little on the utilities—you know, to help with what she used up. My father nodded and said, yeah, that'd be okay, she could start just as soon as he installed a meter next to her light switch.

She unpacked her clothes into the dresser and covered the top of it with a silver mirror and hairbrush set, a few cosmetics, pictures of her kids and grandkids and various knick-knacks she'd collected. She put a radio on the nightstand and hung a small reproduction of Sallman's *Head of Christ* on the wall beyond the foot of the bed and a crucifix midway on the wall beside her so that when you walked by at night, the crucifix glowed there, as if suspended in the dark, and the radio was always on, a little red light just above the tuning dial that seemed permanently locked onto whatever station carried broadcasts of *The World Tomorrow* with Garner Ted Armstrong, during which he railed on and on about the end of the world and how anyone not saved was going to roast in hell for eternity. But of course you could avoid perdition by contributing generously to his crusade, which Grandma did every month, five dollars in cash in a small white envelope addressed in her best Palmer Method script to him at a post office box in Pasadena, California. She was the first person I knew to take religion seriously enough to pay for it, and I asked her once if she did that so she wouldn't be scared. She asked whatever did I mean, and I told her it frightened me to lie in my room in the dark every night, listening to that man yelling about stuff, and she said it shouldn't scare me, it didn't bother her a bit. Scared was what you felt if you didn't believe in the Lord, a being, which, to my young mind, belonged in the same realm as Santa Claus and the witch Grandma said lived in the attic and would come down and get Len and me if we messed in the things that she'd stowed in two suitcases and a steamer trunk in the closet in her room.

But even with all her eccentricities, Grandma's beliefs seemed harmless compared to Aunt Louise's, who came to visit regularly after Grandma moved in with us. She was a tall, handsome woman, with a big smile and a hearty laugh, and anyone who spent no more than a few minutes with her thought she was charming. And she was but for one thing: her insatiable need to save souls. Before the end of every visit, she would recount how, when she was younger, she'd been a wicked wicked woman, a regular drunken Jezebel, but after the death of her first husband, she saw the error of her ways, accepted Jesus as her personal savior, repented of her sins and was baptized, which she never failed to remind us was the most important event in her life. Had she not seen the light, she said she would have been dead by now, rotting in hell, or lying in a gutter—all the while staring at our father the old man, as Len had taken to calling him by then, whom she badgered relentlessly about his smoking and drinking. Why, it said right there in the good book, her hand opened as though she were actually holding it in front of her, present your bodies as a living sacrifice, holy—did we hear that?—holy, acceptable to God. And be not conformed to this world. Romans 12: 1 and 2. The only way to achieve that state of righteousness, in her view, was to surrender to the love of Jesus, be washed in his blood and come to accept him as your lord and master. Again, with her hand opened: He who believes and is baptized will be saved. Mark 16: 15 and 16. It was that simple, and we (meaning primarily our father) needed to think seriously about it, because you never knew what tomorrow might bring. Only the Lord did. The Lord giveth and the Lord taketh away. To die without having accepted the cleansing power of Jesus' blood was to be separated from God for eternity. After all, it said right there: The wages of sin is death. Romans 6: 23a.

You could see her wearing our father down. At first, although it was against his nature, he stopped arguing with her, which had the odd effect of encouraging rather than dissuading her, so he next chose to avoid speaking to her or making eye contact altogether, thinking that she would then have no reason to engage him. But she had locked onto a soul in need of salvation with the tenacity of a dog on scent and pursued him to the point that he began to flee out the back door at the sight of her car pulling up to the curb and to hide in the old shed by the alley until she left, where he perched on a broken-backed chair and smoked and sipped whiskey from a bottle he had stashed there. In the end, however, Aunt Louise's proselytizing forced him into such a corner of guilt that it was decided in the way everything got decided at our house—by declaration of our father—that things needed to change, meaning that he thought we might benefit from a reexamination of our relationship with, you know, finger pointing at the ceiling, but not too emphatically, lest he be considered impolite, and the way we were going to bring that about was for Len and me to start going to church.

It's never been clear why he chose us, when neither he nor our mother or grandmother, who said she got more than enough to think about from Garner Ted, had ever to my knowledge set foot inside a church for any reason other than a wedding or a funeral. And curiously, by the time Connie became old enough to go, the family's need for redemption seemed to have dimmed, so she was let off the hook and, at least while I was around, seemed to have had nothing to do with religion or thoughts about it until she got sick herself.

It's still a mystery why our parents decided Len and I would go to the Christian Church, although I suspect it had a great deal to do with Aunt Louise, who was a zealous member of the Church of Christ, which had split from the Christian Church over the use of musical instruments during worship. According to Aunt Louise, the tenets of her church were written in God's own hand: you should sing praises to the Lord only from your heart, no harp necessary. That was the one true and pure way to express your love. Otherwise you could and probably would incur the wrath of God and end up in everlasting hellfire. The fact that Aunt Louise tended to preach about church dogma with the same evangelical fervor she had for saving souls almost certainly drove our father to the conclusion that the Church of Christ would be the last place Len and I would go. The problem was, however, that he had objections to most of the other churches as well. He thought the Mennonites, for example, were too namby-pamby with all that peace talk and the Methodists were a bunch of goody-two-shoed teetotalers and the Lutherans and Presbyterians were too high-church and stuck up and the Baptists were too Bible-thumping and severe. Which, in our little town, left only the Christians.

So it was settled, and the third Sunday of that September Len and I walked the few blocks from our house to the church, kicking pebbles and mumbling, one quarter each our father had given us for the offering clutched in a tight fist in a pocket. It might have made a better story to say we took that money and ran, so to speak, but there was no place to run to that was open on Sunday morning in Carter, Kansas. Besides, someone might have seen us and told our parents and we would have caught hell for sure, so we continued on and soon reached the corner of Second and Sycamore and the drab shoe-box shaped building with brown cedar shake siding and white trim that sat there. A glass case near the main entrance announced First Christian Church, Dr. James Darby, Pastor. We could hear a piano as we peered up the concrete steps to the white double doors that stood open at the top. I smiled at the thought of Aunt Louise and imagined Len smiling, too, but I couldn't look to see for fear of laughing out loud if he was.

We continued to go off and on until the next summer. We learned about tithing and sharing of talents. We learned about the love of God and heard the story of the prodigal son and how the meek shall inherit the earth. We learned some of the differences between the Old and New Testaments and about Jesus as our friend and personal savior. We learned but didn't want to hear how Christmas shouldn't really have much to do with buying presents. Which Len claimed was a bunch of shit, and where did our father the old man get off telling us we had to go to church in the first place while he sat on his ass at home, smoking and watching TV and wishing our mother would go somewhere else so he could sneak a drink? And so on, until the Sunday Dr. Darby asked Len after church if he'd been thinking yet about baptism, and Len said no, he didn't know he needed to. Dr. Darby went on to explain that the Disciples of Christ—the real name for the Christian Church—didn't believe in baptizing babies. They thought people should make up their own minds about being saved and joining the church, and they usually did that pretty soon after age twelve or so, and Len was at least a couple of years past that, wasn't he? Yeah, he was fifteen, but— Dr. Darby said to go on, he was listening. That baptism, wasn't that where you walk down into that tank and somebody puts a rag over your mouth and you get dipped backwards into the water? Exactly, Dr. Darby said, three times—in the name of the Father, the Son and the Holy Ghost. And Len said that was what he thought and there was no way in hell anybody was going to do that to him. I told Dr. Darby to forgive Len, he probably hadn't meant to use that word, and Len said he certainly had and Dr. Darby smiled and told Len to let him know if he changed his mind, which he was sure he would, since everyone eventually gave themselves to the Lord.

Len hunched his shoulders and pulled in his neck like he was about to be smacked, but I knew it meant instead that he was saying nobody could tell him what he was or was not going to do or when, and that moment marked the beginning of the end for Len and First Christian Church, Disciples of Christ. He started missing church so often for one reason or another that our father finally asked why he bothered going at all if that was his attitude, and Len said fine, he wouldn't, and for some reason that was the end of the conversation. Our father started making excuses that sounded like Len's not attending church had been his idea all along: the boy needed to spend more time on his schoolwork; he had a new paper route and getting up so early in the morning meant he needed extra rest, especially on Sunday; and the best one of all—he was a football player now. To our father the old man, there was no higher mission in life than playing football, and for his son not only to be on the team but to be a starting tackle meant more than baptism ever could, although he curiously missed every game Len or I played.

For a while, the less Len went to church, the more involved I tried to become. I had convinced myself that my increased presence could make up for Len's absence and maybe lessen the degree of God's displeasure, which I believed I had already seen in the accident our mother had on the way home from the grocery store when she smashed a dozen eggs on the floorboard of the car, or the dropped machine tool that broke our father's big toe at work, or the mysterious illness that caused Len to miss nearly a week of school, or the night terrors that woke Grandma Caulkins and sent her running down the stairs two at a time, yelling that she had seen Grandpa, that he had been there beside her bed plain as day and was about to say something, but when he opened his mouth she could look straight through his head to the wall behind him.

If that was God annoyed, I didn't want to see what he might do if he were truly angry, so my spending more time at church seemed a small price to pay to help keep that from happening. And it wasn't such a bad place. I liked the people there, they liked me. I eventually took a membership class and was baptized. I started going to Sunday School before church, then youth group Sunday evenings. I was gone so much that our father the old man actually said something about it, asking what the hell was the matter, didn't I like being at home any more? But he didn't really mean it. That was just his way of saying he'd noticed, which he didn't most of the time, so I took it as a compliment.

Connie would have been old enough then to have noticed, too, and I'm sure that's the period she must have been thinking about when she said that thing about how I was so—what did she call it?—holier than thou. Which seemed so odd to me. On the one hand, if only by sheer exposure, I was probably the most right with God of any of them and was yet still the least right in their eyes. If she'd ever asked—although that wasn't in her nature—I would have tried to explain this to her and why, ultimately, rightness in the sense she meant it was of no interest to me whatsoever.

She was sleeping again, for all I knew in her god's arms. She did look tranquil, and I was happy for that, regardless the source of her peace—the big guy, a furry cat, a teddy bear, it didn't matter. I even envied in some ways her lack of searching, her automatic, uncritical acceptance of that which she called god. It at least gave her—and our parents before her and Len soon enough—something to hang hope on, or despair if things got that bad. You can't hang anything on a question mark.

I touched her forearm, just below where the PICC Line entered. Our father was gone, our mother, Grandma Caulkins— who died one Sunday morning (when else?) as she leaned down to tie her shoe—everybody but Connie, who hadn't long, and she knew it; and Len, who was himself a single heartbeat away from another stroke and another which would leave him living his final days unable to move or speak, eyes fixed on the ceiling of a nursing home room, thinking things no one else would ever be aware of. All of which again rendered me just as helpless, with no answers to give and only the vaguest of nods when Connie rolled her head toward where I stood beside her bed and asked me to pray for her.

The Tale of Ezra

Every Memorial Day was the same: get up at the crack of dawn and load the trunk of the car with a picnic basket and wreathes and newspaper-wrapped bouquets of fresh-picked pink peonies with little black ants still crawling on the blossoms, recheck everything two or three times and finally crawl into the car—our mother, Grandma Caulkins and Connie in the back seat, Len and our father in front, with me between them—and set off on the three-hour drive to Chanute, Kansas, to visit graves in the Caulkins family plot.

Ours was a sacred journey, a pilgrimage that, for reasons I have never fully understood, held far more meaning for my family than Christmas. And instead of hearing the story of the birth of Christ, we were told for the god knows how manyeth time the legend of Ezra.

To have gone to Chanute with the intention of actually honoring the dead would have been one thing, but the decorating of graves never seemed nearly as important as being seen doing it and eventually talking to as many people doing it as possible, until all was said that could be said. Duty done, our mother and father would go off for lunch or a drink or a drive—anywhere, I finally figured out, to avoid another recounting from Great Aunt Hattie of the life of Ezra Caulkins. Grandma would steer Connie, Len and me out the cemetery gate north along a brick sidewalk made wavy by tree roots, pale green grass and weeds poking through the cracks, until all too soon we reached Great Aunt Hattie's house, a tilted, weather-worn structure that seemed less in danger of falling over than fading from view, like an old photograph left too long in the light.

Once we had assembled on her porch, Great Aunt Hattie, bent, shriveled, dressed head to toe in black, would appear behind a rust-smelling screen door that she would slowly open—with a screech, of course, or did I make that up?—and ask in a crackly voice if that was Irene, using my grandmother's name, and my grandmother would say yes and they would more or less hug and we'd all go into the house, its air ripe with the musty savor of wool rugs, yellowed newspaper and an old woman's breath. Grandma and Great Aunt Hattie would sit across from each other at a small table on one side of the room, Connie, Len and me on a scratchy sofa opposite them, and the women would run through the usual litany of Great Aunt Hattie's ailments and who in the family had died since they'd last seen each other, which I imagine was our grandmother's main reason for stopping by.

Before long, we would be back out on the porch, drinking Lipton instant tea out of pastel aluminum filling station glasses that made my teeth ache and eating sugar cookies laced with something, I was sure, that lulled us into a near stupor, so that when Great Aunt Hattie asked whether we'd stopped by Ezra's grave we said we had and she said that was good because it was due to his awful sacrifice that any of us were even there. She would pause at that point, as if making certain we were drugged, and ask whether we remembered the story about him and his family on the trip from Ohio. We would nod that we did, but she would go ahead anyway—we were to stop her if we had questions—about how our great-grandfather, Ezra Caulkins, who along with his parents, two brothers and a sister, left Mt. Vernon, Ohio, the tenth of June 1873 to join a group of five wagons bound for the newly chartered town of Chanute in southeastern Kansas. But they weren't the only ones heading west, she wanted us to know. They were part of a much larger migration—her arms spreading as wide as they could—that had been under way since the middle of the nineteenth century. The first people, she said, were after gold or furs or just the thrill of going somewhere else, but Ezra's family and others like them were looking for free land and new lives in Kansas. Our heads by then were lolling like drunks at a bar as she went on to tell how in the middle of Missouri—whether it was from bad water or food or what—six or seven people, Ezra's whole family included, came down with cholera, she'd heard it called, and died and were buried right there beside the trail in unmarked graves. She always leaned forward at this point in the story and lowered her voice and asked if we could imagine how terrible it would be for nobody to know where they were or how to find them? Mercy. And did we realize how miraculous it was that Ezra survived— her claw of a hand locking onto my forearm—even though he became deathly ill himself and ran such a high fever he had no memory of anything when he emerged from it, other than his name, Ezra? But Ezra what, nobody could say. Why, it was like everybody else had suffered the same amnesia: was it Grimes or Graham or Grimsley or maybe Gormley? They soon gave up trying, she said, and another family took pity on Ezra, suddenly a nameless orphan, and adopted him on the spot, giving him their name to carry with him instead of the one he was born with. And they came on to Kansas and settled, and Ezra grew to be a man and married and had his own family, our grandpa among his sons, she reminded us, and that was the story of how we came to have the name Caulkins.

Great Aunt Hattie would struggle up from her chair then and go back inside. She would come back out in a minute or two, carrying a familiar ornate silver photo frame that held a creased portrait of a man with an angular face and a full dark beard. A taciturn, sharp-faced woman stood beside him in a bonnet and a dress with long sleeves and puffy shoulders. Great Aunt Hattie said they were Ezra Caulkins and his wife, Sarah, with such authority no one doubted the truth of what she said. In the photo, the man's right hand grasped the lapel of his heavy dark coat and his left rested at the back of his wife's neck. He stood perfectly straight, a watch fob looping across the front of his vest, the knot of his broad tie held in place by points of a starched white collar folded neatly down on either side of it. Like his wife, he had a stern, foreboding expression that was so intense it made you want to glance away. Great Aunt Hattie said he looked that way because he felt so guilty. She would pause a few seconds for dramatic effect before going on to ask who wouldn't if he'd been the only one to survive the loss of his whole family—and his name to boot? Not to mention his life—the early part of it at least. That'd be enough to drive anybody to distraction, wouldn't it? And it did Ezra Caulkins, too. We could see it right there, plain as day, if we looked him in the eye, which I always did no matter how many times I'd heard the story and seen the picture. I looked, I stared, I practically burned holes in that picture, and I never saw it, not once, that guilt of his, although I knew better than to say as much. About that or any of the other questions I had about the story—like why they came by wagon train rather than the new railroad, how it could be that there wasn't a shred of evidence, not even a single scrap of paper, as to what his name had been before, what proof Great Aunt Hattie had that the picture she showed was actually Ezra Caulkins and not some snapshot she'd picked up at a flea market, and in the end what difference any of it made, since we were all who we were and the story wasn't going to change that in the least. But no one ever raised an eyebrow that I saw, not with Great Aunt Hattie, and by the time the mantle of official keeper of the legend had been passed on to Connie, it had grown beyond challenge, taking on a life of its own, still independent of historical fact. It had become its own truth, its own justification, as whole and self-evident— and just as unassailable—as any sacred text. As had happened with Great Aunt Hattie, when Connie told the tale, she demanded the same belief in the truth of what she was saying as any fire and brimstone preacher. What she was telling you was, to her mind, largely what made you not only a Caulkins but who you were altogether. It was what made you unique and inter- esting, and although she would never have admitted as much, Connie had always felt a desperate need to be part of something like the myth of Ezra Caulkins—something more grand, more ultimately mysterious than her own life had turned out to be.

Lawn Tractors, Painted Men and Journeys Not Taken

Len was nodding yeah, yeah to Sammo's father, Jim, after Jim started talking about his lawn tractor, a John Deere L110 with hydrostatic drive. Why, it was the best damned machine he'd ever had and might have been the best one ever made, and he meant that, he wasn't talking just for the hell of it. He told us that even with a forty-two inch deck, you could turn the tractor on a dime, and it would speed up or slow down automatically, depending on how thick the grass was or how deep the snow—which was another thing: you could put all sorts of attachments on it, like a plow, or a hitch to pull a cart—and it even mowed in reverse. Could we beat that? Now he knew a machine like that was expensive and not everybody's cup of tea, but he needed the power and maneuverability to mow the runway at the airport outside of Summit, where he lived about fifty miles farther west. He'd been doing that four or five years, and it was a good way to make a little extra money and keep himself out of trouble at the same time, he said, with a glance at Sally, who said that was right and gave him a stubby thumbs up. Len tried to say he didn't know Summit had an airport, but all he got out was he didn't know-know, so I filled it in for him, and Jim said yeah, they did, all right. There were a lot of them out that direction and a lot of planes, too, coming and going. Little ones, Cessnas and the like, bringing people in to check on ranches and small companies, or maybe to visit family, although most of it really was for business. And nearly all of them landed on nothing more than a grass strip in what used to be a pasture, maybe with a corrugated metal lean-to you could pull a plane or two under for protection. Most times, though, they didn't even use those and parked and tethered the planes to the ground in a neat row next to the runway, kind of like in a parking lot, only there weren't any lines to show them what space to use. And there weren't any lights, of course, so anybody flying in had to do it during the day, meaning he, Jim, had to be careful and keep his eyes open so he didn't end up sliced and diced like something on a chef salad. He said before he started working out there he never used to think a landing strip would need much maintenance, either, but it did. Just how much depended on whether the owners took money from the FAA. If they did, they had to follow the same rules as the big boys, like at Wichita. Which was how he got the job at Summit. They'd applied for federal money in the beginning to set things up and got it, so Jim now had a little book that said runway grass couldn't be over two inches high and the apron sixty feet on either side of it had to be kept mowed down to no more than four inches, not to mention the two hundred or so feet at each end of the strip that had to be kept clear of trees and wires and poles and such. Depending on how much rain they got, he could be out there every day or once a week, but never less often than that. Oh, it was a job, all right, and between it and keeping after his own place and a few others around town, he stayed about as busy as he wanted to, and maybe more, but he'd never had sense enough to tell anybody no, even though he was retired now.

Connie had been listening to Jim with as quizzical a look as she could manage with so many tubes and wires running in and out of her. I raised my eyebrows to ask what and she tapped her thumb and fingers together to show she thought Jim was talking a lot. I craned my head closer and she whispered that most of the time you couldn't get more than a couple of words out of him. Like father like son? I wanted to ask but of course didn't and whispered back that he'd probably just gotten excited telling us about his tractor. She nodded and said he did love the thing, and wondered if Len still had his riding mower. I told her she should ask him, and she did, and he said yeah, yeah, but. It wasn't a tractor like Jim's, I think he wanted to say, with the big motor and all the gadgets and extras. His was a plain riding lawnmower, a grey Craftsman our father the old man had gotten years ago at Sears after he'd developed so much leg pain he could no longer walk behind a push model. It had a smaller deck and a smaller engine and you had to use gears to make it run faster or slower. There was even a clutch and a column-mounted lever to control engine speed. But that was all right, Len would have said, because he didn't use it for anything but to mow his own lawn and ride occasionally up to visit Petey when he didn't want to get his car out, something he'd been doing more often since his "spell," according to his daughter, Suz.

Connie said she was glad he still had it, because she liked thinking of him on it, his hair and beard blowing in the wind. It reminded her of the movie about that old man who rode his mower all the way from Minnesota to Iowa—or maybe it was the other way around, she wasn't sure—so he could see his brother one last time before he died. Had I seen it? If not, I should, it was the best thing she'd seen in years. Really, she meant it. The more excited she got, the louder she talked, and by now Jim and Sally and Len were listening to her, and even Sammo glanced up more often from his solitaire game as she went on about how the movie was based on a true story about the brothers, who'd been on the outs for years over something one or the other of them had said or was thought to have said and it grew and grew and got so ugly and twisted neither of them could remember what had really happened. But the feeling remained, wedged between them like a stump or a rock or some damn thing, until the mower man decided he at least was being ridiculous and went looking for his brother in the last place he knew him to be. Which was where he found him—wouldn't have been a movie otherwise, she guessed—and they sat in the brother's kitchen and drank coffee and talked when they wanted or needed to, and that seemed to be just enough to satisfy them both. She said when the mower man got back on his mower and started home she cried like a baby, and if she didn't stop talking about it now, she was going to again, which made Jim take a long look at the roofscape beyond the window, Sally pick up her bag and dig through it, Sammo excuse himself to have a smoke, Len nod yeah, yeah and clean his right pinkie nail on one of his few remaining front teeth. I concentrated on the monitor above Connie's bed, following line after wavy green and red line across the screen, as if somehow by watching long enough everything would make sense.

Nobody said anything for a long while, and, as usual when such silences fell over us, Jim and Sally began to doze and Len drifted off to whatever place he stayed in when he was by himself. Connie's head sagged against her pillow and her eyes closed. She soon became so still I had to watch her chest to see that she was still breathing. She must have sensed what I was doing, for her eyes popped open like a doll's and locked directly on me, and she said not to worry, she was still there and I asked what that was supposed to mean and she said I couldn't fool her, she knew what I was thinking. I said in that case would she mind sharing my thoughts with me? and she smiled and reached for my hand and asked if I had any idea what she'd been dreaming about. I said no and she said Mardi Gras. As in New Orleans? She said where else, and I said for all I knew she could have been dreaming about some hunk in Rio, and she said no, New Orleans had been wild enough for her. She'd loved everything about it, she said — the costumes and/or lack of them, the bands, the floats, the dancing, the boozing, the sheer lunacy of it all. She laughed — a weak, wet croak but a laugh nonetheless — and said she couldn't remember for sure which year it was, but there was this one guy — big, so tall she thought at first he was on stilts, not exactly muscular but not fat either — walking the streets completely naked. He would have been hard to miss anyway, she said, but the guy was painted head to toe in circles of bright blue, red, yellow and green paint, except for his, uh, you know, his...waiting for me to say dick/prick/cock/schlong/peter/penis/ weewee/peepee/junior, but I wasn't going to, and she finally said except for his thing, which was black. Not because he was black, she didn't mean that; you couldn't tell what race he was. But it was black, big and black. How big? I asked, and she said big enough, and I said it might have been a prosthesis, then. She asked if that meant fake, and I said yes, and she said, oh it wasn't fake. It was just big and painted black and hung there like an exclamation mark, like it was holding him to the ground. Otherwise, she said, she was sure he would have floated off into the sky on the next gust of wind, like a gigantic balloon sculpture. I said wow, and she said yeah, she'd go back tomorrow if she could and take me with her, but she doubted I would go. There would always be something to keep me from it, wouldn't there? her eyes fixed on me, in me, like a hook only she knew how to cast and set without my feeling so much as a pinch. It would always be a bad time of year, a bad time of life, I would always have something else to do or somewhere else to be. Africa, Europe, Canada, Hawaii, Mexico? Where the hell hadn't I been? her voice growing louder, more shrill. China, India, Russia maybe? She hadn't heard anything about them. Or the Middle East or South America, either. Why not? What was I waiting for, for chrissake? Everybody knew I'd rather be somewhere else. Anywhere but here. So why didn't I go on? There was the door, goddamnit. I could walk out that door any time I wanted to, it wouldn't bother her one bit.

Jim honest to god had his hand over his hearing aid ear, Sally's face was descending into tears and Len was going but, but-but, but, but-but, like a motor he couldn't get started to save his life.

A passing nurse stuck her head into the room and asked if everything was okay. Connie nodded and, when the nurse had gone, smiled, took a deep breath and, staring straight up at the ceiling, said in a quiet voice that she'd often wondered if she hadn't missed her calling.

A Confession (of Sorts)

She had finished eating a small bowl of banana pudding and a single vanilla wafer and was asking if I thought that was supposed to fill her up. I said, no, but I doubted that was the idea, and she said she didn't know whether it was worse to be hungry all the time or be teased about it. Giving a person that little bit of nothing was plain torture. Just got your taste buds going and it was over. Was that fair? And I wasn't supposed to tell her that life wasn't fair, she already knew that. God did she ever. She sighed and turned her head away, pawing her eyes with the heels of her hands. Sorry, she kept saying, sorry, she didn't mean to be a mess.

I told her not to be silly, she had nothing to be sorry about—unless of course she was referring to what she'd told Mrs. Cox one certain Saturday morning long ago, in which case an apology would be gladly accepted. Good Lord, she said, did I ever forget anything? I told her that sounded like censorship to me, and she asked what the hell I was talking about now, and I said, given my job of faithfully recording her life's story, she would surely want me to include all relevant details. She said sure, as long as they were true, and I said we at least agreed on that. She licked her lips, eyes darting back and forth, like a badger sniffing a trap, and said but true is true, isn't it? and I said oh yeah, as true as we can make it. Okay, then, why did she need to apologize? She hadn't done anything but try to wake me up and couldn't, no matter what she did, and she was just a little kid—what, maybe seven? Yeah, yeah, I said, and scared too, right? Because our mother and father were gone? So was Len, she said, I shouldn't forget about that. Oh, I hadn't, I told her, because that had left me in charge, right? Of her? Of the house, of everything? Wasn't that right? Wasn't that the way it was?

It was a Saturday, and I had slept in, like any normal fifteen-year-old. Connie had been up and around for a while and had gotten bored with cartoons on TV, and according to her version of the story, had tried to wake me to keep her company. When I wouldn't budge, I imagine she spooked herself and ran next door to summon Mrs. Cox, who at the time must have been at least seventy-five and was so bent and twisted her right shoulder humped next to her ear and pushed her head permanently toward her chest. She always wore a babushka—brown or black, no pattern—over thinning grey hair and had two or three moles on her face sprouting coarse black whiskers. If you didn't know her, you could swear she was a witch, but Mrs. Cox was as kind and gentle a person as you could ever meet, and I was angry and humiliated when she appeared in my bedroom, asking if I was okay. I said sure I was, why? sitting up in bed, sheet pulled under my chin, since I, as usual, had slept naked, was something wrong? Mrs. Cox said no, she didn't think so, not now, lips pursing into a wizened smile. I pulled the sheet tighter and looked at Connie, back at Mrs. Cox, at Connie, standing in the doorway behind her, hand to her mouth and fear in her eyes. I thanked Mrs. Cox for coming and for being such a nice neighbor, and as soon as I heard the back door close I got up, slipped on a pair of pants and found my sister cowering behind a chair in the living room. What had she said to Mrs. Cox? Nothing. She'd damn well better tell me. Only that she couldn't wake me up. And? That she was worried. And? That I was dead. I lunged, but she made it to the door before I could catch her.

No, she said, she wasn't sorry about that and never would be. She tongued the spoon to get the last tastes of pudding from it, then swiped the inside of the bowl with her finger, sucked it clean and pointed it at me. Because nobody got hurt, did they? Embarrassed maybe, but not hurt. Hurt was something else entirely. She knew. She'd been hurt. Ron and Shelley and Bo had been hurt. Plenty. By that sonofabitch Mason. I knew about him, didn't I? I asked if she meant that he was crazy, and she said, well, yeah, that, too, but she was talking about the other stuff, and I said you mean carrying a loaded rifle in the trunk of his car? and she shook her head and I said what was this, some kind of guessing game, for chrissake, and she said she was talking about him having a boyfriend. I said, oh that, yeah, I'd heard some rumors—even Len had mentioned it—and she wanted to know what he'd said. Just that people were talking, I told her, and she said, well, it was true, she'd found a whole bunch of letters from another man, saying I want you I need you I miss you—just like some fucking soap opera. Jesus H. Christ.

Mason was her second husband, after Bax, and her third as well, since she'd married him twice, a divorce in between, which is not unimaginable in cases of undying passion or power or money. But I don't think those were at play in this situation. In fact, why she married Mason the first time is still a mystery to me, unless it had to do with her predilection for gathering and protecting wounded strays—dogs, cats, people. He was tall but too skinny to be attractive—scrawny, some people might say—with dangling arms and slightly bowed legs and a stoop to his walk, as if he were trying to lessen the effect of his height the way some women pull in their shoulders or hunch forward when they feel self-conscious about the size of their breasts. His face was hallow, almost sharp around his cheeks and jaw, and he had a constant Alfred E. Neuman what-me-worry smile that made you want to smack him or shake him by the tufts of wild, unruly hair that stuck out from beneath his baseball cap. He was full of tics, some body part always in motion, and jittery, narrow hazel eyes unable to settle on anything for long, like a squirrel, but without a squirrel's ambition. His primary concern seemed not to be how to keep his job at the trailer factory/cabinet shop/filling station (fill in the blank) so much as how to concoct yet another story with Connie about their desperate need for food money from mother/father/brother/grandmother (again, fill in the blank) to tide them over until Mason got paid/until they got their tax return/until the first/fifteenth/thirty-first, when her/his unemployment check would arrive.

That husband.

The one whose last known occupation was traveling the central and near western states maintaining and replacing highway billboards. It was then, Connie told me, that Mason met the other man (she had never said his name, at least in my presence, but we'll call him Travis) in a bar in some dusty eastern Colorado town (let's say La Junta). They had hit it off right away and Mason got the man on with his company and eventually as his assistant so they could travel and stay together on the road. Whenever Mason would come home, Travis would write letter after letter, which Connie never saw until the day she found them in Mason's sock drawer, piled up in plain sight like he'd meant for her to discover them. She was shocked, she said, devastated and cried for two days. She confronted him when he came home one Friday from being on the road. He denied everything, like any normal person would, until she read him a couple of the letters, and he told her that it was true but it was a thing of the past. He and Travis had broken off their affair and Connie didn't have anything to worry about now. She said she started throwing shoes, books, hairbrushes, clothes, whatever she could find, and he put his hands in front of his face and kept telling her to settle down, it was going to be all right—and she was, too. By that time, though, she said she was pitching ashtrays, a lamp, pots and pans, a vase of flowers and telling him that if he had fucking given her AIDS, she would kill him. And he said, no, she, there was no chance of that. He'd been tested and she could be, too, if it would make her feel better.

She said she did get the test, which turned out to be negative, and she was so relieved that she filed for divorce the same day, and when it was granted she told me she was the happiest she'd been since she could remember. And all seemed well with her and the kids for almost a year until the night Mason came over to tell her how sorry he was, how much he missed/wanted/needed her, how he couldn't live without her, and they got drunk, and— imagine her at the SPCA, staring at mongrels in the pen—she started feeling sorry for him (again), and they ended up, if you can believe it, sleeping together that night and the next and setting their new wedding date before he left to go back out on the road Sunday.

She wished someone—I imagine she had me in mind, but, as usual, I wasn't around—had stopped her, you know, hit her over the head, knocked some sense into her, because the miserable bastard didn't change a bit—why she'd ever believed him she had no idea—and, if anything, he was worse than before. He seemed to understand all too well what she was feeling—the overwhelming stupidity and shame at having made the same mistake twice (the guilt didn't come until later, she said)—and, with the brutal instincts of a wolf stalking its prey, he turned her humiliation into a self-loathing that deprived her of the will to leave him again. She said he told her almost daily that she was so fucking ugly she could never find another man, even if she tried, and she should goddamn well count her blessings that she had somebody as good as him. He told Bo and Ron and Shelley again and again how dumb and lazy and worthless they were. When anyone contradicted him, he reminded them that he didn't have a loaded rifle in the trunk of his car for nothing, so they should maybe think twice before shooting off their goddamn mouths— no pun intended, she assured me. To make matters worse, he was becoming an even more brazen faggot—her word, not mine—a world-class cocksucker—pun definitely intended. He hadn't touched her since the night after they remarried and even then she said he had to get drunk in order to go through with it and afterward curled up on the bed and wept. Our father was already dead, thank god, and our mother didn't know about him only because Connie swore everyone to secrecy.

Hold on, you say, wait a minute. This couldn't have happened, I'm making it up. Well, I'm not. I couldn't. You have to trust me. Believe me when I say that Connie was so dispirited she couldn't summon the will to save herself, or ultimately, her children, until it was too late and that she chose the easier path of booze and selective ignorance. You tell me that people don't have to go down that path, that some overcome even greater adversity and survive, and I say, yes, some people do. You also tell me that no one can be as bad as Mason, that there are always mitigating factors influencing people's behavior and why don't I include those? Why don't I write about his alcoholic stepfather and his suspected sexual abuse of Mason that later led to Mason's arrest for shooting bullet after bullet into his stepfather's house, or Huntington's chorea that eventually drove his mother mad, or the demons that must have haunted him about his own sexuality? Any one of those alone could drive a person to do things he might not otherwise, Mason included. It's the stuff of modern literature, after all, the fast-becoming-clichéd extra material novelists rely on to explain their characters' downfalls and egregious behaviors. And these are serious problems, real problems that, were I a stronger, better person, I would use to explain Mason. And I would forgive him. But I'm not that good. I can feel sorry for him. I can pity him. I can wonder at the depth of his sickness and depravity. And this doesn't have to do just with his sexual orientation. I don't care about that. How he lives his life is not my business nor anyone else's. But what he did to Connie is, and what he did to the kids is. The way he preyed on them, beginning in their first marriage, taking them slowly, one after the other, so that none of them knew until later, most definitely is my business.

Why else do you think Bo, years later, blew up at Connie and ran away, accusing her in his letter of allowing those things to happen? Where was she? Why didn't she stop him? She tried to explain, as she told me she told Bo, that she didn't know, hadn't the slightest idea what was going on. And just how, I know you're wondering, again like Bo, could that be possible? How she could live with someone that long and not be aware of what he was doing? How many excuses for him did she have to make up? How many lies did she have to tell herself and others? How many new lies did those lies breed before she became confused about what was true and what wasn't? What was real? And even now could she remember for certain which was which? Was that what she was sorry about—that she hadn't seen it sooner and by not seeing it had appeared to condone it? That she'd lost one son, and the other and her daughter were so wounded they refused to mention Mason, as though he were beyond dead and had never existed? Or was she merely sorry that she'd ever been born?

False Teeth and Trailer Houses

I don't remember when I realized that all the adults in my family had false teeth and that all of them had at one time or another lived in a trailer house. With the possible exception of Grandpa Doolan, our mother's father. I don't know that he ever lived in a trailer, and he didn't have false teeth—none that he would wear, at any rate. He said they hurt his mouth and refused to put them in even at mealtime, preferring instead to gum everything he ate, including steak and pork chops, pieces of which he wallowed around in his mouth until they became soft enough to swallow. But it didn't seem to hurt him. He stalemated me in arm wrestling when I was eighteen and he was in his seventies, and he lived through two wives to be ninety-one, claiming that his toothlessness gave him one clear advantage over everyone else: it made him a champion kisser.

For everyone else, though—Grandma and Grandpa Caulkins, our father and mother, Aunt Louise, Aunt Kate (our father's other sister), Uncle Boyd (our father's brother) and perhaps some of our mother's family whom we weren't as immediately close to—the connection between teeth and trailers held. During one lengthy period, in fact, after Connie became old enough to need her own room, Grandma Caulkins lived in a ten-foot wide, fifty-foot long, two-bedroom 1959 Midwest Mobile Home set on a permanent foundation on the lot we owned just north of our house. Aunt Kate and Aunt Louise lived with her off and on, usually separately and usually between husbands or during some other family crisis. Uncle Boyd had a thirty-foot, one-bedroom trailer—I forget the make and year—on the west side of Carter near the house Len would buy and raise his children in during happier times before his divorce. Our father and mother lived in a more luxurious twelve-wide 1964 American Mobile Home beside a lagoon east of New Orleans, which sounds more exotic than it was, due to snakes and mosquitoes and the fact that this would be the second house they would lose to high water, courtesy of Hurricane Camille.

The same predilection for trailer housing seemed to have carried over to the next generation as well, with the exception of Len, who lived in the aforementioned once happy pre-divorce house, after which he moved to the house we grew up in. But he did work in a trailer factory. And so did I, and so did Mason, for that matter. All of us at different times in final finish, where we put the cosmetic touches on the inside—mirrors, carpets, fancy handles on cabinets, those sorts of things—that drew the attention of buyers away from the half-assed assembly and cheap designs that made the places inherently more dangerous to live in than tents. But it was a job, and like any other job, as long as I didn't think about it too seriously, I could live with myself—the same rationale drug dealers must use, or mafia hitmen, or CEOs. A direct result of the experience for me (and maybe for Len as well, I'm not sure) was a firm vow on my part never to live in one of the damn things, which I should have known better than to make, since at about that same time Grandma Caulkins decided that she wouldn't live with us any longer in favor of Aunt Louise, with whom she felt she had a closer spiritual relationship. The problem with her plan, however, was that she was still paying on her trailer house and was going to lose it if she couldn't find someone to rent it to. All fingers pointed figuratively at me. I was finishing my first semester of graduate school in Wichita and was paying more rent than I could afford from my next-to-nothing stipend and she offered her trailer for half what I was spending. Money once again winning over principle, I said yes. Our father arranged to have the unit moved and installed in a trailer park behind a sleazy stretch of bars on North Broadway that were in competition over who could produce the biggest go-go mamas, starting weight three hundred pounds, to dance Friday and Saturday nights. It wasn't what I would call an ideal location, but it did allow me to go from eating French toast as a special treat on paydays to Spanish rice, with hamburger occasionally mixed in. It was also where I brought my new wife the next summer to join me in marriage and graduate school. We stayed there a year, then fled the country, only to find ourselves living until our house was built in a much smaller caravan camping trailer near the front steps of the school in Africa where we had gone to teach. Grandma Caulkins' ten-wide seemed luxurious.

But Connie was the real trailer queen. She lived in at least three different ones, starting with our father's and mother's in New Orleans. I don't know whether she and Bax ever had one, but she and Mason did on the north side of Carson, behind the Dairy Deluxe, just beyond the city limits because Mason had decided he couldn't live any longer without a horse. Not to mention pigs and chickens and god knows how many stray cats and mangy dogs. It was an El Dorado sixty-foot doublewide they could ill-afford—a decent enough place, if you ignored the shag carpeting, dark paneling and boxy appearance—that provided room for the two of them and by then three kids—Bo from her marriage to Bax and two with Mason—Ron and Shelley— (meaning they had to have had sex at least twice, right?). But lack of money had never stood in their way before, and they somehow talked our mother into giving them enough for the down payment—you couldn't honestly call it a loan since loans usually get paid back—and afterward offered Mason's father room and board in the new house if he would pick up the mortgage payments. So Mason had his house, his animals, his wife and kids. What more could a man ask for?

After Mason came Sammo. He and Connie have had no children together, although to hear them tell it, they fuck like minks. They lived in a trailer soon after they were married— third husband, third trailer?—a dilapidated black and white Windsor ten-wide parked diagonally along with four others in similar shape. A wire fence enclosed a grassless yard beside it, where two dogs prowled back and forth over the same path, barking and growling at the slightest sound or movement.

Inside, the roof leaked badly enough in several places that white plastic five-gallon paint buckets were lined up to catch rain water. Electricity was out in half of the trailer, and only two of four burners worked on the kitchen stove, although it wasn't clear that those problems were related. The furnace was on the fritz, the toilet bowl was loose so water seeped out and buckled the bathroom floor. The whole place reeked of cigarette smoke and spent butts. A console TV in the corner of the living room was on constantly to the weather channel, muted. They'd told the landlady several times about the problems they were having, and she promised to have them taken care of. Sammo said at the time that he was fed up and was thinking of moving, just as soon as he could figure out how to come up with a down payment.

You're right, I am repeating myself. First, Mason and now Sammo and the down payment? Different characters, same circumstances. Both going around and around in desperate circles, with nearly enough but not quite, thinking they've almost got it, they've almost got it, like dogs chasing their tails.

Dogs? Connie'll say when she reads this. What a fucking snot. Have I ever been in a situation where I honest to god didn't know where the next meal was coming from, where to turn for help? If not, then what makes me so goddamn smart? What makes me think I know everything about everybody? And I'm not supposed to tell her it's fiction, I can say whatever I want because it's just a story, with made-up people and made-up lives, we both fucking know that's not true. It's her story, her life, and if I'm going to tell it, I'd better goddamn well tell it the way she wants it. I'll remind her that wasn't our original agreement, which was that I would tell the story as honestly and objectively as I could—but as *I* saw it, not anyone else. And she'll ask if that gives me the right to call people stupid, toothless dogs? I'll throw up my hands and say fuck it then, and she'll say exactly, and that'll be that. Except we'll never have this conversation.

Bearing Tidings

Dr. James J. Jameson III was generally considered the best thoracic surgeon in the region and expected his patients to appreciate his reputation. He was an imposing man with a Roman nose, hollow cheeks and strong jaw and, according to Connie, perfect skin and teeth. Steel grey hair helmeted his head and his clothes had the soft rustle of money. People said he drove a Mercedes sports car through a back entrance of the parking garage in order to avoid encountering his patients outside the hospital.

The first question he'd asked Connie in his office was whether she still smoked, and she said yes, but really not for all practical purposes: she was down to two cigarettes a day. And that, he said, in a nutshell was why he didn't like to treat smokers at all: they obviously didn't care whether they lived or died. Oh, she wanted to live all right, he shouldn't get her wrong about that. If so, he told her, she had to quit smoking now, period, no ands ifs or buts about it, and she said okay, even though she mostly wanted to laugh at buts. She didn't, of course—he didn't seem to be in a joking mood—and he turned directly from her to Sammo and asked him about his smoking. Sammo said he'd cut way back, too, and Dr. Jameson rolled his eyes—he honest to god did, she said—and told him if he had to smoke, it was to be outside. Connie didn't need any of that second-hand crap—she just knew he'd wanted to say shit but couldn't bring himself to do it. He said she was going to have a hard enough time as it was breathing with one lung, she didn't need any extra challenges.

Dr. Jameson examined her then and looked at the x-rays and said he couldn't tell for certain what the situation was, so she would need to have a pulmonary function exam, a brain scan and a PET scan. The first was to determine if she could, in fact, survive with one lung. The second was to see if she had brain lesions, since the brain is one of the primary sites lung cancer spreads to. The third was to see whether cancer had appeared anywhere else in her body. When those tests were complete, they would talk again.

Within a week, he called Connie and told her everything looked good for going ahead with the operation, he was scheduling her for the following Monday. The sooner they got in there, the better, right? And even though he couldn't be certain what he would find when he opened her up, he still felt surgery was the best course of action, because if he did nothing, she would be dead in six months. So of course she agreed. When he put it in those terms, she didn't think she had a hell of a lot of choice.

I've wondered since, as I did then, what was going through Dr. Jameson's mind just before he pushed open the surgical suite doors on his way out to talk to us that morning after Connie's surgery. I doubt that he was feeling sorry—he hadn't promised anything and had done nothing wrong—nor would he have been angry about being duped, since, as he'd said, he wouldn't know what was what until he got in there and looked around. Sad, then? But about what? Us having to get bad news, Connie having to face a dismal future, himself having to deal with failure? No, not failure, not him. Failure was a concept he didn't seem capable of entertaining, ever. I do like to think that he was at least perplexed by her case and perhaps even disappointed in its outcome. But if he was, he didn't show it. He didn't show anything at all.

Our father the old man said he'd wanted to be a doctor for as long as he could remember. He said when he was about seven or eight he used to hide summer mornings in a ditch to wait for Dr. Glickman to drive by en route to his office in Colony, where our father's family had moved from Chanute so Grandpa Caulkins could work in the gas fields. Dr. Glickman drove a Model A Ford, and our father could hear it coming a half mile away and ready himself to jump out of the ditch and race the car the remaining quarter of a mile to town. He always lost, but that didn't matter, he said. He would run along behind the car and by the time he reached the office, Dr. Glickman would have parked and begun gathering his bag and whatever else he needed for the day. Our father would sit under a tree across the street to catch his breath as Dr. Glickman went through his routine of pulling out his watch to check the time, patting his pocket for a key and unlocking his office door to go inside. Within a few minutes, the first patients would arrive, and our father said he would spend the rest of the morning imagining what was happening with them—what Dr. Glickman was doing and saying and recommending as treatment.

He was never able to say for sure where his interest in being a doctor came from, but it was real and didn't go away all through high school and his first semester of college, where he'd enrolled in a pre-med program. But the Depression hit. Grandpa Caulkins lost his job and he and our father began working as field hands, carpenters, milkers at a local dairy farm, whatever jobs they could find, at best being paid fifty cents a day, at worst eggs or cheese or fresh vegetables, maybe an old hen. Eventually our father left home and joined the WPA, intermittently riding the rails, as they say, from Kansas to California and back. By the time the economy showed signs of righting itself, our father had returned to Kansas, found steady work at a dairy and bought himself a used Harley Knucklehead, on which he cruised the countryside, attracted our mother, took her for a few thrilling rides, they both said. Before long, they got married and had us, and somewhere in the midst of all that becoming a doctor faded, entering the realm of what he would do if he could live life over again.

I would be curious to know, even at that, what kind of doctor he would have been. Not what specialty, although I would guess, given his impatience and sense that no one could do anything as well as he, that he, too, might have thrived as a surgeon. So in a different life, and without his being our father, Connie's father, what would he have said when he came through those doors?

How would he have acted? I don't believe he would have been as imperious as Dr. Jameson, since a good bit of that comes from what one learns to expect from life. But on the other hand, it's difficult to imagine him as Dr. Welby, either, the warm, all-wise-yet-forgiving patron of the medical arts. Somewhere in the middle, I suppose, which is where the great majority of us end up, isn't it, no matter how self-confident we are, or how lost?

A Revelation Perhaps

Inoperable. That was what he said, Dr. James J. Jameson III. A heavy, clumsy word that didn't fit well in mouth or mind. One that tormented from the moment he uttered it, like gristle you can't swallow or spit out. In-op-er-a-ble. In=not; opera=work; ble=able to. Not operable, not fixable, not workable. Operant word: NOT.

Late the morning after Connie's surgery, once she had been transferred from the recovery room back to the ward, Sammo, Jim, Sally, Janice and I gathered around her bed, sitting and standing as we could, watching her sleep. If you could call it that. It was more a drug-induced moaning and writhing, tubes and lines undulating away from her in a sympathetic tremor. There was the oxygen tube, with its two little prongs, one up each nostril; the morphine drip hooked to the port in the PICC Line, the clicker for it lying within reach of her right hand; a saline and glucose drip, the bag sharing the stand with the morphine; drainage tubes from the incision carrying fluid and blood to a disposal bag hung on the side of the bed; a catheter line down to another bag at the foot of the bed; and there were monitor lines running from leads on her chest to the blipping screen above her head; a blood pressure cuff on her arm that inflated periodically and released, like someone wheezing. Nurses came and went, a subaltern of Dr. Jameson's stopped by to see how the patient was doing, a respiratory therapist checked her breathing, house-keeping took out trash and swept under our feet. No one talked much, other than to inquire about who was okay, who wanted to sit down, or to announce who was going to the bathroom or on a food or smoke break. People tend not to talk much in the presence of pain. And she was in pain. We could hear it, see it in her face, watch it move in waves along her limbs as we did what we could to distance ourselves from it—watched the nearly mute TV, dozed, concentrated on hallway traffic, played electronic solitaire. Occasionally, a moan would reach a crescendo that commanded our attention, and we would glance in unison at Connie, then retreat to our diversions.

She told me later that she'd been dreaming of snakes, water snakes like the kind she saw swimming in the lagoon beside the trailer park where she lived with our mother and father east of New Orleans. There were always a few around, she said, but whenever a storm approached from the Gulf, they came in droves, inland from the tidal marshes. She remembered dozens of them at a time ribboning the water, some going through the culvert under the highway to the swamp on the other side, others slithering up the bank and across the hot pavement. Every day the highway would be littered with their carcasses, and every day there would be stories in the news of drivers bitten by snakes that somehow got flipped into open car windows as tires passed over them. In her dream, she was the highway and the snakes were crawling over her—water moccasins, black snakes, diamondbacks, yellow-bellies and, oddly enough, woolly cater-pillars, behind them a dark, brooding anvil of clouds pressing the water ever higher, wave after wave crowned with snake-heads flowing toward her. Until then, she said she had not been sympathetic enough with our father, who, some thirty or so years earlier, had had heart by-pass surgery and had become delirious during a difficult recovery and believed he had been abducted by aliens and taken aboard their ship where they were performing medical experiments on him, a situation that made considerable sense, given that he had worked on the Saturn V project which was instrumental in the first manned lunar landing.

Connie groaned, arching her chest, as though into or away from something only she could sense, eyelids fluttering open, closing again as she sagged back against the bed. Sally said poor thing and Janice said it looked like she was waking up and I said maybe a little but it would take a while. Jim and Sammo said nothing.

The evening before, Dr. Jameson had stopped by for his pre-op consultation and gone over with her (and us, presumably, but that wasn't clear) what she could expect. At the end, he asked her how she was doing and she said fine and he wanted to know if she was ready and she nodded at him and tried to smile. He gripped her foot, which was tenting the blanket at the end of the bed and told her that was great, he wished everyone he operated on had that attitude, that kind of pluck. He spoke with the same sense of you-can-will-your-way-through-this-if-you-really-want-to that my sons' high school football coach had used to motivate his players. Those who gave beyond the limit of their endurance and carried on regardless of pain he called gamers. Everybody wanted to be a gamer, to be recognized as one. And, shit yes, Connie was a gamer. Was she ever. She had pluck and game and whatever the fuck else it took for her not to pull out a gun and kill that sonofabitch Jameson and any other sonofabitch she took a mind to, then turn the gun on herself. Which didn't make sense in the least, but neither did much else.

I had to leave before I said or did something I might regret. I was pissed, plain old pissed. At everybody around that bed, at doctors and coaches and idiots in general, Connie included, and at myself. For being there and wishing I weren't and not knowing quite why—she was my sister, after all, and she needed me, or at least said she did, although who knows whether she meant need in an emotional or manipulative sense. Which was precisely the problem, the not knowing, never knowing which prong of the fork she was pricking me with and my resentment over finding myself in such a position to begin with, hating myself for being so easy yet selfish, so available yet distant, so apparently caring—hadn't Sally and Jim both said how wonderful and thoughtful it was for me to have come?—yet indifferent to the point I realized that if Connie weren't my sister, we would have nothing in common, no reason ever to have met, let alone develop any sort of friendship. So, yeah, I needed in the worst way to get the fuck out of there, and I told everyone I was going to the lobby or somewhere to call Len and my wife and let them know Connie was out of surgery and doing okay, I'd be back later. Janice glanced up like a puppy wanting to go out for a walk, and I went over to where she perched on the windowsill and said in a low voice that I needed her to stay there and keep an eye on Connie, if she knew what I meant, and she nodded, tapping her temple with her finger and said kidneys and I said you bet your bippy and left, wishing with all that was within me that I would never have to go back.

A Form of Forgetting

I don't know how well Connie remembers herself as a child. She was cute as hell, even as a baby, with teal eyes—not the ice blue of Len's—blonde hair and an impish smile no one could resist, and I hated her for it. Is that too strong a word? Would resented be better? Or saying I was jealous of her, or that I wished she'd never been born? I was eight years old, running on raw emotions, fueled somewhat, I'm sure, by my overhearing our mother and father say that Connie had been a mistake, not knowing at the time what that meant exactly but understanding full well that if something was a mistake, you could take it back, get rid of it. But no one seemed inclined to do that, and the longer she stayed around, the more people became attached to her and ignored me. My indignation grew to the point that one afternoon I threw a fit and kicked a wheel off of Connie's crib when our mother refused to let me go downtown to a movie with Len and his friends, and I started screaming how much I hated her and Connie and everybody else. Our father must have heard me, even from the garage out by the alley, where he had gone to get into the car to drive to work, because before I had so much as drawn a breath to start in again, the back door flew open and there he was. He looked at the crib wobbling on three wheels, at me, and in one motion, grabbed me by the arm, draped me over his knee and began paddling me so hard I was told his hand hurt for a week.

Anger is a condition Caulkins males seem to inherit as surely as ear shape and nose hair. Our grandfather's temper was notorious. It's said that a cow once stepped on his foot while he was milking her and he got so mad he ran around to face the animal and hit her with his fist as hard as he could, directly between her eyes. The cow's front legs buckled and she went straight down and nearly died. Another time (this account was verified by our grandmother who says she was there), our grandfather was crank-starting their Model A Ford and it backfired, whipping the crank out of his hand and up against his arm. He howled and stomped around the car, kicking and pummeling it, swearing youbitchyoubitchyoubitch until he had ripped off all four fenders and the headlamps and thrown them aside like so much junk.

Uncle Boyd, our father's brother, was a yeller. He married five times, each wife in succession saying he was so prone to sudden outbursts of rage that he was impossible to live with, although he was never accused of striking anyone. After his final divorce, he was arrested for spraying the inside of a diner and his waitress with ketchup because he felt she wasn't paying enough attention to him.

Our father lashed out both physically—primarily at me, for some reason, like the beating I got for ruining Connie's crib or Thanksgiving dinner the year I was twelve when he didn't like the way I looked at him and backhanded me from across the table, knocking me out of my chair and against a wall—and verbally, like when he argued with our mother, usually over money or lack thereof. On Friday or Saturday nights after Len and I (and later, Connie) had gone to bed, we would hear them talking, but never in soft, comfortable tones. Instead, their voices crackled like paper being wadded to throw, always growing louder and louder, culminating in shouts and scuffles as our father the old man tried to get the car keys from our mother who said he had no business on the road in his condition, meaning he had been drinking (again) and she was afraid he might kill himself, or worse, someone else. The fights invariably ended with him getting the keys, and he would stomp out amidst shouting and door slamming and not show up until the next day, contrite, asking everyone's forgiveness, it would never happen again, and would I please, please rub his back, it hurt so much, and I would because I knew he would go to sleep where he was on the floor and it would be over then until the next weekend.

But none of this was real anger. It was pathetic blustering, whimpering, raging at the wind. Real anger is an exquisite pain, a grand emotion worthy of articulation on the highest level. We should sing arias to anger, capture it on canvas, create the most impassioned prose and verse we can in its honor, rather than debase it by the tawdry displays of our father and grandfather and Uncle Boyd, who might as well have worn the cheap neon-colored t-shirt that says Approach with Care: I'm Pissed Already.

Like Connie will be when she reads this. Only she won't get loud and yell and throw things. She'll sulk. And whine and sigh, and call me a selfish shit because all I do is write about myself—mememe, in her best mocking voice—when it's supposed to be her story, the one she asked me to tell, remember. But I don't know how else to do it. For the story to be hers, it has to be mine first. It can only be hers as it comes to me, hers as I remember it. How else, for example, would you ever know that our father thought freeway interchanges, with their layered looping steel and concrete spans, were the most beautiful creations on earth? Because I'm the one who asked him, and he told me, not Connie, not you. Okay, you're saying, maybe so, but what does his aesthetics have to do with her or her life? Steel and concrete, remember, precision, perfection, replicable feats of genius, an appreciation—love—of logic and predictability that totally disappeared when it came to his dealings with Len and Connie and me and our mother, all of whom, with the exception of her, he succeeded in driving from home.

Len was the first to go. He'd started college—pre-engineering, at the insistence of our father the old man, who had decided for him that a career in engineering would provide the job security and income he would need to be successful, neither of which our father felt he had achieved himself. When Len decided enough was fucking enough and dropped out after his first semester, our father the old man wanted to know what the hell was wrong with him, didn't he have any sense, why there were people who would die for a chance to be in his shoes. And so on. And so forth. Len said he didn't care, he was joining the Navy so he could see the world (read: get the hell away from here). Honest to god, he did say that. He trained in Chicago and was stationed first in San Diego then in Las Vegas, where he spent most of his time. That's right, in the middle of the fucking desert, as he said. In the Navy, in the desert. He'd hated it, too, couldn't wait till he got out, and when he did, married Josie, had kids, got divorced and is now— What? It's too easy to say he's dying, although he is, we all are, but he really is, quicker than the rest of us, except maybe for Connie, and with more determination.

I was next. I went to college, majored in English, of all things, then set off to graduate school and a master's degree in more of the same and finally stopped with a second master's degree in, god help me, creative writing. But after the fiasco with Len, our father the old man more or less left me alone. Worthless as he must have considered my degrees and pursuits, he never criticized, never belittled what I did—for two reasons, I believe: first, I married a woman who eventually became a doctor, vicariously fulfilling his dream, and second, unlike Connie and Len, I never went back to Carter to live, thus breaking the pathological family-first cycle that was valued above all else, regardless the cost emotionally.

With Connie, our father the old man reverted to more direct methods. She had no desire to go to college, and that drove him to distraction. He pleaded, bargained, even bribed her with an offer of a car, if she'd agree to go. But nothing changed her mind. She had Bax and he was all she wanted. Then. And now? Who knows. Now, nothing would make a difference, nothing would bring back what she is going to lose.

Care and Feeding

As soon as I came in the door, she asked if I could smell soup, pizza, fried catfish, red beans and rice, lasagna, fresh bread, cheddar cheese so sharp it burned your mouth, vanilla ice cream with chocolate syrup, hot coffee, apple pie, turkey and dressing, a big juicy steak on the grill. God she was hungry, hungrier than she'd ever been, when were they going to give her something to eat, or didn't I care either, like everybody else? We should all be ashamed, little children starving to death, ribs sticking out, flies buzzing around their faces, jesus, oh, sweet jesus, click-click on the morphine drip, her eyeballs like peeled white grapes rolling up, lids closing, Nurse Kim, back on duty, her body knifed over Connie's bed, saying not to worry, lots of patients hallucinate after surgery, she would come out of it soon, and Sammo saying he for one had heard enough, he had to get the fuck out of there, and when no one, not even Sally told him (again) not to use that kind of language, he got angrier and stood, barely managing not to throw down his electronic solitaire game and said all right, all right, if nobody gave a shit he didn't either, he was fucking going outside for a fucking cigarette. But I held up my hand and said before he did, could I ask him something, since I'd gotten there later than he, and he cocked his head to one side, long hair hanging like a dirty dark curtain, and said okay but I should hurry up, he didn't have all day, and I asked whether he thought she realized, a quick glance at Connie, and he wanted to know if I meant that they hadn't gotten it all, and I nodded and he said yeah, hell yes, she knew, and I asked how he could be so sure, and he said because he was, that was all. You could just tell when you'd been with somebody long enough, you could feel it, you didn't have to goddamn talk each other to death to find out. Everyone stopped what they were doing or not doing and watched Sammo the way you did someone you have suddenly realized is crazy and potentially dangerous to you or himself. Jim, Sally, Janice, even Nurse Kim, who was standing now at her full height, eyes narrowed. I wanted to ask her now if she thought Sammo would come out of it the way she'd said Connie would, whether any of us would and how she went day to day dealing with cases like Connie's and people like us, whether she relied for support on her family, her husband, if she were married, her god, whispering give me strength, lord, as we all did at one time or another, reflexively, without thinking what we'd said/asked/prayed for, devout and secular alike, because believe in it or not, you occasionally needed something, someone out there to solicit help from or to blame. Like Sammo. Poor sap had no idea what to think or do besides smoke. Not that he didn't care for Connie. He did. You could see it in the near tears in his eyes, you could feel it, like he said, even if maybe he couldn't or didn't want to say it. But he somehow showed her he loved her enough that she called him her rock, didn't she? Enough that she looked at him with a lover's eyes. Enough that their hands touched gently, with affection. Even though I couldn't tell how he did it, I appreciated what he had given her, and when he repeated that he thought yeah, she knew, she knew all right and pushed past me toward the door, I simply said thanks and stepped aside.

What If

It should have been be a comforting picture but wasn't—Connie lying there, resting peacefully—because if you take away her breathing and the hospital bed and the lines connecting her to this and that, you'd have pretty much what she'd look like dead. At times, as I'm drifting off to sleep, I find myself in a similar pose, hands folded, fingers interlaced on my chest, head back slightly on the pillow, legs straight out—like a corpse, I think, like every corpse I've ever seen, stiff and posed, instead of in a more natural position with my arms cocked behind my head, say, or lying on my side, hands pillowed under my cheek—and I jar myself awake so I can shake the feeling that I'm on view, people filing by to pay their final respects, and focus instead on the wagon wheel shadow cast by the streetlight through the round window at the top of the bedroom wall, until I can clearly see and count and recount the number of spokes—six—satisfying myself that I am in my home in my bed next to my wife and am not dead nor, as far as I know, even close to it.

I wish I could have as easily controlled my vision of Connie, shaken my head and said okay, that was enough, it was time to get on to something else. But I couldn't. No matter what I did or thought, it lingered as a backdrop, like a stupid song lyric or a bad taste and brought back strange memories of long, sultry summer afternoons at the local Carnegie Library, where I sat hunched on the floor in the stacks, poring over book after book on paranormal psychology and their endless plates depicting séances with non-corporeal beings hovering about, or the recurrent nightmare I'd had around that same time about Grandma Caulkins in a coffin at Moreland's Funeral Home in Carter. It was always at night, after hours, and I always entered the building without opening a door that I knew of, and once I was inside everything became hushed and muffled and the air smelled of flowers in first wilt, and I somehow, without walking as such, moved through the empty vestibule to a short flight of stairs and up them to a small, dim room where I knew someone was, although I never remembered who. The door always stood open, and I stopped at the threshold and saw the casket and heard from somewhere else—a different room, a different dream, perhaps?—a soft swell of eerie, mournful music, and I made myself stretch out as tall as I could and peer over the edge of the casket, and I saw Grandma's face, powdered and grey and dead, just like Grandpa's had been, her wispy white hair teased around her head, hands folded. I could hardly breathe, and movement was out of the question, and I kept wondering what she was doing there because I had just seen her in her room on my way to bed, and her eyelids flickered and her mouth began working, as though she were trying to moisten her lips enough to part them, and her hands unfolded, her left floating in my direction, until it turned palm up, its finger beckoning me toward the casket, and despite myself, I began gliding forward, as though propelled by some other force, and her head lifted from its satin pad, eyes locking on me, and I mercifully awoke, a scream stuck in my throat.

I don't think of myself as morbid, and gloomy as the scene with Connie might appear, it wasn't unrealistic. Her odds of living were not good. I knew, I'd looked up the figures before I came, since that way I could think about them and not her or her kids or Sammo or Len or me, for that matter, not to mention everyone else who knew and cared for her. I could make a silly game of her condition and sound like I had control because I could cite specific studies done at specific medical centers that produced specific numbers and percentages that in the end all pointed to the same basic conclusion: fewer than ten percent of all people diagnosed with lung cancer survive more than five years. Which means that ninety percent die, as in stop living, despite their treatment regimen. And Connie will get the best. Even with an inoperable tumor, Dr. Jameson will remind us of what he said right after surgery: that she most likely will benefit from aggressive treatment under the care of an oncologist, whom he will recommend. In light of her age and the possibility of enhanced quality of life—no mention of the word cure, mind you—she will be administered a multiple drug chemotherapy cocktail (hence, the need for a Porta Cath) with concurrent radiation treatments twice a day for three weeks, which has in other cases provided improved benefits for the recipient but also has carried greater health risks. Small-cell lung cancer (the type Connie has) is quite responsive to treatment, so most patients experience immediate shrinkage of their tumors. A fair number achieve complete clinical remission. Connie will be one of them and consequently will be recommended for prophylactic cranial irradiation, during which doctors will administer radiation therapy to her brain to discourage the development of tumors there, because that is where the disease reappears at one time or another in virtually all lung cancer patients and will in her case as well. Connie will live longer than anyone suspects, given the initial extent of her disease, but she, too, will succumb.

And then what? That wasn't something I'd talked to her about—what she wanted done after she died. I had assumed she and Sammo had thrashed that out between them, but I didn't know, and it worried me. For one thing, there was no place to bury her. The family plot at Chanute was full, with Grandpa and Grandma Caulkins there, our father and our mother, Uncle Boyd. The final two spots had been penciled in with Aunt Louise's and Aunt Kate's names, although they had been living in Texas for years and rarely returned to Kansas. I had no idea if Connie felt any other place was home enough to be buried there, nor did I know what she felt about cremation.

On the other hand...if I were to tap into the rarely summoned optimistic side of myself, I would have remembered what Dr. Jameson had said—Dr. James J. Jameson III, mind you, son and grandson of physicians, graduate of Carleton College, Harvard Medical School and a surgery residency at Johns Hopkins Hospital—that same Dr. Jameson had said Connie had pluck, hadn't he? And hadn't he implied that pluck counted for a lot in these cases? And maybe it did. Maybe I hadn't given pluck the credit it deserved. Maybe if she had enough of it, she could in fact make it into the top ten percent, the ones who survive five years. And if five, why not ten, or fifteen, or twenty? By then she would probably have outlived Len and me and could die of a heart attack or Alzheimer's like everyone else. So, why not imagine for a moment that she does live, that she experiences what she would call a miracle and spends the rest of her days thanking god for every breath she takes? Why not imagine that Sammo doesn't kill himself out of despair and he and Connie live happily ever after in contentment and financial security? Why not imagine that we could begin taking deep breaths that aren't depressive sighs, that we could smile at one another and really mean it, that we could come to love each other in a way that we could express more deeply than saying loveya; love you, too? Why not imagine that because of her new lease on life and the attitude changes it brings in her that this story can end other than I've been thinking it would? Or not.

On the Lighter Side

Once when I was a kid, maybe eight or nine, our father's sister, Aunt Kate, who at that time was known for her loose and reckless personal life, had been drinking vodka all afternoon (a form of liquor that made her predictably unpredictable); and she told me a joke that she thought hilarious. I laughed at her laughing and she thought I was reacting to the joke, even though I had no idea what it meant, so she said I should go share it with my parents, which I did. When our father and our mother heard it, they tried not to laugh but couldn't help it. They finally asked where I'd heard such a joke, and I said Aunt Kate had told it to me, which she of course denied and asked what they took her for, some kind of pervert? They all laughed again and had quite a conversation about what was and was not appropriate to say around a child, Aunt Kate offering that most everything was okay, except maybe for the F-word, she'd never really liked the F-word, if they knew what she meant. She just got tired of F-this and F-that, and our mother and our father agreed, and after a while they all quieted down and our father and Aunt Kate had a drink together.

The joke doesn't seem as funny now:

—What did the woman say after riding her bicycle along a cobblestone street?

Answer: I'm never going to come that way again.

I told you.

There were other jokes as well. Some still bring a smile, and some are plain stupid: For example,

—Do you know why the chicken crossed the road?

Answer: To get to the other side.

Admit it, you're laughing or at least smiling, aren't you?

—I scream, you scream, we all scream for ice cream!

—Why did the elephant wear sunglasses?

Answer: So he wouldn't be recognized.

—What do you get when you cross a snowman with a vampire?

Answer: Frostbite.

—Why did the elephant cross the road?

Answer: It was the chicken's day off.

See what I mean?

—Knock-knock!

Who's there?

Madam.

Madam who?

Madam foot is caught in the door.

Drum roll, please!

—Do you smoke after sex?

Answer: I don't know, I never looked.

Go on, now, laugh behind your hand.

—What is black and white and red all over?

Answer: A newspaper.

—What is black and white and goes Thump! Thump! Thump!

Answer: A nun falling down the stairs.

—What did the elephant say to the naked man?

Answer: How do you breathe through that thing?

I'll stop for a minute while you catch your breath.

—Student writing home: No mon, no fun, your son.

Father writing back: Too bad, so sad, your dad.

—Mommy, Mommy! Why is daddy so pale?

Answer: Shut up and keep digging!

—An attractive young woman walks into a bar and approaches a middle-age man. She tells him that for $200 she'll do anything he asks. Anything? he says. Anything. Okay, then, he says, paint my house.

Tell me you still have a straight face.

—Bumper sticker: Jesus saves. . .passes to Moses, shoots, SCORES!

—Knock-knock!

Who's there?

Dexter.

Dexter who?

Dexter halls with boughs of holly.

I warned you, didn't I, some of them were stupid?

—Bumper sticker: Support your local undertaker—drop dead!

—Where does a 500-pound gorilla sleep?

Answer: Anywhere he wants.

—Want to know how to lose ten pounds of ugly fat?

Answer: Cut off your head.

Stupid and tasteless.

—Knock-knock!

Who's there?

One shoe.

One shoe who?

One shoe come home, Bill Bailey?

More drums, please.

—A guy goes to his doctor for a check-up. After some tests, the doctor comes in with a grave look on his face.

Doctor: I have some bad news and some really bad news.

Patient: Well, give me the really bad news first.

Doctor: You have cancer and only six months to live.

Patient: Then what's the bad news?

Doctor: You also have Alzheimer's disease.

Patient: Thank god, I was afraid I had cancer.

Keep going, it gets better.

—A customer asks his waiter how the cooks prepare the chicken. The waiter says they don't do anything special; they tell them right off that they're going to die.

But. . .

—Whenever I feel blue, I start breathing again.

And. . .

—Despite the cost of living, have you noticed how popular it remains?

One final thing to remember. . .

—If the world didn't suck, we'd all fall off.

The Reason for Spring

The last day of my visit, I arrived at the hospital early in order to spend as much time as possible with Connie and to catch Dr. Jameson when he made his rounds, the timing of which was unpredictable at best, coming either before surgery or just after or in between, depending, although on what no one seemed to understand. I was determined not to miss him, however, and when Connie, who had just finished breakfast (such as it was, she said, followed by a sardonic curl of the lip), began asking if someone would go to the vending machine to get her a snack, I opted out and offered Sammo money instead, if he didn't mind. He looked at me, at Connie, at me again, as though unclear what was being asked, until she said please in her sweetest girly voice and he stood stiffly, inch by inch, like a seventy-five-year-old, dropping his electronic solitaire game on the chair as a marker. She said she wanted something good, something gooey and chocolate, and he said he'd see what he could find but that he was going to step outside first to get some fresh air. She told him all right, but not to take forever, she was hungry, remember, and she didn't need to hear any smartass remarks about that, either. He shook his head and hitched his pants and had no more than cleared the doorway into the hall when she turned to me and said that as bad as he was at times, she didn't know how she could ever get along without him, her eyes suddenly brimming with tears, or how he would be able to get along without her. I said I didn't think she needed to worry about either thing happening any time soon, and she said she hoped I was right. She hoped we all grew old and crotchety together, Len included, and I said I did, too. Really? she asked, and I said what the hell was that all about, and she said nothing, she didn't mean anything, she was just being stupid, and I said, no, she had to tell me what she meant. She said she didn't want to argue my last day there, she wanted things to be peaceful for once, and I said it seemed a little late for that.

She teared, chin puckering, quivering, bottom lip dancing a jerky rhythm against her upper. I sat back, took a deep breath, which I let out slowly so it wouldn't sound like a sigh, and told her I was listening. The problem was, she said finally, and this was what she'd meant, she supposed: it was hard to tell whether I cared—about her or Len or any of the rest of them—and if she was wrong and I did, she still couldn't tell how much. She sometimes got the feeling that I really didn't like them—the way they looked, talked, acted, what?—and would just as soon not be around them. I told her I had no idea what she was talking about and she said it wasn't just her, other people had noticed, too, and had said things to her which she'd tried to explain away, like I wasn't a snot, and I wasn't trying to avoid them. I said that was exactly right, I wasn't, and besides when I did visit—from halfway across the country, I added—did any of them make even the slightest effort to come see me while I was there? Hell, no. Not me or my wife, I told her. What was it? Did we have some damn disease or something people were afraid they'd catch? Did she remember the times we'd flown or driven in to see our mother and our father when they were still alive and we'd been told by them that Len, for example, who lived five or six blocks away at that time—and her, Connie, too, for that matter, although to be fair, she did live fifty miles from Carter—were waiting for us to come see them, instead of vice versa, which would have seemed to me to have made more sense under the circumstances? Did she remember that? And, besides, I was there now, wasn't I? Hadn't I come when she'd asked? (Begged, wheedled, cajoled might have been better terms to use, although I wasn't going to.)

Yes, she said, and then added but—the word dangling like a bauble before a kitten—I was going to leave, wasn't I, like I always did? and I said that, yes, according to my plane ticket I was, and she told me I could change it and I said, yes, for a hundred bucks I could and would if I thought it necessary, but given that things were looking up for her and the fact that my wife was off in a couple of days for a week-long business trip and that I needed to get back to my own work, I wasn't going to. She rolled her head away, a pained expression on her face, what remained of her lines and tubes clinking against the bed rail for emphasis, and I told myself to be calm, since I knew the next question long before she asked it in a barely audible voice: when was I coming back? I said I didn't know and she said she hoped it would be for something besides a funeral or to gather around another sick bed, and I agreed and she added as a calculated afterthought that when I did, I might want to consider staying more than my usual day or two, a ripple of a smile passing her lips to signal that she knew I knew no matter how long I stayed it wouldn't be long enough. Even if I lived there, at her beck and call every minute of every day, it wouldn't be enough. No matter what I did or said, it would never be enough.

I didn't say what I was thinking. That wouldn't have done any good and I told her instead that I would see what I could do, although I couldn't guarantee anything. She said she understood, she just wanted me to know I was welcome any time for however long I could manage, but I didn't need to worry, she wasn't planning to die any time soon. I said I hoped not—that word again, that troublesome, troublesome word—and she said she, in fact, was going to outlive us all, if we weren't careful, and I said that wouldn't surprise me in the least, and she hesitated for a moment but said nothing.

And into the silence shambled Sammo, as though he'd been standing in the wings waiting for a cue to make his entry. Connie reached out to him with a flourish fit for a returning hero and asked what he'd brought and he gave a Snickers bar, which she held up to the light, turning it over and over, before unwrapping it halfway and nibbling back and forth across the end like a squirrel eating a nut, finishing only moments before Dr. Jameson appeared with Jim, Sally, Janice and two surgical resident doctors in tow and told Connie he hoped that was a dietetic bar. She gave him a chocolate grin and he said maybe they could make an exception this time. It could be her celebration bar, because, if no problems appeared, and he didn't expect any, he was sending her home tomorrow. The residents nodded and we smiled in unison. Dr. Jameson raised his hand—I swear he did—as if to stop us from applauding, gathered the residents to him and commenced with his examination. He opened Connie's gown and talked about the incision, then asked her how the pain was, which she answered with a shrug, and he said good, good girl, that was exactly what he wanted to hear. Residents gathered around him, he leafed through several pages of her chart, and said yeah, he believed everything was looking good and that was what they were going to do, all right. Someone would be around tomorrow morning to perform a discharge physical and write up instructions for her to take with her, but as far as he—they—were all concerned, she was good to go.

Sally held a tissue to the corner of each eye, Jim smiled vaguely, Janice wiggled all over like she had to pee, and Sammo looked up from his solitaire game, bit his lower lip and asked if we shouldn't maybe find out first what Connie would like. Dr. Jameson peered at him, head slightly cocked, as though such an idea would never cross his mind, gave everyone a final nod and walked toward the door.

I followed him into the hallway. Dr. Jameson, I called, without shouting. His head jerked slightly and he picked up his pace. Dr. Jameson. The resident to his right touched his arm and he stopped, glancing over his shoulder.

I—I—goddamnit, I told myself I wouldn't do that—I was wondering—I swallowed and he blinked, held his lids closed a second, looked back at me. I told him, my voice now calm, that I was leaving after lunch to return home and was wondering if I could get an idea of how things were with Connie. How they really were—out of her hearing, if he knew what I meant. He pulled the clipboard under his crossed arms even tighter to his chest, raised his chin and said, he'd already told us she was excellent, so what more—? And I said but, now dangling the word in front of him, and he said, yes, and I said but was that true? Was that really the case? Dr. Jameson glanced at the residents, who glanced at their feet, and asked if I were implying that he wasn't honest with his patients. I said of course not. It wasn't that at all, but I had heard medical people sometimes wanted to put the best face on things, and he said I could rest assured he wasn't one of them and that when he said someone was excellent, the person was excellent. And Connie was. She was healing fine and was regaining strength. I asked about her prognosis, and he said that was for her and her oncologist to discuss. As far as he was concerned, she was excellent. He didn't know how he could make it more clear than that. Everything was excellent.

Act Two

Len

Begin Again

Len balanced the picture on his stomach with his left hand, glancing from it to me to it over and over, his brow knitting and unknitting, mouth working—at words, I was wishing, but it was more likely a piece of food dislodged from a snag of a tooth. He looked good for someone who, after a series of what were called cerebral events, lay in light yellow pajamas paralyzed on his right side and speechless on a nursing home bed. His hair and beard were trimmed the shortest I'd seen, whiskers a mere shadow of grey across his face, so that what you noticed most now were his eyes—ice blue, blueonblue, as Connie said, the bluest blue you ever saw. Sinatra had nothing on him.

I asked if he'd ever seen the picture and he shook his head and laughed huh-huh-huh—three short, quick grunts and no more—which he did in response to nearly everything, making it difficult to know whether he thought something was funny or was being dismissive or sarcastic or god only knows what else. I told him Suz had given me the picture after she'd found it while cleaning out his house, getting it ready to sell. (He had to have known as well as the rest of us that he would never go back there to live, but I saw no reaction from him.) I said the picture was in an old chest upstairs in the East Room—just like the White House, huh?—and he frowned but whether about the reference to the White House or the chest, I wasn't sure, so I said it was that one our father the old man had made out of two by twos and some of that god-awful cheap blonde paneling he had left over from remodeling the kitchen. It was about a two and a half foot cube with screw-on wooden legs you always had to keep tightening so the thing wouldn't wobble—did he remember it now?—and he nodded that it was coming back to him (or so I chose to think). I could see it clear as anything because the East Room was my room and the Middle Room Grandma Caulkins'. The West Room was his until he moved out to join the Navy and, as he put it, ride some Waves, the meaning of which I pondered incessantly as I lay in my room on hot summer nights, the whump-whump of the whole-house fan in the window beyond the foot of my bed mixing with the apocalyptic rantings of Garner Ted Armstrong on Grandma's radio and the rude braap of semis as they jake-braked for the city limits at the north edge of town.

The picture is a four by six inch black and white studio portrait of our mother in her early thirties, maybe, and Len and I when we were about ten and six. Our mother has flowing dark curly hair and is wearing a dark dress with light daisies and appears to have on lipstick, which emphasizes her playful smile and the glint in her eye. It's easy to see why our father the old man was attracted to her. Len and I are smiling as well—me with the gap-toothed grin I've always found annoying even as others have told me how cute it is, how sweet and little boyish—both of us cleaned up, dressed up in white shirts with broad, pointed collars, Len's opened over a zipper jacket, mine out over a V-neck sweater. We've each had a recent haircut, parts and waves made possible most likely by Brylcreem. Our mother leans slightly forward between us, our heads haloed in an oval of light, she and I gazing directly at the camera, Len a bit to the left, as though something there has caught his attention at the last second. A close look at our eyes, mouths, chins and especially noses, with that distinct Doolan flare at the end some people are unkind enough to call a bulge, leaves little doubt we are related. The picture is framed in an embossed mat that is now covered with jagged water stains. In the bottom right-hand corner, our mother wrote: With all our love from Ruby and boys, presumably as a gift to our father, who, I hope, appreciated it.

I also wanted to ask Len whether we really were as happy as we looked in the picture. I'd studied it for hours after Suz gave it to me, trying to get a handle on a time and place I don't remember inhabiting, although I must have since there I was, a much younger version of me with my mother and brother, so I hunkered down all the more, searching the photo for any clue, any nuance to help explain it, the way an archeologist might scrutinize a newly discovered artifact, which could, given the right interpretation, provide the key to understanding a previously inexplicable culture.

He ran his finger back and forth over the inscription below the picture, and I said wasn't that something, what did he make of it, did he think she'd meant what she'd written? He pinched his brow and ducked his head, one eye squinted shut, either to say that of course she had and I was the dumbest ass he'd ever known, or he had no idea because he could no longer read but had no intention of letting me know that, gesturing in the exaggerated way he had to cover for himself as people with severe tics learn to do to disguise their random motions—a well-placed hand to the head, as if scratching an itch, or a palm to the cheek, as if thinking. But I suspected he still could read some things, like the clock, for example, since he seemed to know it was now eleven-thirty, time for the aides to come take him to the dining room for lunch. He began shifting in bed, making nonsensical sounds with his lips and tongue, eyes darting between the clock and the empty doorway as he listened carefully to every voice, every footstep from the hall, and at each false alarm wagged the finger of his left hand and shook his head no, as if scolding time itself. When they did come, he drew his right arm onto his stomach with his left hand, tilted his chin up and looked away from them, pretending he couldn't care less they were there while they went about their business of changing and cleaning him and slipping under him the harness they used to lift him into his wheelchair, laughing and joking that they needed to hurry up and finish since his favorite waitress had been asking where he was and they knew he didn't want to disappoint her. Once settled and adjusted in the chair, he shooed the aides out of the room, and, using his left arm to push the wheel and his left foot as a rudder to guide the chair, he started for the door, then stopped suddenly, reversing himself in a single motion, and pointed toward his bed. I asked if he'd forgotten something and he made a sour face and gave me a curt nod, like I should have known not only that he had but what it was he wanted. He motioned again and I asked if I should turn off the TV and he tried to say no, I swear he did, and I asked if he wanted his robe, a pillow, a blanket, and he grew more exasperated with me at each failure, until I tumbled finally to the last thing there and, of course, the most obvious—the picture. I got it and tried to put it on his lap, but he shook his head and pointed at me, and we started again toward the dining room, with me striding along just behind him, holding the picture chest-high in front of me, facing out, like a relic-bearing celebrant in a Mummer's parade.

The dining room was down the hall to the right, round tables scattered like flat brown rocks along a shoreline, white heads and bent bodies around them so much flotsam left by the ebb tide. No one appeared to notice as we marched toward a table near a bank of windows that looked out over the loading dock and the street beyond. Chucky Riggs, according to his place card, was parked to Len's right, Hector Branson directly across the table. The fourth chair was empty, and that was where I sat. A young woman, barely twenty, I imagine, brown hair captured under a net, pretty but for acne not quite hidden by makeup on her face and neck, bounced toward our table on squeaking tennis shoes and asked in a perky voice if I were joining them— meaning everyone, I assumed—for lunch, and I said no, that wouldn't be necessary, and she asked if I was sure and I said I was and she said okay, I could suit myself but the food really wasn't bad. I wanted to tell her, but didn't of course, that it wasn't the food and it wasn't Len. I knew him, I knew what to expect. It was the rest of it—the empty motionless stares, the cacophonous throat-clearing and coughing, choking, the overwhelming absence of the human voice other than an occasional too-loud reminder to eat your lunch now, that was good, remember to swallow.

I was still holding the picture and asked Len what he wanted me to do with it. He pointed to the middle of the table so I put it there but he shook his head and stirred his finger in the air until I asked if he wanted me to turn it and he nodded in that what else could he possibly have meant way, slowly up and down like an oil well pump, until I wanted to yell fucking stop it, I got the point, I was a dumbass, all right, a dumbass, but I didn't then either, I never did even though I should have for my own peace of mind and put the picture down close to where it had been in the first place. I asked him if he was happy now, and he gave me a smug look, raised his left eyebrow and I swear twitched his head in the direction of another aide—shorter, cuter, with a disarming smile—who was wheeling a white cart toward our table. She stopped, said hello and after looking at a chart, put little white paper cups of pills in front of Chucky, Hector and Len. She wanted to know who was in the picture and Len pointed to himself and to me, and she said oh, so I was his brother. Len nodded the same oil well pump nod as before but without the dumbass part because of her, and she leaned closer to get a better look, her elbows on the table, her rear end level with Len's face and well within reach. He was doing everything he could not to stare or touch—at least that was what I was hoping—and she straightened and asked if that was our mother and Len smiled and she said how neat that was, how cool and put her arm around his shoulder and gave him a hug, drawing him tight against her left hip and releasing him with a reminder to take his pills before he forgot.

Len had never been a big eater, but he dug into lunch with enthusiasm, scooping the spoon in his left hand against the high rim of his plate—first a bite of vegetables, which I had never seen him have, a bite of peach, all of the bread, butter spread on it with the back of his spoon, two-thirds of his meat and all but a smidgeon of potatoes. He declined coffee when an aide came to take his dishes and tipped his head for me to fetch the picture as he released the brake on his chair, backing himself away from the table.

Instead of going directly back to his room, he took me on a tour of the home, expertly propelling himself around as we explored a sitting area with a fish tank, looked out at the garden, saw the library and several other rooms, passed the nursing station where everyone cheered and Len laughed huh-huh-huh and turned finally into his room, where he maneuvered himself backward into a space beside his bed just big enough for the wheelchair and set the brake. I said wow, would you look at him and he puffed his chest out, thumb tucked into his armpit, head bobbing side to side, the way he was in that picture of him holding the biggest fish of the day, after an outing with our father and Grandpa Doolan. Whether he'd caught the fish or not, I don't know, but he got to hold it, and that was what mattered. Someone let him hold it.

As soon as I settled into my own chair, a stiff-backed, vinyl covered imitation Queen Anne's across the bed from him, he began wagging his finger at me, the TV and the remote, in that order. I cocked my head and he repeated the gesture. I asked if that meant he wanted me to turn on the TV and he gave me his whatdaya think, dumbass head shake. I told him no, he could do it himself. He had to when Suz or I or somebody else wasn't around, so he could now. I held the remote in his direction until he shrugged and took it and hit the power-on button, channel-surfed his way straight to *High Noon*, roared a mighty yawn and slouched forward, head drooping, as though once having reached a safe haven he hadn't the energy to hold himself up any longer. I called his name, called it again, and he jerked his head back and seemed to be watching the movie, although his eyelids were drooping and fluttering, about to close, his head going forward with them. I said Len sharply, a flick of a sound, a pinch, and his head flew up again, one eye glaring at me like it was my fault he was so miserable, and he rubbed his face with his left hand and shook his head until his cheeks flapped. He opened his eyes as wide as he could and tried to watch. God help him, he tried, and I watched him watch and began wondering what thoughts, if any, were going through his brain, what sights and sounds, what images and where they were being processed, whether in the frontal, temporal, parietal or occipital lobe, and whether those lobes were really blue, red, green and purple, as I'd seen in brain maps, little lights going on and off like miniature explosions inside them whenever there was activity, or whether they were all the same pinkish hue because of so much blood flowing to them, and whether the exposed brain really felt to the touch, as I'd read, like a peeled avocado?

But I doubted there was anything normal about Len's brain now. A doctor at the VA hospital where he'd been before coming here showed me a picture of a normal brain and then one of Len's, his whole left cortex covered with a translucent film, like a cataract—everything gone, everything, the doctor had said, no feeling, no speech, no memory as such; why, he was lucky to be alive. So with Len, when he saw, heard, felt, tasted, smelled, instead of small flashes in specific areas of specific lobes was there more of a massive emission, like newsreel images of infrared storm sightings, huge thunderous flares of energy, wantonly violent, without form or meaning or pity? I wonder what Len would say, if he could, about how lucky he felt?

These moments were the worst, when I was no longer talking, asking questions, telling stories in order to fill his silence, to give him words, sense, meaning to give back to me. But the more I wished him awake so I could speak, the harder he seemed to sleep, his chin pressing ever more heavily into his chest, jaw slackening, eyes darting beneath his lids, the fingers on his left hand twitching, as though he were trying to grab hold of something. And I looked away, ran away in my mind, from him and in him every other person in every other room in every other wing of that home, my brother a cliché of infirmity itself, a ball of saliva welling on his lower lip, set to drool down his chin.

The Forgotten Child

I was born four years and one month after Len. Sounds simple enough when you say it, doesn't it? I was born. I was brought forth? Men tend to idealize the process as a noble event, but from what I've seen and most women have told me, it involves pain— exquisite pain. Although the intensity of childbirth varies from person to person, according to medical literature, every mother goes through the same stages of labor and delivery: the first begins with uterine contractions at intervals of three to ten minutes and a concurrent gradual dilation and effacement of the cervix, which forms the neck of the uterus, the inverted pear-shaped organ holding the fetus. Once the cervix has dilated ten centimeters, the second stage of labor begins, with strengthening contractions that come every two to three minutes and last a minute to a minute and a half, a process that can continue up to several hours and ends when the baby's head crowns or shows through the opening of the vagina. The final stage begins after the birth of the baby and ends in five to ten minutes, when the placenta is delivered. By then, mothers are exhausted, which seems reasonable to me, considering that the uterus is normally a hollow organ that is two and a half to three inches long but during pregnancy stretches to twenty or more inches and has strong enough muscles to force a baby anywhere from five to ten pounds and eighteen to twenty inches long out of it and through the vagina, which previously has accommodated perhaps a single finger/group of fingers or an erect penis rarely longer than six and a half inches and a mere four and a half inches in girth. Think about it. Coming through that narrow canal is a child with a head averaging thirteen and a half inches in circumference, which would be roughly the equivalent of expelling a croquet ball—all bald and red and slathered in juice—through a space meant for nothing bigger than a hen's egg. Is it any wonder there is pain? Is it any wonder some women, after such cramping and clamping and rending of flesh say to hell with it, they're not going to go through that again, ever, despite the elation they are also supposed to feel over having birthed a child? And add to that postpartum depression women have always been vulnerable to and some succumb to—the darkness, the gloom, the despair following what should be an inherently joyful event—and it's a miracle that the species perpetuates itself.

I have heard and have no trouble imagining that if our mother had had her way, Len would have been an only child. And what if he were? Would his life have turned out differently? Would he have become a self-centered, spoiled brat everyone avoided, or, just as easily, an introverted, creative type, a musical prodigy, say, playing classical piano concerts for enthralled audiences worldwide, our mother and our father among them, neither of whom had ever touched an instrument let alone played one, sitting in awe themselves, perhaps wondering why they had been chosen to bring forth such a child and thanking god that they had, since otherwise they would never have known the likes of him? Or, as a third possibility, might he have been neither and ended up one of those great underachievers people like to talk about, the kid who had it all and didn't do a damn thing with it, squandered it like the prodigal son, but didn't come back home until it was too late?

As it happened, Len didn't turn out to be an only child, although it apparently took our mother three years and four months to get over his birth enough to consider having me. I imagined at one time her decision was precipitated by the fact that not long after Len arrived our father the old man began working two jobs—he did have a new family to support, after all—and was rarely home. When he was, I doubted he paid much attention to baby Len, or to his wife, for that matter, except when driven to by lust, after which he would leave her alone in bed where she would fall asleep to the glow of light from the kitchen and the chink of a whiskey bottle on glass. In my mind, that situation drove her deeply enough into despair that she came up with the idea of having me as a perverse sort of revenge on our father.

In another imagining I had our father as such a doting dad that his only concern was for the happiness of his new son. He didn't work all the time and instead played with Len to the point of excess, tossing a ball back and forth in the yard or pulling him in a Radio Flyer wagon or taking him fishing on lazy Sunday afternoons or curling up with him in a chair to read another chapter of *Mr. Popper's Penguins*. In that version, our mother grew more and more jealous of our father and Len and soon came to want me in order to have someone of her own.

Later I uncovered the real story—or, truth be told, most likely patched it together from this source and that. But it's the one I find most plausible, given the circumstances and people involved. It seems clear that I still wouldn't be here if our father hadn't moved the family to California so he could work at the North American Aviation plant in Inglewood, making bombers for the war—a verifiable, historical fact. He loved the job, I was told, and it was one the government felt was important enough that he and his co-workers were exempted from the draft. He also loved the people he worked with and lived around. He loved California and said he'd never been happier. If he'd had his way, as I understand it, they would never have left. But our mother apparently hated California with equal passion. To her, the people seemed even then far too strange—give her a good old Kansan any day. When our father saw beauty in the mountains, she saw fires that could destroy them all. When he commented on the blue sky, she pointed out a dingy layer of smog beneath it. When he ahhed about a sunset over the Pacific, she reminded him that those same clouds could bring deadly storms. If a truck rumbled by on the street in front of their house, I was told she would grab Len and cower in the middle of the room, waiting for the walls to crack and the ceiling to fall. On the odd days our father was able to drag her to Redondo beach, she wouldn't so much as get her feet wet for fear some creature would wrap its loathsome tentacle around her and pull her into the deep. She became so miserable, in fact, that she told our father one evening after dinner she was taking Len home and he could decide on his own whether he was coming or not. As luck would have it, I'm told, workers at the Inglewood plant had been informed that a new facility was being opened in Kansas City, Kansas, and the company was looking for workers who might be willing to move there, given the right incentive. Our father, without telling our mother (I never did say our family resembled the Cleavers, did I?), signed on for the move, which of course allowed him not only to pocket a healthy bonus but also to accept our mother's ultimatum and make it look like a sacrifice on his part. And that was how, I was told, the fledgling family returned to terra firma. Our father was happy—or at least acted like he was and never once mentioned that he wished he was still in California—and our mother was so ecstatic she forgot that she didn't want to become pregnant again. By the time I was born, the North American plant in Kansas City was producing a new B-25 bomber every ten minutes.

From what I can gather, Len was none too thrilled about me. Even before I came on the scene, he seemed to realize something was different about our mother. That she was rounder and waddled when she walked, that she grunted more when she got up and down. I imagine he followed her so closely with those blue-blue eyes that she finally asked what was bothering him and he walked over to her and put his hand on her belly and our mother told him a baby was growing there, a little brother or sister for him to play with, wouldn't that be fun? Picture the pause, his little hand on her pregnant belly, before he said that was all right, he didn't need anybody—or something to that effect—she could send the baby back.

Judging from some of the pictures Suz gave me, our father and our mother might as well have done just that. There were dozens of snapshots of people playing, laughing, touching, sometimes mugging for the camera, like Grandma Caulkins with her hand up, trying to turn her face away, or like our father in a line of men posturing beside someone's car, all dressed in khaki shirts and trousers, all with dark, plastered-down hair, all hoisting a beer bottle and cigarette in the same hand to salute the photographer. Not to mention the plethora of shots of Len—standing beside his bicycle, for instance, in his plaid jacket and cap with earflaps tied in the up position, or posing in his high school football uniform or later his Navy or Co-op uniform, or sitting in his '58 Chevy, or standing under a tree with Josie and eventually Suz and Sonny, in the days Sonny was still talking to him. A few photos of Connie were mixed in as well, mainly from her cute, curly childhood, and one or two apparently obligatory, guilt-assuaging pictures of me, but never me alone like the others but always with someone else, next to them, being sized up to them, as though I was an extra brought in to balance the shot or a neighbor kid who'd wandered across the yard while the photo was being taken and left immediately afterward with a seeya, yeah, seeya around, so that forty, fifty years later people scratched their heads and asked now that guy there, who the hell's family did he belong to?

But I got used to it, first with Len alone and then with Len and Connie chumming it up and me hanging around the edges like the ugly/crippled/retarded brother being constantly overlooked/looked around/looked through. But in the end it wasn't as awful as you might think, because without my knowing it, that very exclusion—or was I excluding myself, you might wonder—prepared me to do the one thing no one else had been able to—go away and not come back. Len tried to, but he didn't make it any farther than Vegas before slinking home, and I'll bet he never even saw a Wave let alone rode one.

Places

For me—always me, as Connie would say—the most pleasant aspect of the trip from Chicago to middle Kansas is the plane flight: lift-off, the weightlessness of becoming airborne, shivering through overcast and light winds, banking, bursting brilliantly into sunlight, clouds thinning, rippling like white sand at the bottom of a tidal pool, giving way to a rare, perfectly clear view of the earth gliding past thousands of feet below, rivers and their tributaries like rhizomes bristling with root hairs, fields, farms, fences, hills and valleys, grids of highways, byways, railways connecting dots of small towns that dribble across the land with remarkable regularity, as though dropped into place every few paces by some ambling giant marking his return route.

One of the last in the string is Carter, where I lived for more than ten years, where I grew up, you might even say, or at least the part I remember of growing up. The town comes into view while making a final descent into Wichita, and from that height, I can clearly see the glimmering metal roof of a machine shed on the south edge of town, two sets of grain elevators—one by the Rock Island tracks to the west, the other by the Santa Fe tracks farther east—the swimming pool, the park with its half-mile circular track, the high school and football field, a glint of sun where Deever Creek joins Morgan Creek, and even our house— or so I imagine—now neglected and weather-beaten on a barren double lot that was once bathed in the shade of matching columns of Chinese elm trees.

It was called the Murphy Place when we bought it, although nobody named Murphy had lived there within memory and no one could say for certain who they were, other than, you know, the Murphys, them Murphys, who quite possibly built and were the first inhabitants of the house. It may have been those very Murphys who installed the oil lamps, marks of which were still visible on the living room walls, fired the furnace with coal and later converted it to natural gas without ever installing the ductwork necessary for it to be a whole-house source for heat, leaving the upstairs, according to Len, colder than a dead witch's tit. The Murphys probably also added indoor plumbing by walling off the north end of the kitchen and cutting a doorway through it, making the only bathroom in the house almost literally a water closet.

We got the house, as I understand, with help from the Red Cross, since we'd recently been victims of one of the worst floods ever to hit central Kansas. I was seven at the time and Len was eleven and Connie wasn't anything yet, and we moved in with what clothes we'd been able to salvage and a chest freezer that Suz or somebody told me is still working—or was at least when Len was taken from the house. About the same time as our move, whether shortly before or after I don't know, our father started working second shift at Boeing Aircraft in Wichita, which meant, figuring an hour and a half commute each direction, that he left home at one-thirty in the afternoon and returned around twelve-thirty the next morning. We hardly saw him during the week, and on weekends he busied himself with handyman chores around the house or more massive projects like tearing down the old barn by the alley or converting the screened porch on the back of the house into a breakfast nook. He reroofed, reguttered, repainted the house, rebuilt the front porch, utility room and bathroom, resodded the lawn, reclaimed the brick sidewalks from weeds, rerouted the sewer line away from the apple tree. He retiled and recarpeted floors inside, refinished woodwork, repaired the living room ceiling, replastered walls upstairs, replaced broken windows, rewired and replumbed most of the house.

In its heyday, I imagine a real estate ad featuring the house might have gone something like this:

A HUGE COLOR PICTURE OF IT AT THE TOP OF THE PAGE

followed by

Vintage Victorian four-bedroom, one-bath home on tastefully landscaped tree-lined double lot. Lovely wrap-around front porch with swing. First floor includes country-style, eat-in kitchen, full utility room, large open living room, bath and sought-after main level bedroom. Upstairs features three bedrooms, with a westward facing sunroom and whole-house fan for ventilation. Large walk-in closets. Attic access for storage. Half basement, inside entry. Hardwood floors and carpeting throughout. Newer electrical and plumbing. New roof, fresh paint. Detached two-car garage with built-in work bench. This charming home must be seen to be appreciated.

I don't know about lovely or charming—comfortable, maybe, inviting enough that we hosted an occasional gathering of the tribe there, usually around a holiday—Thanksgiving or Christmas, the Fourth of July, Labor Day—with all kinds of aunts, uncles and cousins, Grandma Caulkins (even when she wasn't living there), Grandpa Doolan, friends, neighbors and sometimes their relatives as well. Everyone brought at least one dish of food. It wasn't a true celebration without beef roast, fried chicken, ham, mashed potatoes and gravy, potato salad, green salad, green and yellow beans, peas and carrots, jello, pies and cakes and ice cream and enough beers and Cokes and Dr. Peppers to send people pissing in the yard. There's a photograph, apparently taken toward the end of one such get-together, that shows people sprawled on the porch and lawn in the heat of a summer evening, with barely enough energy to raise an arm in recognition of the family driving past, who are waving back and thinking, I imagine, what lucky folks, what a great party and wouldn't it be nice if they could join the fun, maybe even sit in on the under-shirt-only penny-ante poker game our father, Uncle Boyd, Grandpa Doolan and any other interested uncles were playing huddled around a table in the breakfast nook at the back of the house. They had by then graduated from beer and cigarettes to straight whiskey and cheap cigars, the lights as dim as they could get them and still see the cards. The back door and a couple of windows were open to the screech of cicadas rising and falling with a regularity that you either blocked out or went mad from. There was complete silence at the table, however, marked by an occasional cough or thunk of a tumbler or ping of a cigar against a metal ashtray. Communication was by gesture—two fingers meant two cards, a single knuckle rap on a hand turned face down meant pat—followed by a final intense focus on the money in the middle of the table, like fishermen concentrating on that single point at which their lines enter the water, thinking magically that by staring hard enough and long enough they can finally catch the big one they've been after their whole lives.

From the outside looking in, like those folks driving by in the car, you'd have thought we were the Rockefellers or somebody, who could party at will and never have to worry about money. The truth is, those were two or three times a year events, and everybody who came brought their fair share of food and drinks. There was no way in hell we could have afforded to pay for bashes like that ourselves. According to our mother, we could barely make ends meet as it was, a subject that came up without fail the evening of the last Friday of every month, after Len and I and Grandma Caulkins had gone upstairs and Connie was down for the night. Our mother would say she needed more money for food and our father would tell her he already gave her everything, what more did she want, he wasn't a miracle worker. She would mention that maybe he could spend less on beer and whiskey, that would help, which brought his usual refrain: he worked hard, goddamnit, and he provided well for her and his children and she should goddamn appreciate it. Not every woman had it that good, and she knew he was right. Could she please explain then, his voice rising, what made her so hell-bent on taking away one more thing he enjoyed, one more thing that gave him a little pleasure? A whining groan now that asked why in god's name she wanted to do that to him, why him? By that point, Len and I would usually be hugging the railing at the top of the stairs, and Grandma Caulkins would be in her room praying for her son's foolish soul loudly enough we would be sure to hear.

But one night their voices were different—more immediate, not as loud, like dogs with bared teeth and their ears laid back. Len and I glanced at each other, and even Grandma Caulkins had grown silent, waiting. The keys, he wanted the goddamn keys and if she wouldn't give them to him, a thump, our mother saying he wouldn't dare, the smack of someone's hand hitting something, her clenched voice saying all right, if it was that goddamn important, the sprinkle of metal on the counter or the floor, a growl, a lunge, a squeak from her as if she were trying not to scream or cry out, and I was up and heading down the stairs before Len could grab me. I slammed open the door, fists clenched, shouting for them to stop, just stop it before I saw him standing over her, the keys a shiny clump on the floor near the back door. She was trying to tell me it was okay, she'd slipped, but blood was pounding in my ears so loudly I couldn't make sense of what she was saying, and our father the old man was righting himself and turning to face me, a sneer on his face, and was saying I should come on, come and get him, while his feet stabilized and he doubled his fists like a prize fighter. Hell yeah, if I thought I was big enough, he'd take me on, may the best man win. If it was me, there was the goddamn door. If it was him, well, then we'd know, wouldn't we, who was boss, because I didn't have to goddamn like him, but I would respect him or I would not be living in that house a minute longer. Did I understand? huh? huh? did I? I told him yeah I did all right, but that didn't change the fact that he was never and I meant never to lay a hand on our mother again. He asked what the fuck I was talking about, she slipped and fell, like she said, what the hell did I take him for anyway? What kind of a man did I think he was? And without waiting for an answer, he turned, picked up the keys and lumbered toward the door with one last hurt glance back at us, as if he were the victim and we had it all wrong.

Len never would have done that. He was always quieter, more shy about confrontation—about everything, really. I mean, he used to have me call girls and pretend to be him and ask them for dates, since nobody, not even our mother, could tell us apart on the phone. I would say hi and Marilyn (or whoever) would say hi and I would say I was Len Caulkins, how was she doing, and she would say, good, everything was going okay—you get the idea—until I would finally ask what she was doing Saturday night, would she like to go to a show, maybe, or get a burger or ride around or something and she would usually say yes because bashful as Len was girls seemed to be attracted to him. He was nice looking, now that I think back on it, not James Dean, maybe, but of average height and build, with a lock of hair curled ever so slightly onto his forehead in a way that made any girl who saw it want to fix it for him and in the process peer a bit deeper into those blue Sinatra eyes. But even with all that to his advantage, what appeared to attract girls the most, I believe, was his very shyness, which made him seem at once strong and vulnerable and protected him, unlike the rest of us, from saying stupid or offensive things just to hear himself talk.

The same silence that worked with girls, however, frustrated our father to the point that he, himself, would become nearly speechless. He could ask Len how was he doing and Len would tip his head ever so slightly to his right and, without making eye contact, say he was okay. Our father would ask if that was all—okay?—as he tried to get within Len's field of vision, and Len, bringing his shoulder up to match the quick tilt of his head—a half-shrug, you might call it—would say he guessed that was about it. The blood would start to rise in our father's face, his eyes hardening on Len as he tried to get Len to look at him and tell him more than he was capable of telling; and under the increasing pressure both of them were feeling, Len would bring forth what our father considered his most egregious sin—the full, two-shouldered, head-ducking shrug, along with a nearly inaudible dunno, at which our father would stammer goddamn and son and just when was it he did plan to know something, anything?

Child behavior experts would have told our father to back off, lay off, let the boy come around on his own. As you can imagine, our father was as unable to do that as Len was to answer with more than shrugs and one-word responses, and the favorite son (child) gradually became persona non grata. Len was too much like our mother, according to our father—he would rather watch than do, listen than talk, right? and he was too willing to stand there and let things happen, rather than make them happen. Where the hell was the determination, the drive, the ambition? that's what he wanted to know. Any son of his—he would say but not finish, since the implication was clear and the damage already done. When Connie was born, our father moved on to her, passing me by completely. She became favorite daughter (child) and he our father the old man.

The fact is, he had enough ambition for all of us and devised one crackpot project after another, usually with an eye toward getting rich sooner rather than later. Right after we moved to Carter, for example, he went into partnership with Uncle Boyd in a filling station on the highway that passed along the north side of town. Len even worked there for a while evenings and weekends and nearly lost a finger trying to fix a drive belt on one of the gas pumps. As I heard the story, he was removing the old belt when the pump unexpectedly started running and trapped his finger under the belt as it passed over a pulley and, according to our father and Uncle Boyd, slashed it to the bone. By the time I saw the finger, it was wrapped in a huge bandage with a metal splint on either side of it, and Len had to sit quietly in a chair, his whole hand elevated, like a prince or a king holding court. And you would have thought he was one, too, the way our mother waited on him—did he want any more milk or cookies, was he feeling okay, maybe some ice to numb the cut, anything, anything at all, he should just ask.

But something happened with the filling station. I don't know what except that it involved a huge argument between our father and Uncle Boyd. One story I heard had to do with money missing from the safe—and this from Connie, who, if you remember, was all too familiar with the subject of ill-gotten gains. She said a good deal of money was involved, in the hundreds of dollars, with the implication, if not outright accusation, that Uncle Boyd had taken it. He of course said that was bullshit, our father had the same access to the safe as he did. Our father asked just how stupid Uncle Boyd thought he was and Uncle Boyd said obviously stupid enough to blame his own brother for something like that, the person closest to him on earth, with the possible exception of our mother. The mere mention of her sent our father into a spitting and cursing rage because, according to another story—I don't know who I heard it from—the blowup that day really had to do with her—our mother—and him—Uncle Boyd—for our father, according to what I heard, had convinced himself that the two of them were having an affair. It was plain as the nose on his face, the way they batted their eyes at each other and smiled and could hardly keep their hands to themselves, billing and cooing around like a couple of turtle doves in heat. Uncle Boyd, who had been changing the oil on a car, stepped out from under the lift, slowly wiping his hands on a red cloth, and asked our father what the hell he'd been drinking, he wanted some for himself if it was that good, and our father said this wasn't a laughing matter, but Uncle Boyd laughed anyway and our father told Uncle Boyd he'd better get the hell out before he did something he'd regret, and if he ever found the two of them together again. . . . Uncle Boyd shook his head and said she was our father's wife, for chrissake, he knew better than to mess around there. Besides, he had plenty of other women to choose from, and our father asked what that was supposed to mean, was there something wrong with our mother, wasn't she good enough for him, which sent Uncle Boyd stepping lightly backwards out the door, as if worried our father truly had gone off his nut and might suddenly produce a knife or gun. Early the next morning, after both of them had been able, under separate roofs, to sleep off whatever was ailing them, our father went to see Uncle Boyd and must have patched things up enough that six months later they had sold the filling station and leased a pig farm.

From what I heard, neither of them knew much about farming or pigs. Our father had milked cows as a young man and may have bucked bales or planted and harvested for local farmers—as had Uncle Boyd—but neither of them had any idea of the economics of farming—how to manage that much money or the land itself, for that matter. And pigs? They're smelly, rude and so smart as to be unruly. They love to lie around in mud mixed with their own shit, if you don't clean it up, and catching one is nearly impossible, as Len and I found out.

Each sow births two litters a year, for a total of maybe twenty piglets. Several of these will be males, and as we were told, too many mature boars spoil the pack. They're nasty and aggressive and their meat is inedible by humans because it smells like a pigsty. Castrated males are easier to control, make less noise and are quicker to fatten for slaughter. But you only have three weeks to do the deed. Beyond that, they're too big to handle.

Which was where Len and I came in. On cuttin day, as our father and Uncle Boyd called it, we would go out to the farm early and round up all the male piglets, isolating them in a separate pen as our father sharpened his knife by spitting on a whetstone and slowly rubbing the blade in a circle on top of it, stopping every few rotations to test its sharpness against his thumb. People normally used a surgical scalpel or a special castration knife, but our father and Uncle Boyd thought that was a needless expense—good god, they were pigs, not people. When everything was ready, Len and I were to catch the piglets, which average ten to twelve pounds and even that young are stronger and quicker than you might believe. Once we finally grabbed one, we would hang the grunting/squealing/squirming animal upside down between our thighs and spread its hind legs while Uncle Boyd applied an antiseptic to its scrotum and our father poked around with his fingers until he found a testicle, made an incision almost the length of it and squeezed, popping the organ out through the cut. He severed the cord but not the blood vessel and tossed the testicle into an ice bucket beside him so it and all the rest could be taken home, fried and feasted upon by our father, Uncle Boyd, Grandpa Doolan, Grandma Caulkins, and even our mother, all of whom would, mouths full, explain to Len and me that we didn't know what we were missing, we should sit down and try some, young ones were always the best.

One Saturday we all drove out to the pig farm as usual, and our father and Uncle Boyd were about to lean against the fence, as usual, to finish their Irish coffees and smoke a cigarette before we started working when our father's arm shot out, finger pointing, and he said what the fuck as we, too, then saw first one, and another and another young pig wobbling around, covered with purple blotches. Uncle Boyd took his hat off and scratched his head, saying nothing, and our father climbed the fence and went inside the shed. We soon heard a hoarse, bellowing cry that ended with goddamnit and an announcement that they were dead, all dead, or might as fucking well be. The veterinarian they brought in said that the pigs had died from hog cholera, or swine flu, and probably could have been saved—or at least a good many of them—had the disease been caught soon enough (a not so subtle hint that farming should maybe be left to full-time farmers who knew what they were doing). The carcasses needed to be cleaned up, the buildings burned and the grounds sterilized. Even then, starting again there, in that place, might not be such a good idea. At least it wasn't a poker hand he would feel comfortable betting on.

Our father decided instead to move on to selling real estate, enrolling in a correspondence course in electronics and collecting full sets of this and that limited edition medal struck at the Franklin Mint right there in good old Philadelphia, all part of his unending effort to amass money, lots of money, and short that, respect.

Most people, I imagine, would have been content with what he'd accomplished in his real job at Boeing, where, as a member of the Apollo 11 team, he helped put the first man on the moon at 9:52 p.m., July 2, 1969—you know, one small step for man, one giant leap for mankind? He even got a certificate commemorating the event made out to him personally and signed by the General Manager of the Launch Vehicle Branch of the Boeing Company. I don't know where they kept the certificate in New Orleans, but after his ills began and they moved back to Kansas, he hung it on the living room wall of the house in Carter, the only thing there besides a sentimental print of a covered bridge in some anonymous bucolic setting. I have the certificate now—part of the things Suz sent me—dusty and dog-eared, resting slightly askew in its cheap frame on a bookshelf in my office. I've been tempted to rescue it—dust it off, clean it up, dress it in a shiny new frame—but I always stop short, probably for the same reason I'm hesitant to do anything with the picture of our mother and Len and me. Sometimes it's best not to mess with things, to leave things as they are, or, perhaps, were.

I know I should be more proud of the old man's accomplishments, and I am to a certain extent. But they all came later, you see, after Len and I were gone and Connie was on her way out of the house and the damage had already been done. Still, you're thinking nobody can be that bad, right, and if I can't say something good about a person, I shouldn't say anything at all, isn't that the way it goes? So okay, let's do that, let's back up and say for the sake of honesty and complexity of character (and favorable future literary reviews) that he's not all bad, that he's not wholly the sonofabitch Len once called him and does have humanity and humor enough to mitigate his peevishness. One of his favorite jokes, after all, was about the guy who died and his family and friends were at his funeral and the minister asked for people to come forward and offer recollections of the deceased but no one stepped up and the minister told them not to be shy and still no one came forth and the minister said surely someone had something to say about the man, and a member of the congregation finally rose to his feet and said, yeah, there was maybe one thing worth mentioning: he wasn't as big a jackass as his brother. Or there was the bumper sticker he liked to tell about: Don't bother me. I'm living happily ever after. Or another story he'd heard but couldn't remember where that went more or less like this: the problem with life was the way it ended. What kind of bonus was death? No, it was all backwards. You should die first, then live in a nursing home and get kicked out when you're too young. You should get a gold watch and go to work for forty years until you're young enough to retire and party and do all the drugs and alcohol and fucking around you want, and you go to high school and grade school and become a little kid with no responsibilities. You finally turn into a baby and go into a womb and float around for nine months and finish it all off with an orgasm. Huh? Huh? Now wasn't that a better way to go out—a goddamn orgasm? Couldn't do any better than that, could you? And he would laugh and cough and laugh some more, until he almost made himself sick.

Len at Home with Len

That morning I found him in a blue striped short-sleeve shirt, grey flannel pants and corduroy slippers, sitting bright and sassy in his wheelchair, and I opened my arms and said would you look at that and he lifted his chin and slicked the hair back on the side of his head, and I asked him if he had a date or what and he poked his finger at me to say I was right, that was it. I wanted to ask him who he would be with, where they would go and what they would do. Given the way I'd seen him look at some of the women who worked at Twin Oaks Manor, I wanted to ask him whether he still got horny, what with the stroke, and whether, given the paralysis on his right side, he could still get an erection, or even half of one for that matter. Which got me thinking about how that would be possible physically and what it would feel like if you could and how people paralyzed from the waist down had sex at all, even though I'd read that everything was just the same—tension, urgency, even orgasm—as long as they didn't get hung up on function and had a loving and gentle partner who was willing to experiment. I tried to imagine Len with a woman old enough to know what she was doing, what she was giving, probably someone widowed or divorced, someone familiar with pain and loss who would come to his room late in the evening when things had quieted down and sit on his bed and hold his hand and stroke his face and kiss him, saying his name over and over, and unbutton his pajama top and her blouse so he could touch her breasts with his good hand as she rubbed up and down his torso, lower and lower, until he quivered with pleasure and she stood, slipping her pants down enough he could curl his hand into the warmth between her legs and go to sleep with her scent on his fingers.

There had been at least two women in his life post-Josie and pre-stroke. Fran at The Main Street Grill for one—more on her later—and Grace for another. I heard about her from both Suz and Connie and read about her in the love letters Len had written her off and on, which she must have given back to him when their affair was over. They were in a neat pink-ribboned bundle he'd put in an upstairs dresser drawer where anybody (in this case Suz) could have found it. She told me she opened the bundle, read the first letter, tied it up again and sent it to me to do with as I pleased, she never wanted to see it again. Which only whetted my curiosity and I untied the bundle immediately. In the snapshot that fell out of the first letter, Grace appeared to be a slightly younger, shorter, perhaps plumper Josie, which would have been enough to have stunned Suz even if she hadn't read how he was driven mad at the thought of lying naked next to Grace, or how he couldn't get the memory of her kiss/touch/smell out of his mind, or how she was the only woman he'd ever really loved. The letters were all basically the same sexual infatuations that would have put to shame a seventh-grader in need of hormone modification, and all at one point or another mentioned Bill, Grace's by every indication willfully oblivious husband, who seemed not only to tolerate her carrying on with Len but to encourage it. He sent her off with Len to Kansas City for a bowling tournament and a baseball game. Another time, they went to Colorado, then to Texas and would have gone on to New Orleans, if they hadn't run out of money. On several occasions Len spent the night at Bill's and Grace's house, particularly after partying into the wee hours beside their above-ground pool. Bill always slept on the sofa and rose early to fix coffee and breakfast for Len and Grace and anyone else still there. There was no mention of Grace ever staying overnight at Len's house in Carter, although Len did write pressuring her to do so by saying things like okay, then, maybe next week when Bill would be on the road again (he was a long-haul trucker), or she hadn't kept her promise yet and when was she planning to, or what was the matter, was she worried what the neighbors might think? Len seemed to expect her to leave Bill sooner or later and live with him, since there were constant references to when was she going to tell Bill to get lost, they could be so happy together. But for some reason Grace didn't leave Bill, and she decided that if she in fact wasn't going to, then what she and Len were doing was wrong. A long silence ensued. The letters stopped, the visits stopped, and Len took to his house and himself, but for daily outings to The Main Street Grill and Fran, for whom he seemed to have an even deeper, yet so far as anyone knew, unrequited love.

He rocked back and forth in his wheelchair, short quick motions, like a dog wagging its tail, and I was tempted, wiseass that I am, to say what is it, boy, what do you want, you want to go out, when in fact that was exactly what he had in mind as he directed me with flips of his head to get behind him and push. A flip to the left as we went out of the room, finger pointing straight ahead to keep going, raising at a right angle beside his ear to stop, another head flip to the left and along a short hallway with an exit door at the end. We stopped there and he nodded twice toward the door. I asked if we were supposed to do that. He wheeled himself around with his good arm, brow scrunched, and I said maybe we should at least tell somebody so they'd know where we were. He stroked his chin and peered at me with those blue-blue eyes as if trying to determine how anybody as dumb as I was could still be breathing, then dropped his stare and turned the chair back toward the door.

I expected an alarm to sound but none did. We rolled down a short sidewalk, around the corner of the building, and joined the main walk that ran the length of the grounds. Bright sun, blue sky, a cool but not cold breeze, daffodils dotting the lawn, and I said it sure was a nice day and Len's head went up and down twice, then began rocking side to side like a metronome. I leaned closer and could hear him humming hmmm hmm-hmm hmm-hmm hmm hmm-hmm hmmm hmm-hmm hmm-hmm hmm-hmm, a monotone chant not unlike his huh-huh-huh laugh that in any other context I would have found irritating. But not there, not seeing him that happy. It was all just too absurdly perfect, and I tousled what hair he had and hummed along with him until the sidewalk ended at a curb with no wheelchair ramp. He swung his head as far around toward me as he could, and I asked what he thought, and he nudged his chair closer and closer to the curb until I tipped it back and bumped it and him down onto the street where he dug the sole of his corduroy slipper into the pavement, swinging himself ninety degrees due east, and jabbed his finger in front of him to tell me he wanted to cross the street. I asked if he was sure that would be all right and he locked his left arm against the chair, hoisting himself to a half-standing position, peered long and hard toward the Rock Island tracks and points beyond, lowered himself back onto the seat, and with his head now craned at me to be sure I was paying attention, raised his arm, forefinger extended, and thrust it in the direction we were headed, Wagons Ho as clear as if he'd said it aloud. When I didn't begin pushing immediately, he wheeled himself forward, good foot dragging as a rudder, but was soon stopped by a wash of sand and gravel from a recent storm. I caught up behind him and told him he'd better be careful or he'd end up in a heap with a scraped nose and me in a hell of a lot of trouble, since I didn't think I was supposed to have him on the street to begin with and if we went much farther, who knew, the home might have me arrested. His head snapped parallel to his left shoulder, brow knit in his for chrissake you can't be serious expression, and I said it was true, he might even read about it in next week's *Chronicle*: Chicago Man Held for Kidnapping Brother from Twin Oaks Manor, and he rolled his eyes and shook his head and laughed huh-huh-huh as he once again pointed east.

I had a good idea of where he was trying to go, but couldn't for the life of me imagine what he expected to find when he got there. Had some vision or smell or sound weaved its way through all those misfiring synapses in his brain and emerged as a memory of home, of the life he'd led post-Josie until he was carried out years later by an EMS crew? I tried to imagine what was going through his mind and it came out something like this—from things he'd told me and I'd seen first-hand and other things I knew because he was my brother: I imagined he was seeing himself waking at six o'clock sharp—without benefit of an alarm since he'd always gotten up then—sitting on the edge of the bed and smoking a cigarette, walking into the living room and turning on the TV on his way to the bathroom—something our mother always did for the company and to catch the weather forecast for the day, as if it made any difference. In the bathroom, he'd finish his cigarette on the toilet as he listened to someone talking about rebels fighting somewhere over something, followed by an ad and more news, another ad, until he finally couldn't tell one from the other, and would flush the cigarette butt, wash his hands and face and try to decide whether to shave. What the hell. He'd been thinking about growing a beard anyway, except Josie had once told him she'd never kiss a man with whiskers. As if what she said would make any difference now, and it was a fucking lie to begin with. And that would get him thinking about the night at the Rod and Gun Club, when everybody was drunk on vodka and beer and Ray Johnson was sitting on a bench behind a table wagging his red beard at Josie like a feather duster, and Jim Reilly was walking around with a rolled-up towel stuffed down his pants so it would look like he had a huge cock, and everybody was laughing and cutting up and saying they'd never had a better time, and that's when she said the thing about never kissing a man with a beard, first to Phil, and later on to him, Len, after he'd asked her what the hell had been going on over there and she told him it was none of his business, they were just kidding around and she could say any damn thing she wanted to to anybody.

Finished in the bathroom, he would go to the kitchen and fill a saucepan half full of water and put it on the stove, measure two teaspoons of instant coffee into a mug and one of Coffee-mate, shake another cigarette from the pack, light it, and smoke and finger his chin until little bubbles formed on the bottom of the pan and he'd pick it up and swish the water around three times, no more, no less, listening to it hiss against the hot metal and pour it into the mug, swirl a spoon exactly twice so as not to overdo it and carry the cup back to the living room where he'd sit on the couch inhaling the fumes before drinking because it smelled good, felt good, cleared his head, like he was an attic or something, Josie had said, when she'd meant addict. About halfway through his cup of coffee, he'd decide to shave after all and stub out his cigarette and gulp the rest of his coffee and trudge back to the bathroom where he'd wet his face, squirt menthol lather onto his fingers, work it into his beard, pick up his razor and stop as always, wondering why he shaved the right side of his face first and never the left, why he always put his right leg into his pants first, why he wiped himself with his right hand, slept on his right side, sat to the right on the couch, why he did any of the things the way he did them. He told me he had once tried moving the razor to his left sideburn, but it had felt so awkward he was sure he would cut himself, not because of the position, but because of the thought of doing that side first, nothing more, and for a moment he would just stand there staring at himself in the mirror, asking himself how the hell things had ever gotten to such a point. He almost always wore the same clothes—clean but unvarying—blue jeans, a plaid short-sleeved shirt, white socks, cowboy boots, and by seven-thirty, even if he wasn't hungry, he'd drive downtown to The Main Street Grill where he knew Fran would be on the lookout for him. She owned the place and had named it The Main Street Grill because it was located on the corner of Main and First Streets in an old bank building, a strange as hell place, he told me, since you had to climb fourteen steps—he counted them every day—from the street to the front door, big bumpy limestone walls rising in front of you, up and up and up until you felt surrounded by them, both sides and over your head, heavy and solid and not one bit inviting, like the picture he'd seen once of a tomb over in Greece or someplace, but he could never tell Fran that, since she'd have a hissy and say tomb her ass, did he see anybody dead in there?

There were almost always the same customers sitting in the same seats whom he would greet the same way as he walked to the counter and swung his leg over the third stool from the right end and sat down and smiled as Fran sashayed over and told him it was a good thing he'd shown up, since she'd about been ready to send old Hank out to look for him, and he said, even though Hank was sitting two stools away, that she should know better because Hank, cop or not, would likely have trouble finding his way out the front door. They'd all laugh and Fran would go off to place Len's order without asking—eggs sunny side up, bacon, hash browns, toast and coffee. She'd always ask how he was doing when she came back and set the plate in front of him, and he'd say fine, why, and she'd say she just worried about him was all and he'd tell her not to and besides if she was so concerned she knew how to make it better. That was part of a game they played. If she wasn't in the mood, she'd go on about her business. If she was, she'd tell him the only way he was going to get better and stop moping around was to get the hell out of Carter, what was holding him there now anyway, and he'd say he would if she'd go with him, run away with him, and she'd ask where he had in mind and that day it might be Mexico, and she might say she'd heard you had to be careful what you ate there and you couldn't drink the water, and he'd say they could live on love and she'd say she'd heard people got awful skinny doing that. By then he'd be finished eating and light a cigarette to have with a fresh cup of coffee and he'd watch her tend other customers, pushing herself up on her toes and twisting just a little with each step, giving her hips a nice sway, which he imagined she was doing only for him. He told me that by then he always felt good he'd come and thought if it wasn't for old Fred back there in the kitchen, he might do more than look at her. So say he did, I told him once, say old Fred dropped dead and he and Fran got together and had a blast, what would there be to stop them? And it always came back to Josie and how it hadn't seemed anything could stop them either and didn't for twenty-some years, until she pulled that bullshit with the divorce papers and that goddamn restraining order, handing them to him just like that, out of the blue, and he wasn't to let the door hit him in the ass on his way out. What was to keep the same thing from happening to him and Fran some morning at breakfast when Fran for no good reason he could think of would say how she couldn't stand it anymore, couldn't stand him, nothing about him, not the way he looked or acted or smelled, none of it, and she wanted him out, immediately, no buts about it? What was to keep that from happening again?

The next thing he knew, he said, Fran would be back with the coffee pot, refilling his cup and saying he must have been thinking again. He'd ask her how she could tell and she'd say she just could and she wished he could be happier. He'd turn away then, as he said he always did when somebody pushed him that way, and look at the cigarette machine, like he was studying it, like he was trying to decide whether to kick the sonofabitch in or not, his eyes filling with tears, because what he really wanted was to grab her and hug her and cry, cry like a little baby or a big baby, it didn't matter, just cry because it seemed like it'd feel so good. But it never seemed the right time or place—when was that ever going to be, he wanted to know?—and he always ended up clearing his throat and reaching for a section of the newspaper to hold in front of him until she went away.

He told me everything would always be back to normal by the time he was ready to leave and she'd meet him at the register and tell him the meal was on the house. Six days a week she'd do that, even though he'd always say it wasn't necessary and she'd say it was her place and she'd do any damn thing she wanted to and he'd shove a five dollar bill across the counter anyway which she'd hesitate to take but finally would and ring up the sale.

She'd always ask him what he was going to do that day and he'd
shrug and she'd tell him, as usual, that if nothing came up, he
should drop back in around dinner time, they could use the extra
help, and he'd say sure, thanks, he'd see what happened.

There would always be a few cars on Main Street, he told me,
generally people coming in to the grocery store, the feed store,
the hardware, though you had trouble finding even a screw in
there sometimes, since it was half antiques now. He'd always
thought that if he had the money he could start a store himself, a
general store, sell a little bit of everything—clothes, hardware,
tools, you name it—and he figured he could make a killing
because there wasn't anything else like it in Carter, except so
many people had gotten out of the habit of buying in town, going
to Newton to the big discount stores or down to Wichita to the
malls, he wasn't sure it would work. But it was something to
think about, something to help kill time as he'd make his rounds,
driving north toward the highway, stopping in at the Quick Pik
for cigarettes and a chat if anybody was around who he knew but
there usually wasn't, only the Appleton kid behind the counter
talking on his cell phone to his girlfriend, arguing with her really,
as they always seemed to do, which would make him nervous
enough he wouldn't hang around even for the air-conditioning
and left as soon as he got his change.

Then he'd always head a half mile west to The Baitshop and
Fat Louisa, who laughed all the time—if you said hello, she
laughed, goodbye, kiss my ass, it didn't make any difference
what, open your mouth and she'd already be grinning. She had to
be crazy, he said, a little bit at least, and he couldn't see why old
Merrill kept her on, except she was steady and got her work done
and that might be about all you could really ask of a person,
unless he was getting a little on the side, but she'd probably laugh
then, too. Think how hard it would be to nail a laughing woman,
he said, a fat laughing woman. But most of the time Bob Jenkins
would already be out there, loading up on beer and bait for the

river where he was going to spend however long it took to catch him some of them big goddamn catfish he'd been hearing about, a V of red flesh pointing down from his open collar to the middle of his chest that somehow caught Fat Louisa's attention and set her off on such a laughing gig Len always left before he did or said something he might regret.

His next stop would always be the Co-op where he worked for years until he got canned for some reason he never talked about and where he went now for a couple dollars' worth of gas, enough to get him by the next day or two no more than he'd been driving. Back when he worked at the trailer factory in Newton and drove a round trip every day he'd use a tank or two a week, and Sam, who managed the Co-op kept a regular account in his name so he could gas up and go, be off with a wave, just like on TV and pay at the end of the month. Now he'd be lucky to get as much as a thank you when Sam took his money and ducked back inside before Len could say anything.

That was the way it was everywhere now, he told me—the grocery store, the bowling alley, Randy's Garage, you name it— people would take his money all right, but act like they were stealing it or something, like they might catch something from it, bad luck or something and it would be best to have it out of their hands as soon as possible. When he was first laid off everybody seemed to have lots of things that needed doing—hauling this and that, cleaning, repairing, painting and such, but not now, now it was all dried up, like he'd already done everything that needed doing or it would be just too painful or too embarrassing to have him around, since he'd been one of them not so long ago and who knew, maybe even passing the time of day with him— let alone having him around working—could just possibly, not that anyone actually believed such things in this day and age, but could just possibly bring the woes that were plaguing him down on all their houses.

So I imagine that was his normal day, the way he spent his

time, since he had more time than money, and he would usually end it going back to The Main Street Grill and seeing Fran again and helping her and Fred with the dinner crowd, eat dinner himself and help them close up, get twenty bucks for his efforts, drive back to the Quick Pik to buy enough beer to put him to sleep, get up the next morning and start all over again.

But then something happened that wasn't normal at all, and I know this, I don't have to imagine it, because he told me word for word about how he skipped dinner at the grill one evening, thinking it was too damn hot to eat anyway and a cold beer would taste mighty good after all his travels and how he pulled in the driveway behind the house, did an old man's climb from his pickup, one leg at a time, scooting to the edge of the seat and hauling himself upright, as tired as if he actually had done a day's work, slammed the door and turned to go inside. It wasn't until then that he realized what he'd done, that instead of going back to our father's and our mother's house where he'd been living, he'd gone back home, to his home, his and Josie's house, out of habit, since it was probably against the law even for him to be standing there. He looked around to see if anyone was watching and walked over to the bedroom window where the shade was down, but for a narrow slit at the bottom and he could see the room was dark, the covers on the bed kicked back over the edge of the mattress from what must have been a restless night, or an active one, and there was something on the floor he couldn't quite make out, clothes, maybe, but none he recognized.

He climbed the steps he'd built up to the porch, noticing for the first time how crooked they were and thinking how odd it was that you had to be away from something for a while to see its flaws, because when you were around it all the time, you accommodated yourself to it, like you did to people's irritating habits. He knocked a couple of times, pushed the button for the bell even though it hadn't worked for years, and when no one answered, he tried his key in the lock and just as he'd expected, it didn't work.

All the windows he could see were down so he went to the back of the house where the door was locked as well and the windows closed, but by then he was sweating and his heart was racing and he felt like a goddamn burglar, except how could he be a burglar when he was trying to get into his own house, the house he'd paid for and thought he was going to have his whole life and even die in? Then he saw that the cellar doors didn't look right and he lifted one and it swung open and, glancing around one more time to see if anyone was watching him, down he went as quick as anything into that dark, dank cellar and felt his way to the stairs to the back porch where he knew the door would be unlocked, as would the one into the kitchen and he thought maybe she wasn't so goddamn smart after all.

There was baloney in the meat drawer of the refrigerator and he made himself a sandwich just for the hell of it, even though he wasn't sure he could eat it all, and opened a beer he found there, which was strange since Josie hardly ever drank beer and it wasn't the kind he usually bought. There were dirty dishes in the sink, greasy pots and pans on the stove, and the place smelled like a litter box. There was a rip in the upholstery of his recliner, the TV remote had dead batteries, the bathtub was filthy, the toilet smelled like piss, hair was all over the sink and floor, and a bottle of Mennen aftershave was in the medicine cabinet in place of his Old Spice. He found jeans in the bedroom, crumpled up near the foot of the bed, like somebody had been in a hurry to get undressed, men's jeans with fancy stitching on the butt that he wadded up and threw back on the floor, wondering what the hell old Romeo had worn home then, if he'd gone home, that was. But maybe he hadn't, seeing as how there were a couple of pairs of men's underwear in the dresser, two shirts and another pair of jeans in the closet. The bastard. In his house, in his bed with his wife. The bitch. He threw a lamp against the wall, ripped the covers off the bed, cut the crotch out of the jeans with a pair of scissors he found, laid them, legs spread, on the bare mattress, ground his boot heel into the remote control, smashed the aftershave in the sink and scrawled FUCK YOU in lipstick on the bathroom mirror because he couldn't think of anything more hurtful to write.

Then he said that somehow he was back home, on the couch in his real home and not hers, thinking how stupid he was, how fucking stupid, a beer in one hand, a cigarette in the other as he waited for old Hank to come and arrest him for breaking and entering and destruction of property and god only knew what else. But maybe nobody had come home yet and found the mess, or maybe when they did, they decided not to say anything and just go on about their business—whatever business they were up to—not caring enough about him or what he did or thought even to be pissed off. That's what hurt most, if I really wanted to know, the not giving a fuck about him, how he felt, whether he was alive or dead or anything else.

He told me he opened the fridge for another beer, decided against it, and even though he wasn't particularly hungry, grabbed a chunk of cheese, which he regretted because of the taste it left in his mouth. He rummaged around in the pantry until he found the bottle of Old Grand-Dad he kept for special occasions, like now, the one day in his life he'd done anything different than usual and would probably go to jail for. He drank to jail and Josie and our father the old man and our mother and to me and Connie and finally to Fran, after which he put the bottle down and, drunker than anyone should be that early in the evening, drove to The Main Street Grill to see her.

The dinner rush—if you could call it that—was over, he said, and Fred was washing up in the kitchen and Fran was running totals on the register and she looked up at Len and said it looked like he was getting a head start on the evening and he said yeah, he guessed you could say that and she asked if he wanted something to eat and he said no, all he wanted was her. She told him he was sweet, and he said no, he meant it, she had the prettiest eyes and teeth and hair and ears, not to mention— She put her hand to his mouth and said he'd best stop right there, and he said he couldn't, she was all he could think about and why couldn't they— She told him he really was sweet and even kind of cute but what would something like that mean to him? She wasn't going to leave Fred and wasn't going to do anything else to hurt him and besides she said having a quickie with Len would be like putting a Band-Aid on a hemorrhage because he needed more than that and she didn't have it to give. So why didn't he just go on home now and sleep it off and come in for breakfast tomorrow like he usually did and they would start over from there? And she leaned across the counter and pecked him on the cheek, like his mother might, or his Aunt Louise, and he backed away, hand to his face, like she'd slapped him.

She was still calling after him as he clomped down the steps, which he didn't count, and lit a cigarette at the bottom, got into his pickup, rolled down the windows, started the motor and sat, hands on the wheel, staring down the street and thinking what a goddamn mess everything was and how there was no goddamn way he could go back home, not to either one now, not yet anyway, and he flipped the cigarette butt into the gutter, took one last glance at the restaurant where he knew Fran would be peeking at him from behind the curtains, put the pickup in gear and swung a U-turn in the middle of the street. He drove up Main, he told me, passing old Hank in the police car and a couple of other people he knew and at the end of the street, where the highway intersected it, he looked west toward The Baitshop and east toward nothing in particular and thought what the hell, what difference did it make now where he went or how long he stayed? Fran was right, he told me, he could drive all night if he wanted to, all day tomorrow, even go to Kansas City, it wasn't that far, go up and stay over, maybe take in a Royals game, eat at a good steakhouse. He had enough cash for an emergency, a credit card, and there was an all-night truck stop at Florence where he could get gas, a six-pack and cigarettes; so what was stopping him, why didn't he just turn the wheel and head down the road?

And just then he said a car pulled up behind him with a bunch of kids, and they honked and yelled for him to move it or milk it, and he turned around and gave them the finger, he told me, and said up yours even though he knew no one could hear him.

He didn't leave that day, of course, nor ever, except for his four-year stint in the Navy, even though, as Fran had said, there was nothing to keep him from it. And now that he couldn't even if he'd wanted to, he was in an odd manner running away toward a past that may never have existed, with me as his accessory, old Hank looking for the two of us wannabe fugitives, road banditos on the loose in Carter, Kansas, neither of us having harmed anyone or stolen anything, but for me perhaps, wheeling a dying shell of a man home.

Once we were across the tracks, which, needless to say, weren't designed for wheelchairs, we had fairly smooth sailing. With enough imagination, we might have seen ourselves in a prairie schooner, its sharp prow and white canvas gliding over endless miles of tall grass. But the truth was, our ship was more of a raft, Captain Len Caulkins alternately pointing us in the direction we should go and waving at passers-by, who gave us the usual one finger lifted from the steering wheel salute or, if overcome with emotion, a single toot of the horn. And to a person everyone smiled, understanding without having to be told exactly what was going on.

The old man's house was six, maybe eight blocks, from Twin Oaks and we made it there more quickly than he, or I, might have liked, since after I asked him if he wanted me to take him in and he gave an adamant shake of his head no, we hadn't much else to do than park under the meager shade of an elm tree as sick as he was, he in his chair and me cross-legged on the ground. We stared at the back door through a rusty screen—expecting what?

I wondered. Somebody, something to appear? A squatter? A ghost? A whole parade of them, in fact? Did he see himself as part of it now and perhaps had since the day Suz had found him paralyzed on the couch? Had he realized, through the firestorm in his brain, that the moment he was carried out by the ambulance crew was the beginning of a long and torturous end for him and that he would never return to his home? But that may assume more lucidity than he was capable of, given that his days at the time consisted of drinking from morning to night with Petey and then maybe or maybe not going to the Carter Inn as he'd begun to do after his breakup with Fran for the only food of the day and home again to drink himself to sleep.

Saying nothing and with nothing to say, I got up after a long while and stretched and asked if he was ready. He nodded that he was and as we started back, I asked if he wanted to take a spin downtown for old time's sake, no, or maybe roll past the park and around the track, no, or head out to Petey's, no, or wheel past his old house, the one he'd had with Josie, double no, with a flip of his hand to shut me up, or else.

In Retrospect

I don't know for certain what kind of strokes Len had, whether ischemic or hemorrhagic, whether from a blockage, clot or otherwise, in a blood vessel in the brain or a major artery leading to it, or from another vessel bursting and filling the brain cavity with blood. Both cause serious damage—that is, the deaths of millions of neurons by interrupting the normal flow of blood to them—resulting often in paralysis, loss of speech, hearing and sight, trouble breathing, eating, sleeping, eliminating, emoting, comprehending, thinking, judging, behaving, to mention a few consequences, and, in the worst circumstances, deep coma or death. So, as you can see, it doesn't matter which kind of strokes he had—medically or technically, biologically perhaps, but not in real terms since he was the way he was and wasn't going to get better.

His demise started gradually enough with his falling once in the doorway of the Carter Inn and once after Petey drove him home and he was stepping up to the curb, saying on each occasion that he'd stubbed his toe or tripped, which seemed a reasonable explanation at the time. Suz even discovered one of his boot soles had torn loose and was flapping with each step, so she bought him new shoes I don't think he ever wore, preferring, as he did, to repair the boot sole with duct tape. In hindsight, he was most likely experiencing transient ischemic attacks that involve momentary blockages of specific areas of the brain, during which a person might get dizzy and pass out or fall or suffer sight or speech problems. But the symptoms disappear after a few minutes or no longer than twenty-four hours and leave no permanent damage to the nervous system. So it's easier to ignore what happened and say you tripped or bumped into the door frame instead. The problem is, many people who experience transient ischemic attacks go on to have full-blown strokes within a year, all of which fits Len's case to a T, if we play Monday morning quarterback—the falling, as I've said, and subsequent slurring and stuttering and loss of strength on his right side, his concurrent descent into depression (brought on by both deteriorating health and heavy drinking) and stubborn refusal to seek help until that near final big bang that left him captive on his couch. So looking back, sure, all the signs were there, and we did try, remember, to get him to go see a doctor, talked till there was nothing more to say. And I don't know how much anything we could have done would have affected what eventually happened—the second massive stroke just after he was hospitalized and the even larger one at the VA hospital in Wichita, which left him permanently paralyzed and speechless. So I doubt we could have changed any of that, but on the other hand with earlier treatment he might well have had less severe nervous system damage and maybe have had a better chance at recovering the faculties he lost.

But that's said with benefit of an informed hindsight that could just as well have been applied to our mother and our father. If they had chosen to go their own ways, for instance, rather than to have gotten married so that none of us would have been born and Connie would never have married Bax so young nor Mason—nor Sammo the rock, for that matter—and none of what happened between Mason and her sons and the loss of Bo from her life would have come to pass. Len wouldn't have been the bastard to Josie and their kids Connie said he was when he'd been drinking—remind you of anyone else?—and he wouldn't have then driven Josie so far away she felt she had no recourse but to divorce him, and he wouldn't have then begun what you could argue was a deliberately self-destructive nosedive that, to his mind, I imagine, he was pulled out of against his will just short of a pitiful but decisive crash. I would never have met my wife nor sired my sons and we might all have remained, if you believe in such things, hanging in the cosmos, perfect Platonic ideals (orgasms?) of lives waiting to be lived.

Whatever Can Happen Will

I hadn't been home more than a couple of weeks and had finally gotten back into a work routine that was allowing me to make real progress on a writing project—this one, in fact—when Suz called me from a hospital emergency room to tell me that Len had been taken there with pneumonia which had probably been caused by his inability to swallow well and his consequent aspiration of food particles and other foreign substances into his lungs. He was on antibiotics and oxygen and was being suctioned regularly by respiratory therapists—thugs, he would have called them if he could—and was in general responding to treatment. But the real problem, she said, her voice dropping, quavering, was that when they did a routine chest x-ray to see how extensive his infection was, they discovered something else—a huge tumor at the back of his throat which was squeezing his esophagus, making it difficult if not impossible for him to swallow. That made him more susceptible to the aspiration pneumonia he now had and would lead ultimately to his choking to death on his own secretions. Dr. Hawkins, the surgeon who had been asked to consult on Len's case after the tumor was discovered, said that operating was out of the question because of the size of the mass and Len's generally rotten shape, although he might not have used those exact words. But because Len was not, as the doctor said, completely fried—that is, was still alert and seemingly aware of what was going on—he couldn't just leave him to, well, choke to death or suffocate and he thought it more humane to transfer Len to Newton's regional medical center, where he could be cared for by Dr. Khulhoff, a radiation oncologist whom Dr. Hawkins thought so highly of he would, if necessary, send his own mother or child there for treatment. I asked Suz how she was doing with all this and she said Sonny was with her, thank god, and they both thought Dr. Hawkins' advice was good, did I? I said sure, since otherwise the only alternative seemed to be, like the doctor said. . . She was quiet for a while and finally said no, she and Sonny had talked about it and they'd decided they couldn't just watch him, you know, and if there was any chance of making him even a little more comfortable, they wanted to do it. I said great, they had their answer, did they want me to come out? She was again quiet, then said I'd just been there, so she didn't think it would be necessary, they'd be okay—she and Sonny—and I asked if he really was being helpful or had merely happened to have been around that day. She said no, she'd called him directly and he'd come right away and had even offered to drive her to the hospital, and I said that was nice or something snide like that and her voice hardened as she explained that she wished people wouldn't be so judgmental about Sonny, he'd been over some rough roads and was a good person at heart and was trying to do the right thing now, even with their dad, which was going to take time and a lot of patience under the best of circumstances. And we also had to remember, as the old saying goes, chickens come home to roost, like it or not.

Sonny's Story

What happed with Sonny and the baby isn't nearly as exotic as Ezra's tale. You remember it, don't you, how he became a Caulkins and all the death and intrigue Great Aunt Hattie reveled in? That tale? No, I like to think this one follows more fittingly an occasion years earlier when I was running errands on a hot, humid day with my two sons in the car, the older maybe eight and the younger six, and as the afternoon wore on and the heat rose, so did our tempers until at some point over a remark or incident I no longer remember I yelled at my older son— although I contend it wasn't a yell so much as a raising of my voice. He in turn punched my younger son, who, after we had parked in our driveway at home, got out of the car, walked resolutely up to our front door, opened it and kicked our waiting cat.

When Sonny kicked his cat—is that maybe too cavalier a notion?—he was living with a person whose name I may have once heard but promptly forgot. So for the purposes of this story let's call her Miranda, or Mandy or Randy for short, you choose. She was ginger-haired, as I've been told, not pretty nor plain, a gaunt, anemic-looking, girl-woman with the squint-eyed, hard demeanor of someone three times her age who nonetheless drew our Sonny in and held him so tightly that he became a virtual pawn—some say slave—of this Miranda. She even went so far as to name him the father of her child, although that remains an open question, given, first, the absence of blood-typing or, even better, DNA testing and, second, Miranda's apparent propensity to dress in tight jeans and tank tops and hang out with bikers. But to most people the question of whether Sonny was the child's father paled next to the fact that, to their minds, nothing would have happened that night had Miranda been home where she belonged and not riding off on that bike like the floozy she was, leaving poor Sonny—their description, not mine—tending a child she said was his, neither of them yet twenty years old with no plans to marry and no idea how to raise a baby. So it was clear, to them at least, that Sonny wasn't the only one at fault. And many of them went even further, suspecting that he was the victim of a story concocted by Miranda and her biker buddies, wherein they had innocently left him alone with the baby to go for a ride and upon their return had found the child motionless in his crib and Sonny so drunk and drugged that he had no idea what he'd done.

But let's step back a minute to reconstruct what really went on, try to imagine events through Sonny's eyes that hot, baked-earth night at the height of summer. Saturday night to be exact, international date night as a friend calls it, and everybody but him had one because the woman who'd said over and over not to worry, she loved him more than life itself, was going out without him. Just a quick ride from Hutch to Newton with her friends— you know, the feel of the wind in her hair, the tremor of the bike beneath her. He wouldn't mind staying with Joey, would he? She'd pay him back just the way he liked, a sultry girl-woman glance and a full-mouth kiss, her tongue stilling his as he silently watched her turn and head out the door, slender but fine hips sashaying goodbye, looking fit enough, well, to fuck. That was all, that was it—fit enough to fuck. And he knew that was just what she intended to do as she climbed on the bike and snaked her arms around Darrell, thighs clutching his butt, not even a glance back in Sonny's direction as the Harleys rumbled off into muggy night air he could feel caress then prickle their skin as they plunged ever faster through it, bugs pinging the windscreen like BBs, tires slapping tar strips on the highway. Joey's gurgling cry rose from somewhere in the house behind him, but Sonny, working on one of his own, couldn't/didn't want to hear it and he went to the refrigerator, took out a beer, any beer, he could care less, and popped the top, drank it straight down, got another, a third. He could still hear Joey and found a bottle for him—at least she'd had the decency to get one ready—put it in a pan of water on the stove, rolled himself a joint, sucked the smoke as deeply as he could, holding it until his head was about to explode, and felt instantly better, except for Joey's hiccupping cry and the image of Miranda on her back under some tree, Darrell standing spread-eagle over her, unbuckling his belt with one hand, holding his beer and joint in his other, laughing that stupid fucking laugh of his, Miranda stoned enough she was laughing, too, just because he was, because that was all it took when you were high, somebody so much as grinned and you were giggling like a maniac. Only Sonny wasn't laughing, wasn't even smiling, no matter how much he drank or smoked, and if he'd caught a glimpse of himself—the flushed skin, scowling brow, pinched mouth and mean as hell look—he'd have been taken aback by the strange yet familiar face he saw, frightened by the anger he'd not have seen before but had experienced as a flash, a mini eruption in that place between body and brain, an emotional retching that inevitably left him feeling more unsettled than purged as he stepped back from a hole he'd put in a wall with his fist, a lawn mower he'd kicked so hard it had flipped over, a dent he'd made in the dashboard of a car that wouldn't start. Rages he'd justified by thinking at least it wasn't a person, although he was undecided what he might do to Darrell or Miranda, the two of them sucking and grunting, Darrell's big belly flapping against her flat one, a grimace on his face, as if she were squeezing his balls a little too hard, her mouth twitching, eyes wild, like a cat's right before it bites you. The bitch, the bastard, dirty little fuckers, a whip snapping out of the darkness, flicking a hot tongue onto their flesh at the exact moment they came, a yip and a yowl in unison, not from passion but pain as the whip snapped again and again and they scrambled to avoid it, naked and on their knees, shielding themselves with their clothes, begging him to stop, not realizing how lucky they were he didn't own a gun. Water boiled around the baby bottle, and he burned his hand retrieving it, swearing dirty cock-sucking sonofabitch as he stomped toward the room where Joey lay crying, arms and legs flailing like a cockroach on its back, like a goddamn cockroach, except cockroaches didn't drive you crazy with their bawling and they didn't shit and piss their pants and eat just so they could do it all over again and you could clean them up all over again because their mothers were off fucking around with some blowhard good for nothing bastard of a so-called friend, Darrell by name. He wished Darrell had a girl he could fuck so he'd know how it felt—turnabout was fair play—or maybe he could fuck one of Miranda's friends, or her sister, Georgie—nobody was closer to Miranda and nothing would hurt her more. He could fuck her in their bedroom and leave her panties behind to make sure Miranda found out. None of which quieted Joey and in fact made him cry harder, or appeared to, and Sonny lifted him from the crib and started to change him but forgot to put an extra diaper over the boy's penis and got piss all over his face, in his mouth and eyes, and he began thinking how that was just like Darrell, to kick a man when he was down, piss on him when he couldn't defend himself and how, when his head was turned at just that angle, Joey looked more like Darrell than anybody, definitely more than himself, he kept thinking as he finished changing him and stepped back and wondered how strange it was that he'd never noticed the resemblance before. He approached Joey again and there Darrell was, sure as hell, mocking him with that just-fucked-your-girl-and-was-she-ever-nice curl to his lips and something happened, something snapped, and he picked up Joey and took him to the kitchen and tried to feed him and the milk must have still been too hot because it set off a screech of hurt and hunger Sonny was

unable to curb no matter what he did—pacing, patting, talking—
until he jiggled the boy, telling him to stop crying, be quiet, shut
up, jiggled possibly a little harder, shut up, shut up now, he
meant it, and a little harder until the crying began to subside and
soon stopped altogether.

No matter what did or did not happen that night, one fact
remains: a child was injured badly enough he was hospitalized
in serious condition and Sonny was arrested without protest. He
said to Suz and his father and perhaps to his mother that he did
what they'd accused him of (not must have, mind you, but did)
and deserved whatever punishment the court gave him. He told
them that they should all be thanking their god or lucky stars
that he hadn't killed Joey, which he apparently nearly did, came
this close—were they aware of that, did they realize he was an
almost murderer?—because if he had, they would be looking at
a totally different situation.

But as it turned out, since he had no prior criminal record, not
so much as a traffic ticket, the judge noted, he was given the
lightest possible sentence—two years in a nearby minimum
security prison and a stern lecture about self-control. But to a
family that, despite its inadequacies, had never seen any of its
members in jail (with the exception of the night Uncle Boyd
spent behind bars for plastering a waitress with ketchup,
remember?), Sonny's internment seemed a huge mistake, a bad
dream that featured an otherwise decent kid with an angelic
singing voice in prison fatigues swabbing hallways and sorting
laundry. No one quite knew what to think or how to act, so we
each fell back to what was most familiar and comfortable. I
wrote. Letters, dozens of chatty, uncharacteristically cheerful
communiqués about my life, my wife's, my sons', my thoughts,
feelings, opinions on virtually everything, including the weather
and what Sonny should and should not be eating. Connie, Earth
Mother to us all, out of frustration over not being able to visit
Sonny often enough—she lived in the same town—finally went

so far as to get a job at the prison so she could see and talk to him every day and thereby control the flow of information from and to him. Suz visited and called when she had the time but generally, survivor that she was, went on about her life. Josie fretted about how he was and what people might think but couldn't do much to make herself or him feel better about the situation. Len drank even more and never once visited or called or wrote his son and would not discuss Sonny's incarceration, other than to say things like once a Caulkins, always a Caulkins with the same fatalistic sigh he also used when excusing his lifestyle by summoning up the "fact" that no male Caulkins family member ever lived past sixty-five anyway, so what the hell difference could it make what he did? The same attitude contributed to the notion that the Caulkins family had only bad luck, if any at all, and were not able to save money, grow tomatoes, keep a houseplant alive, or for the most part, sustain a marriage. We were, according to that view, a miserable lost lot with no real chance of redemption.

When Sonny got out of prison, he and Suz and Josie in general took up where they had left off, not once, as far as I know, talking about what had happened, the same as they'd never really talked about anything before, tending instead toward chit-chatting, laughing at silly things, gossiping, carrying on with life as usual. Relations with his father, however, were a bit cooler, as in more reserved, remote, practically non-existent, which some people thought was inevitable given that Sonny had always been, as Grandma Caulkins so generously put it, more of a mama's boy. Meaning that he tended to defend Josie when she and Len argued, as happened, according to Connie, more and more frequently in the months leading up to the divorce. Twenty years earlier, Len would have found himself, or me for that matter, right in Sonny's place, cowering just out of sight but ready to leap into action when our father's drinking spilled over, as it inevitably did, into yelling and finger shaking and saying things he would later wish he hadn't but was too goddamn proud or stubborn or stupid to admit he was sorry for. Except the drunken, raging maniac Sonny was witnessing was his own father transformed into, as Connie again observed, that bastard, our father the old man, the one person Len most detested and feared becoming.

Maybe Suz was right and those scrawny-assed chickens had finally hauled their carcasses home to roost—on Len's and Sonny's heads, scratching, pecking, shitting, there for the duration, like bad hats. Imagine, if you can, this scene unfolding: after two years of complete silence that had hardened into an impenetrable concretion of heartache and misunderstanding, Sonny, a born-again Christian who had been saved in prison by—his words—the ever-loving grace of God through Jesus Christ his personal savior, taking it upon himself to seek out and forgive his father, whom he found in an alcohol-induced stupor sitting in a tattered nylon and aluminum lawn chair outside the back door of his house—he no longer allowed anyone in but Suz. Imagine as Sonny approached for their pre-arranged meeting, Len rising, a cigarette in one hand, a beer in the other—Busch Light, because it was less expensive and, being light, allowed him the delusion that he could drink more with less effect, although the only thing he was now after was numbness—and them shaking hands, half-hugging, Len gesturing toward another equally battered lawn chair opposite him across the wobbly fieldstone walk that led from the house to the garage. Asking if Sonny wanted a beer—there was a red and white cooler behind Len's chair in the late afternoon shade of the apple tree—and Sonny saying no. A smoke? No again. Len leaning forward then, elbows on knees, saying, yeah? Sonny saying yeah in return and Len asking how he was doing and Sonny saying fine, as fine as he could be, he guessed, finer than he'd been in a while anyway and Len allowing as how he bet that was right, a drink, a drag on his cigarette. Imagine Sonny telling his father the reason things were fine was that he'd changed, his attitude had changed, and Len, not being in the best frame of mind, asking what that meant, which had to have been like that Dutch kid pulling his finger out of the dike—Sonny taking a deep breath and, leaning forward himself, starting the story of his salvation at the guidance of another inmate who had also found the Lord and, through Him, the path to righteousness and new life which was open to all people because all were sinners in the eyes of the Lord. Everyone, but everyone, could be saved, due to the loving kindness, the forgiveness of all-merciful God through his Son, Jesus Christ. Including him, Len. Did he know that? Did he know he could walk at the right hand of God, that all he needed was to renounce sin and accept Christ as his savior? Was he ready to do that? Was he ready to confess and be baptized in the Spirit and receive the gift of eternal life through the sacrifice of God's only Son, Jesus? Imagine the look on Len's face, that shit-eating goofy smile he got when he was so overwhelmed he couldn't respond— or wouldn't give his tormentor the satisfaction of seeing him try to—and consequently saying nothing, doing nothing but tipping the beer can to his mouth to drain it, taking a final long drag on his cigarette and—aggressively cocking his head for good measure—dropping the butt into the can to make sure Sonny understood that the beer, the butt and the both of them were indeed finished.

Cleaning House

I suppose Connie first got the idea the day she showed up at Len's house unannounced. He still had a phone then and you were supposed to call ahead so he could meet you outside the back door, as he'd done with Sonny, or on the front porch where he'd set up two other ragged lawn chairs if it happened to be raining. Even the day Connie came, he saw her soon enough that she said he tried to block her way in by standing spread-eagle across the doorway, saying no, no over and over. She told me she asked him what the hell was going on, did he have a body in there or something and he laughed a little, not because he thought what she'd said was funny but more like he was trying to remember if there was a body there. I said come on and she said no, that's really how he acted before he finally stepped back, shaking his head, and let her through. And was she ever sorry she'd made such a big deal about getting in, because at that point she couldn't leave like she wanted to and had to pretend nothing at all was wrong and that she was instead going into Sammo's mother's house—Sally kept a spotless, perfectly ordered home. If she hadn't, she said she would have broken down then and there—a sigh and a long pause to be sure I had time to absorb the magnitude of the sacrifice she'd made—because, voice dropping a notch for dramatic effect, I just wouldn't have believed what kind of shape the place was in. I couldn't have. Our mother and our father would have died all over again if they'd seen what she had, they honest to god would have. I knew I was supposed to ask her some bullshit rhetorical question at that point—what did she mean the shape it was in? It couldn't have been that awful, could it?—or say something comforting along the lines of sorry she had to go through something so terrible and we all appreciated it, we really did. But, of course, as usual, I said nothing, and she told me she didn't blame me, she wouldn't know what to say either, and went on, as I'm sure she'd been planning all along, to describe the foul, rotten, ugly, sour, everything all at once stench that hit her as soon as she stepped inside the back door. She couldn't tell exactly where it was coming from, she said, since the whole breakfast area off the kitchen where our father had enclosed the old screened porch—I remembered it, didn't I? A question so snide I could only clench my fists and grit my teeth—well, it was filled with green lawn bags, those real big ones? and they were all overflowing with beer cans, Styrofoam food things, garbage, and god only knew what else. The kitchen counter and sink were stacked head-high with dirty dishes, she wasn't kidding, and the stove and refrigerator were so sticky with grease and grime she couldn't bring herself to touch them. And the floors—had she mentioned them? The kitchen was bad enough, all filthy and stained and clogged with dirt and hairballs around the edges, but it was nothing compared to the living room, which was totally covered in dog shit. I'd heard her right, dog shit. Mound after mound like little anthills all across the carpet, because Len never let that poor dog out, afraid that he'd run off and never come back, which you couldn't blame him for if he did. And the smell—jesusgod. Take the kitchen and mix it with dog shit and piss and smoke and stale beer and, she supposed, dirty clothes and sheets and the reek from a bathroom with a toilet so plugged with cigarette butts and who knew what else it wouldn't flush and a sink and bathtub so filthy and crusted they made her skin crawl. On top of that the whole place was brown, like it used to be when our father and our mother smoked all day every day, only worse, if I could imagine that, like he'd brewed big buckets of tea and used it to paint the walls and ceilings and windows, dipped the curtains in it. What she wanted to do, she said, was go outside and throw up and get in her car and drive away. But she knew she couldn't, so she marched herself right over and sat herself down on his couch, the same as if he had told her to make herself comfortable.

He finally strolled in from the kitchen, she said, and asked as best as he could if she wanted a beer, and she said no, she hadn't had one in years—something she told everybody, no matter who, when the subject of drinking came up—and he said fine, whatever, but if she didn't mind, he was going to have one himself, which he brought back and put on the end table beside the chair he always sat in by the TV. When he got settled, he lit a cigarette, and she told him she would rather he didn't smoke around her, since she had just been through treatment for lung cancer. And right then, quick as a flash, his head jerked, she said, twitched, whatever you want to call it, the slightest little movement she doubted anyone else would have noticed but her, because she knew him inside out and backwards and always had, always knew what he was thinking, sometimes before he did. So it was clear as the nose on her face, even as he stubbed out that cigarette in his ashtray and said he was sorry, that he'd forgotten she had cancer. Plain forgot—could I believe that?— which hurt her and made her mad, sure, but scared her more than anything, because she thought if he could forget that as close as they'd always been, what kept him from forgetting to put out a cigarette, maybe, or turn a burner off, or check to see if the pilot light was on in the hot water tank or furnace?

She said they talked a while longer, if that was what you could call it, and watched a little TV, with her trying to make it as normal a visit as possible. When she told him she had to go and got up to leave, she said you'd have thought she'd handed him a hundred dollars, the smile that broke out on his face. He didn't thank her, didn't invite her back but did walk her to the door like a real gentleman and held it open for her, grunting in response to her goodbye.

She said it was while she was driving home—crying so hard, according to her, she nearly ran off the road a couple of times— that she decided what we—all of us—should do—and that was to go back over there and put that place in order. Len's house, she meant. Clean it up, fix it up, whatever, so he could have a decent place to live again. Knowing Connie, I don't imagine she thought to ask Len what he thought, nor would she have worried that, miserable as things seemed to her, he might not cotton to the idea of having his home invaded by a band of do-gooders, even if they were, for the most part, his own blood. No, my guess is that as soon as she got home, she talked to Sammo and called Suz who was to call Sonny and talk to her husband Morris, a master carpenter and general all-around handyman, and then call her, Connie, back so they could set a date for getting done what needed doing. Think Patton/Eisenhower/Hannibal/Mao combined and you get the idea. Even sick, once Connie was smitten by a cause, resistance was futile.

I became the money man, since I couldn't be there in the flesh. I had already made three trips to Kansas by mid-year and really did need to attend to my own affairs. I realize that some people, perhaps you included, regard both writing and teaching as doing next to nothing anyway, occupations that leave their performers with more time on their hands than they know what to do with. So why couldn't I be there? you/they might wonder. Why wouldn't I go help my brother? Was it selfishness? I don't think so. Lack of will, then, or decency? Was I just plain lazy, or, as Grandma Caulkins might have suspected, afraid to get my hands dirty—physically or metaphorically? None of these reasons seems quite right to me, and I imagine, when I'm honest with myself, that it was simply easier to send money than myself. I certainly wasn't the first person to do such a thing. The faithful of the Middle Ages bought indulgences from the Church to pay for their sins, rather than doing penance and good works. In more modern terms, people make annual contributions to UNESCO or CARE so they can more easily flip past pictures of starving children in the *New Yorker* and *Atlantic*. So I was generally disposed toward sending money anyway when Connie called to say that she and Suz and Sammo had gone to Len's house and told him what they had in mind—I doubt that anything was discussed as such—and then had walked through, pad and pencil in hand, making a list of projects and materials needed, including a drainpipe for the kitchen sink, a water heater, vent piping for the furnace, a toilet and bathroom sink, hoses for the washing machine, glass for several broken windows, not to mention nails and screws and caulking, buckets and mops, cleaner and disinfectant—she was sure they'd forgotten something—and when they got finished and looked at everything, they were pretty overwhelmed because none of them had the kind of money they would need, and, well, somebody—that shadowy, vague, blameless somebody—suggested that they, meaning she, call me and see maybe if I could help them out a little. (I swear I'm not making this up, even though it sounds like I scripted it word for word.) They knew it would be hard for me to get there but that I'd want to be involved—Len was my brother, too, after all—and they thought, you know, and I asked how much they needed and she said they'd figured five hundred would cover everything nicely and I said, all right, okay, because it was being used to help Len, I'd send it right away, who should I make the check to? She said to put her name on it, since that would be the simplest thing. I said, sure, fine and wrote the check that afternoon, put it in an envelope, sealed it, stamped it, mailed it and figuratively gave myself a pat on the back.

A couple of weeks later it was Suz on the phone with me, saying that she and Morris had gone to Wichita to buy a new water heater and had installed it and it was working fine. The problem was, they'd paid for it with their credit card, and Suz had called Connie to get the money to cover the cost. Connie hemmed and hawed around and finally told her she was sorry but she didn't have any money, and Suz said what did she mean she didn't have it and Connie asked Suz what part of nothing she didn't understand. I said wait a minute, how could that be, the check I'd sent had cleared the bank with her signature on it. Suz said all she knew was what Connie had told her—the money was gone. Gone? Yeah, she said, Connie had told her it was gone. But didn't that mean she must have had it at some time or another? I said and Suz allowed as how that was the way it sounded to her, and I asked if any new stuff had appeared at Len's, like the sink and bathtub, and she said not to her knowledge, and I asked about drainpipes and windows and paint, and she said she hadn't seen anything of that, either. I said so if Connie had the money in the beginning and now didn't and there was nothing new at Len's, that meant— I didn't really think that, did I? Suz wanted to know, and I asked what else she would call it, and she said she didn't know. I said I supposed we could assume something horrible had happened, some dire emergency had come up, but even so, weren't you still obligated to ask, to get permission before you took someone else's money and used it for yourself? Suz said she supposed that was true and I said what if Connie had taken the money from a store or a bank or somebody's bedside table, for that matter, and Suz said she'd probably have been arrested and I said exactly, but this was even worse as far as I was concerned because it was money for her own brother, for chrissake, after she'd been the one who'd set up such a howl about his living conditions. Neither of us said anything for a while, and I wondered if Suz was thinking the same thing I was, that Connie might have set the whole thing up, used all of us as part of her scheme to get her hands on extra money, since—and I don't think Suz knew any of this—it wouldn't have been the first time she'd resorted to histrionics to weasel money out of our mother and our father, Mason's father, Sammo's parents and anyone else she figured she could tap. When Suz spoke again, she asked what I was going to do—about the money, she meant, and I said I didn't know, did she have any suggestions? Not that she could think of, but she wanted me to know that the whole thing made her sick, and I said I knew exactly how she felt. And it wasn't just about Connie, because frankly she wasn't sure how she and Morris were going to cover the cost of the water heater, since it wasn't something they'd budgeted for. I said I wished the rest of it could be that easy. She should tell me how much it was and I'd send a check. She said that wasn't right, me paying for things twice, and I told her that wasn't her concern, but I did need to know the amount so I didn't have to guess and maybe short-change her. She said all right and told me then, exactly to the penny, and I sent the money that same day.

I also made sure I called Connie before I started feeling sorry for her. She picked up on the second ring, as if she'd been camped out by the phone, waiting. I said her name—that was all, nothing else—and she said yeah, she knew, she knew in that fucking woe-is-me voice that made me grit my teeth so hard they ached. I could see her sitting on the far side of the round table pushed against the wall by the kitchen doorway. It was the nerve center of the house. From there she had easy access to the phone, the newspaper, mail and the bathroom. They ate there, paid bills there, entertained there and might even have had sex there, for all I knew, although I doubt they did so much of that since Connie'd gotten sick. And I could see Sammo sitting across from her now, smoking, urging her on with a nod or a flip of the bird meant for me as she talked, trying to explain how sorry she was but they were desperate and didn't know what else to do—a hiccup in her voice to let me know she was either crying or close to it—and they had no choice but to use the money to buy food or not eat, which may have been a real enough situation, except it was something I'd heard over and over, like a mantra, when she'd call to say she hated to do it, she really did, but they didn't know who else to turn to. I asked what she meant they had no choice, I'd always helped them in the past, hadn't I? Hadn't I? She said yes, I had, but. But what? Come on, but what? She said it was hard to talk because I was so angry—another hiccup—why was I so upset? I told her I couldn't believe she asked me that. Didn't she think there was anything wrong with what she'd done? That wasn't just my money, I said. It was for everybody to use for Len, so she'd taken Len's money—did that make sense to her? It wasn't only me she needed to think about, because a lot of people's feelings had been hurt and now nothing was going to get done at Len's and she had only herself to blame for that. I said I was sorry to be so hard on her because I knew she had other things on her mind, but she had to understand what she'd done. She said she did now and wished there was something she could do to make up for it, she really did—her voice quavering and teary. But it was like she couldn't help it. Like she had some goddamn addiction or something. The money was there, and she needed it, and, well. Anyway, she said after a deep breath that sounded for all the world like someone taking a drag on a cigarette, I should have known better. Oh, really? I said. Sure, she said. What did I expect to happen? I knew her as well as anybody in the world, and she never would have trusted herself with that much money. So why on god's green earth would I? Think about it. Of all people, why would I?

The Best Medicine

He could still laugh, even with cancer massed at the back of his throat like a band of assassins that had slipped unnoticed into place and were, now that their subject had been identified, preparing their last lethal assault. It may have been that very ability to continue finding humor in things that, if not saved, then prolonged his life, or so I assumed the day I talked to Dr. Hawkins in the hallway after he had examined Len and he told me he wasn't going to lie and tell me how great everything was, because it wasn't. The tumor was big and getting bigger and would eventually choke off Len's trachea and esophagus—Dr. Hawkins' thumb and index finger forming an O that slowly closed into a solid fist. Under normal circumstances, given everything else that was wrong with Len, he wouldn't recommend treatment beyond making him as comfortable as possible, meaning unlimited morphine when the time came. But Len wasn't, in Dr. Hawkins' words, a totally lost cause. Just look him in the eye and you could see that there was still plenty going on in there—the way he smiled and flirted with the nurses, the way he stuck out his tongue when the pulmonary therapist came in to do a deep lung suctioning, the way he took notice, for good or ill, as soon as a family member appeared. And because of that, because he was at the moment nowhere near being brain dead, Dr. Hawkins was going to recommend radiation therapy to help shrink the mass—not cure, he wanted me to know, they weren't suggesting that. I said no, no, I realized that and he led me then by the arm a few steps down the hall to where we had even more privacy and said look, he knew this was awful for everybody, especially since Len had brought it on himself and was going to die sooner than later because of it. But that shouldn't mean he ought to strangle on his own spit, should it, and know all along what was happening? There was death, he said, and then there was death that left some self intact, and he preferred the latter whenever possible, like now. He'd already talked with Suz and Sonny and they had agreed with him that they should go ahead with therapy, which was why he had scheduled Len's first session with Dr. Khulhoff the next morning. He was sure I would agree that the sooner they got started, the better, although he did want me to know, as he'd told Suz and Sonny, that the therapy was not without risk. Len could die during the course of it from any number of things—hemorrhage, metastases to other organs, or just the final straw-that-broke-the-camel's-back stress on an already dilapidated body—but the alternative was simply too damned awful to contemplate. So what he was trying to tell me was that it was going to be tough—Len was going to be sore and maybe even sick and we were going to have to work hard to keep up his and our own spirits, to keep him smiling, if we could. I said, yeah, I thought I understood and asked if he'd heard the one about why Cookie went to the hospital and he said no and I said because she felt crumby. He shook his head and tried not to smile and said exactly, that was it, his hand on my shoulder, that was just the ticket, just what the doctor ordered. I looked at him for a second and he smiled again and I gave him a thumbs-up and he said thanks, would I mind if he stole my joke? It wouldn't be so bad, he didn't think, especially for a surgeon.

Len was half asleep when I got back to his room—literally, with one eye closed and the other, though glassy, trained on the TV—and I said hey and he blinked the open eye and I asked him if he knew that dog was god spelled backwards, and there was a silence even within his silence, both blue-blue eyes now watching me, which I suppose prompted me to ask if he'd heard what one eye said to the other eye. No? Well, it said between you and me something smells. He snapped his head toward the open door, the hall, pushed himself up a bit as if looking for someone, and I said why did the gynecologist go to the ophthalmologist? He glanced back at me now, wary, unsure what to think. Because things were starting to look a little fuzzy. Ha, did he get it? Things were looking a little fuzzy. He coughed up a wad of mucous he tried to spit into the little wastebasket that had been put on his bed for that purpose but couldn't get it out, and I wiped his mouth and hand with tissues and he nodded that that was more like it, more like the me he recognized, so I asked him if he knew why men couldn't get mad cow disease and he closed both eyes as if to shut me up and I said they couldn't because they were all pigs. And I said no, he had to look at me, he had to listen. This was what the doctor had ordered, goddamnit, and he was going to listen and he was going to laugh and he was going to get better because of it, did he hear me? What two things in the air could make a woman pregnant, huh, what two things? Her feet, did he get it, in the air, her feet could get her pregnant because— Laugh, goddamnit, goddamn you, laugh. Connie didn't either and he could see what shape she was in. But maybe that was my fault, too, since I hadn't really tried with her; didn't know I was supposed to—and now look at him and look at me, for all I knew. How long before I would be there like him? So we were going to laugh. Even if it killed me, we were going to laugh. Had he heard the one about nursing homes giving Viagra to the old men living there as a way to keep them from rolling out of bed—holding my forearm and hand up stiffly and lowering it onto his mattress, back up, onto the mattress as a demonstration. Like a peg, I told him, to keep a log in place, a telephone pole, did he get it? Because that was all it was anyway, right, a pecker was a peg, only smoother, maybe, no splinters, but still a peg, a squash, a cucumber, jesus, I was killing me. I was a regular sombitchin laugh riot. Single-handed. But I was nothing compared to the whole act I had in mind, with Connie juggling money, Sonny miming Mr. Preacher Man, Sammo grinding an air organ while his monkey threw its shit at people, Suz singing, Jim jumping through a lasso and Sally pushing her puppy in a pram, Janice twisting herself into a human pretzel, his nurses doing the cancan, he himself—yes, Len the man—in a top hat and moustache directing it all from his bed with his good arm, everybody joining in to laugh and make each other laugh until they felt like crying, Dr. Hawkins bringing down the house with a grand finale joke: What was the difference between a brain surgeon and God? God didn't think he was a brain surgeon. Drum-roll, cymbals, curtain.

So what did he think, was it good, was it a go, had laughter cured what ailed him? Was he ready to take up his mat and walk—or, if nothing else, smile?

A Real Mouth-(and Head-)ful

It couldn't have been planned that way, or at least I don't see how, since Suz and I had been there all morning and just happened to have been sitting side by side in matching chairs between Len's bed and the windows. We were facing the door to the room and the hallway outside, hands folded in our laps—I swear they were—faces that I imagine now must have appeared blank of expectation, as Len was asleep and we were deeply into whatever thoughts we were having, like people waiting for a church service or class to begin, and suddenly a person was standing opposite us on the other side of the bed, having materialized from a burst of energy that we felt more than saw. He said his name was Dr. Khulhoff, with a K, and extended his hand. We told him who we were and why we were in Len's room. He sighed, licked his lips and pulled the medical chart he was holding even tighter to his chest. He said he was sure Dr. Hawkins had told us he would be taking over Len's treatment and we nodded and he said good good, why didn't we just begin at the beginning then?

He drew up another chair at the foot of the bed, checked to see if Len was still asleep, and started explaining that the throat was a tube maybe as big around as your two thumbs put together which ran five inches or so from the back of the mouth to the entrance to the esophagus, here, and trachea, here—his first two fingers splitting in an upside down V. Did we get the picture? Now that tube part we called the throat was divided again, for our purposes, into two parts—the pharynx, or upper throat and the hypopharynx, or lower throat. It was the lower part that we were concerned with, the wall of the throat just behind the larynx, or Adam's apple, looking for all the world like Mr. Rogers as he pointed his own out to us. That was where Len's tumor was, a notoriously hard place to examine with a scope or a light and mirror, which was one reason patients and doctors many times didn't know anything was wrong until the person with the cancer had trouble breathing or swallowing or talking. By then, as in Len's case, the tumor had gotten so large and was so advanced— meaning it had most likely spread to other tissue and maybe even other organs—that treatment options became more limited. Surgery, for instance, wasn't going to do Len any good and he was too weak physically to stand the strain chemotherapy would put him under. Which was where he, as a radiation oncologist, came in. Meaning he was a last resort? Suz asked. He smiled and said in a way, yes, he supposed you could say that, but we shouldn't get the wrong idea and think he was suggesting that he could somehow bring about a cure, because, as Dr. Hawkins had surely told us, that was no longer a realistic expectation.

We said we understood that and Dr. Khulhoff said good good and went on to explain that everything they did from this point on would be palliative, did we know what he meant by that? We said sure and he raised his finger and right then—I swear this is true—a gurney rolled into the room, an orderly at each end, like they'd been waiting for just that prompt. They lowered the metal railing on Len's bed and pushed the gurney next to it. Dr. Khulhoff said we were probably wondering what was going on and we said yeah and he said they were getting ready to transport Len to the radiation department. We said why so soon and he said there quite frankly wasn't any time to waste. They had had a cancellation and had decided to push ahead immediately with Len's initial examination and measurements for the thermoplastic mask that he would wear during therapy sessions. He realized a mask might sound kind of strange, but he wanted to reassure us there was a method behind their madness. A mask helped stabilize a patient's head during treatment and also allowed technicians to mark precisely on it rather than the patient's body the points at which they wanted to aim the radiation, thus permitting them to administer a more powerful dose with each treatment, the idea being to destroy the tumor while leaving surrounding tissue as unaffected as possible.

Were we following him? Good good. The plan at that point, then, was to give Len one treatment a day for five, maybe even six or seven, weeks, depending on how he was bearing up and how effective the therapy was. But if everything went okay, Dr. Khulhoff said, Len would be released back to the nursing home where his condition would be closely monitored. For what? I asked. The question seemed to befuddle Dr. Khulhoff and he said, after a rather long pause, changes, new developments, to see how he was doing, whether he was remaining stable, or— Suz and I waited, but he didn't finish, and I said, all right, now that he'd brought it up, what about OR? What would happen when OR came, like we knew it was going to, and he said there was no way to say for certain, it just depended (again), an answer that Len would have heartily approved of, being, as it was, the equivalent of a verbal shrug strong enough to cause our father the old man to grumble in his grave.

One of the orderlies cleared his throat and Dr. Khulhoff, eyes

closing for a moment—a silent prayer in thanks for being inter-
rupted?—told us he was sorry but we would have to wait outside
while they transferred Len to the gurney. We went to the hall
where Suz said she was tired and thought she would go on home,
what about me? I told her I was going to stay a little longer and
she tipped her head why, but I didn't say anything, since I didn't
know why, except I wasn't ready to leave yet, and she said okay,
she might see me tomorrow, and I said sure and she was gone.

It wasn't long before the orderlies drove the gurney out of
Len's room with him on it and Dr. Khulhoff right behind, and I
asked if I could walk with them, and he said that would be fine,
although I wouldn't be able to stay once he was taken into the
examination room. I said I realized that and he said good good,
and I said I just kind of wanted to, you know, and he said no
problem. Really. And he took me by the arm.

We went down several halls and connecting passageways and
finally came to a smallish reception area inside double doors
marked Radiation Lab where the orderlies stopped the gurney
and signed a couple of papers on clipboards at the reception
desk. Dr. Khulhoff talked to them for a bit, nodded good good,
shook my hand and left. One of the orderlies then stayed with
Len while the other went into a windowed room with Venetian
blinds and came back out in a minute, saying they were ready.

Nobody seemed to notice—or care after all—as I walked
alongside the gurney into the radiation lab. Two women in blue
coats introduced themselves as Rene (without the extra e or
accent mark, she pointed out) and Kathy. They would be, as they
called it, working with Len during his therapy. And just who, if I
didn't mind saying, was I? I told them I was Len's brother, and
they glanced at him, at me, and said oh absolutely, no doubt
about it, thenosethemouththeeyes, a strong resemblance, and I
wished I had brought the picture of our mother and Len and me
to show them. But they were already on to other matters,
pointing out to me the table where they were going to put Len

when he came for therapy, a narrow, light blue bench above a single arching foot, a pedestal, really, nothing more, with a headrest you might see in the Egyptian collection in a museum of natural history. Only this one was metal and was designed, they were saying, to hold his head and neck rigidly in place, along with the straps they lifted up from below the table, like flight attendants demonstrating how to put on your seat belt. He would also wear the mask they were going to fit him for in a few minutes and then actually make with gauze and plaster of Paris applied over his face. They would first cover his skin with plastic, of course, and give him a straw to breathe through. Once the mask had hardened, which took only a few minutes—it was an amazing process, Rene said—they would mark on it the precise target for the radiation beam, remove it and that would be that until he came back for his first treatment, when they would refit the mask, give him a shot or two of radiation, take it off and send him back to his room.

I asked if they had a mask I could look at and they glanced at each other not knowing quite what to say or do, as though no one had ever made such a strange request, and finally either Rene or Kathy said she thought they might have an old one and disappeared into what must have been a supply room and came back with a mask in hand. It was of a woman's face, not older than fifty, it didn't appear, with prominent cheek bones and chin and a Roman nose. I raised it to my own face, which it didn't fit, of course, but I still got the idea of what it would be like to lie beneath it on that table, voices, maybe Rene's and Kathy's, maybe not, telling me what to do and not do, the clicking buzz of the radiotherapy machine. *Star light, star bright, first star I see tonight. I wish I may, I wish I might. . .*

I removed the mask and they wanted to know if I was okay and I said yeah, I was fine, why were they asking, and they said well, I just looked kind of— I said honestly, I was all right and, by the way, did they happen to have any idea whose mask that was and what had happened to the person. They said no, they didn't remember, they honestly didn't, but even if they did, they couldn't tell me because of patient confidentiality and all. I said sure, I knew they couldn't and that was the way it should be, but I was just wondering, because seeing it made me wonder, and they nodded and said they could understand how it might. I said something then about how hard it must be at times to do the work they did and they nodded again and said it was but it had a lot of good things about it, too, like when people got better or got well altogether. I said yeah, I imagined that was true, and they started easing me toward the door, saying how nice it had been chatting with me but they really did have to get busy with Len and I couldn't be there when they did. I said sure, I knew that, but just one last thing, and I went over and clasped Len's good hand and said he needed to behave himself and do whatever Rene and Kathy told him to and that I would be checking with them later to see if he had. They smiled, one of them stroking his forehead and cheek, saying she was sure there weren't going to be any problems, none at all, and she hoped I had as pleasant a day as possible.

Retracing the hallways and turns, I made my way back to Len's room and sat a while beside his empty bed and saw for an instant his mask lying in the well his head had made on his pillow, grey, eyeless, lifeless, and I began wondering what the clinic did with the old masks they'd made, whether they moldered away in that storage room off the radiation lab or were smashed or ground up or just pitched out with the rest of the trash. Why weren't they on display as a group or scattered around the hospital in shadow boxes, the kind you might see framing more famous faces in a Musée de Thanatopsis or a Gucci antique shop, or better yet as a rotating memorial for the mothers and the fathers, the Connies and Lens and mes of the world, the Suzes and Sonnys and Jims and Sallys and Sammos and Janices and all the rest on a wall in home furnishings at the bigass

Walmart Superstore across the road from the hospital, where copies could be had for $24.95, including a name and brief biography of the person represented, a final fusion of buying and selling and living and dying as it was always meant to be.

A Table for Two

Suz and I found the calling card the next morning, a pale yellow slip tucked under the corner of the Kleenex box on Len's table tray, announcing that Martin J. Fox, Pastor, Shady Grove United Methodist Church, had stopped by, a penciled note on the back saying he hoped to catch Leonard next time. I asked Suz if she'd ever heard of the guy, and she said no, but, and I said but what, and she said but nothing, forget it. I asked Len if he'd heard of him and he shook his head and I said okay, then, had he seen anybody come in, and he shook his head again, this time with more agitation. So I let it drop, as I usually do, by saying yeah, the Reverend Martin J. Fox must have been one of Leonard here's best buddies. Right, Leonard? I mean, who the hell ever called him that? None of us, for sure, and not our mother even at her maddest, and not our father the old man, either. So the only person I could think of might have been one of his girlfriends when things were getting hot and heavy—oh, Leonard, Leonard, LeonardLeonardLeonard, something like that—and Suz snorted and told me to stop it, which only egged me on with Leonard this and Leonard that, as I danced around the room acting silly, making people laugh even if they didn't want to, just like the doctor ordered.

We didn't notice until too late the tall, lanky, maybe thirty-five-year-old man in a navy-blue short-sleeve polo shirt and tan khakis standing in the doorway with a black leather what looked like poker chip box in one hand and a Bible in the other. He smiled and introduced himself as Reverend Fox, Marty Fox, but most people called him Marty or Reverend Marty. He'd come by earlier, there was his card, nodding to the table tray, and Suz and

I said sure, sorry, would he like to come in, and I scooted my chair over to him and he sat close enough to the bed that he could reach out and touch Len, which he did, saying he was pleased to meet him finally and that he was Sonny's pastor. I glanced at Suz, knowing now what the but was all about and she nodded yeah, that was it. He said Sonny had asked him to make a call on his father, so he hoped it was okay to interrupt for a few minutes and have a few words with Leonard. I blushed, wondering how much of my performance he'd heard, and told him it was Len, everybody called him Len, like he was Marty instead of Martin, explaining the obvious but unable to shut myself up. He said fine, great, Len it would be then, squeezing Leonard/Len's right arm. He grimaced and Reverend Marty snatched his hand back, knowing he'd done something wrong but wasn't quite sure what. I told him not to worry about it, it had happened to all of us one time or another because nobody expected it. Sonny had probably told him that Len had had a stroke and now had cancer, and he said yes. I said the problem was that the stroke had left him paralyzed on his right side, which would make you think he was numb there and that when you touched him, he wouldn't feel anything, right? Well, from what I'd heard and read, I told him, it was just the opposite and even the slightest stimulation could cause him incredible pain. Reverend Marty frowned in a wow that's interesting way and glanced at Suz then back at me, and I said the condition had one of those long medical names—Central Post Stroke Pain, or CPSP for short, and was caused when nerves got messed up during Len's stroke, or series of strokes, as it turned out. Instead of working the way they're supposed to now, the nerves randomly fire off signals, kind of like the distributor or timing belt on your car going haywire, and those signals that do get sent out are interpreted as pain, so when he, Reverend Marty, touched him, Len felt pain rather than pleasure. A hell of a thing, wasn't it, the way something like that could get so screwed up? and he said yes, it was, it was indeed, and he would be more careful from now on, thanks for the tip. And by the way, was I a doctor or— I said, no, just an interested layperson. Good, he said, that was really good, I should keep it up and, oh, just to be sure, Sonny had told him that Len couldn't talk, but he could hear and understand, was that right? I said it was and he should pay close attention to his eyes and his left hand. He seemed to think about that for a bit and said thanks and turned his attention to Len, asked how he was feeling and whether there was anything he could do for him. Len shrugged like did the rev have something specific in mind or was he just talking and Reverend Marty leaned closer then and asked if Len wanted to join him in prayer. Len looked at me and Suz and the rev and nodded that yes, he would, and Reverend Marty reached for Len's good hand and bowed his head and said we knew God to be a God of forgiveness, mercy and compassion and that day we needed Him to bring all those qualities to us, to be with the sick and afflicted of the world, to comfort them and ease their suffering, and we especially needed God to be with Len and us and Sonny and his family so that we might find that same comfort and peace and love God gave us through His Son, Jesus Christ, who bore our sins on the cross and died that we might have life everlasting, amen.

Len was gazing at Reverend Marty like the prayer had truly touched him and he didn't want the moment to pass, Suz was trying to figure out what to do with the hands she'd folded in her lap and I was eying the door, thinking what I would say as I excused myself. But before I could Reverend Marty leaned back toward Len and told him he couldn't imagine how hard it must be to lie there in bed day after day and wonder what next was in store for him, not being able to express to anyone the pain or anger or frustration he was feeling, or for that matter, the fear and that what he would like most in the world was a big old hug. And he realized, Reverend Marty did, that maybe the most difficult thing for Len was to keep his hopes up, to know that people loved him and he wasn't alone. To know that when all else failed, and it ultimately would, God would be there for him, like no other friend or relative or lover could ever be, that God would hold him and sustain him and give him peace. He believed that, didn't he? Len nodded and Reverend Marty said that was what he thought, that was what Sonny had told him—that he'd talked to his dad and asked him directly, the way you have to sometimes, if he was right with God, and the answer was yes. Was that right? he asked Len, did he feel God's loving presence? Len shrugged and Reverend Marty said he would take that as a yes, and Len shrugged again and the rev said he was glad to hear that because what he would like to do now was see if Len might care to partake—one of those oddly reverend words—of communion, holding his little black box out like an offering. Len pumped his head and Marty the Minister smiled and opened his black box across his knees, taking inventory of a row of wafers, two what looked like shot glasses, a small silver thermos and a pair of folded white napkins, and began thumbing through his Bible. Before he began, though, he turned to Suz and me to say Methodists practiced open communion, meaning anyone, a member of that denomination or not, believer or not, could participate, would we like to join them? Suz declined, as did I, begging the reverend's pardon instead to say he should be aware, if he wasn't already, that Len wasn't allowed food or drink by mouth because he couldn't swallow. Reverend Marty thanked me for telling him and gazed out the window while Len glared at me to make sure I knew what an idiot, what a moronic good for nothing dumb shit I was not to realize how perfect it would have been to have choked to death on the body and blood of Christ, what could I have been thinking? Reverend Marty cleared his throat and pulled a pamphlet from his hip pocket, something titled more or less communion with the sick and shut-in and said aha, exactly as he'd thought, although strictly between us, it was what he had decided to do anyway, sanctioned or not, which was to offer the bread and cup to Len and upon his acceptance take the sacrament himself as a surrogate. Did that sound okay to Len? He nodded again.

Reverend Marty opened his Bible then, holding it in one hand, but didn't read from it, presenting it rather as authentication of his version of the Last Supper when he said Jesus said, take, eat, this is my body; take, drink, this is my blood; do this in remembrance of me, the rev lifting a single wafer from the tray, holding it between him and Len and asking Len if he accepted it as the body of Christ, Len nodding, and the rev asking if Len accepted his—the rev's—taking of the body for Len, nodding again. Reverend Marty chewed the host slowly and swallowed and poured a shot glass full of what I imagine was grape juice and went through the same ritual, asking if Len accepted it as the blood of Christ, and so on until Reverend Marty drank it and wiped the glass clean with one of the napkins and put everything away, closing the clasp on the box. Len had by then rolled onto his right side as close to the bed rail as possible, his eyes closed so that you might have thought him to be sleeping but for the slight tremor when Reverend Marty put his left hand on Len's good shoulder and thanked God for the bread of life and the cup of salvation, food for our journey to the heavenly table where we would feast on God's love and glory. He then lowered his head and voice and asked for the Lord to bless Len and keep him and make His face to shine upon him and give him peace.

Silence, total silence, in the room, in the hallway—not even the sound of a breath—or so I imagined, perhaps, as Reverend Marty rose and gathered his things and came first to me and then to Suz and shook our hands without speaking and slipped out the door, Suz, too, shortly thereafter, a blown kiss, a wiggle of her fingers and a mouthed tomorrow? although she must have forgotten that couldn't be, since my flight out was later that evening and nothing short of calamity could make me miss it. She would remember later on her way home and feel sheepish about it and vow to call me but not get around to it right away, just as Connie would after she thought about refusing my offer to bring her to see Len. I'd told her I would come get her that day, but she'd said no, she was too tired, too plain old worn out and hurting, if I knew what she meant, and she hoped I would understand. I'd told her it was up to her, and she said how sorry she was, but she really couldn't do it, and I thought for a moment how much she, in her Earth Mother I'll-nurture-you-to-death way, might have enjoyed the impromptu service given by Reverend Marty and how she would more than likely not have hesitated a bit about partaking of communion and how Len would have smiled and held her hand and been all cozy with her, and that would have been just one more goddamn thing. It made me angry that she could make me angry during my few remaining minutes with our—my—brother. I took several deep breaths, letting each out slowly, calmly as I glanced at Len, who hadn't stirred, eyes closed, face relaxed, off in some place that allowed him, god help me, the slightest hint of a smile—some place away from Josie and Suz and Sonny and Connie and Sammo and me, of course, our mother and our father the old man, anybody who wanted something from him or had something to say about what he had done or should have or have not done, a place of rest and, I hoped, tranquility, from which I realized I would rather he not return. I watched a moment more, but only a moment, before creeping heel to toe, heel to toe— Indian-style, we used to call it—to his bed, kissing my fingertip and pressing it to his cheek.

HomeGo

The young woman next to me on the plane—matching bright blue hair, eyelids, finger- and toenails, studs in her nose, tongue, halfway around each ear and god knows where else—was white-knuckling the armrest of her seat, either because she was petrified at having to sit beside such an old fart or because she was petrified period, so I started talking to be talking, so to speak, to help put her at ease. I told her about our students in Africa and how they got so excited when a school holiday was coming up that they wrote HOMEGO!! HOMEGO!! across every blackboard and all over the sidewalk of the school veranda, and how funny it was—to me at least—that even after all these years the phrase still crossed my mind when I was heading home from a trip. How about her, was she going home, too, and she said, no, just the opposite, actually, and I said is that right, and she said yeah, she was on her way to Europe with friends from her school, tipping her head vaguely toward the back of the plane, and I said Europe, huh?, and she said yeah, Paris, she thought, and maybe somewhere else as well, she couldn't remember, and I said wow, that was really great, trying not to say neat, since my sons had cautioned me how nerdy neat made me sound. Just then a flight attendant closed and locked the cabin door and the young woman's hand trembled on the armrest, and I said of course one of the ironic things was that when I used the term homego I was usually on a plane and I doubted that any of my students had ever flown, and she said she hadn't either. I said never and she said never, and I said no wonder she was nervous, and she smiled a tense little smile and I said I could still remember my first flight, from that very airport, in fact. She gave me a sidelong glance and said no way, and I said it was true and told her how scared I'd been when right after we took off—at least that was the way I recalled it—the pilot cut back power to the engines and the plane dropped, or felt like it was dropping, and I thought okay, that was it, I was going to die. She looked at me like I'd somehow opened the top of her head and seen her thoughts roiling around in there, especially the ones having to do with flying and dying, so I quickly said once that part was over, it wasn't so bad—a few bumps and a couple of banks to get going in the right direction and before long we were at cruising altitude and I could see the ground and the sun and the tops of clouds and got so lost in all that I didn't even realize I was flying. She rolled her eyes and reached for her ear-bud headphones and I said maybe it wasn't quite that simple but that I did think she was going to have a fine time. She was quiet as we lumbered out to the runway, maybe listening to me maybe not as I explained our position in the queue, the length of time between take-offs, what the pilot was saying over the radio, how taxiing wore off more tire tread on planes than any other aspect of flying—that sort of thing—and then we made the turn, straightened and within seconds were pushed back into our seats as we hurtled down the runway. I suggested that she close her eyes and think of a pleasant, faraway place, maybe being there with someone special, and she smiled for real and lay her head back, her blue eye shadow matching the blue in her blouse, and I glanced up at the exit sign, lest she catch me and think I was ogling.

Once airborne and stabilized, she and I settled into our respective worlds. I read, she listened to music that escaped her ear-buds in occasional tinny waves, like a metallic perfume that was at once grating and reassuring, until roughly halfway through our flight when, predictably, we crossed the jet stream and began bouncing and shuddering enough a flight attendant announced that the captain had turned on the seat belt sign and we should remain seated, if we were, or return to our seats immediately and stay there until the captain determined that it was once again safe to get up and move about the cabin. We bumped, smoothed out, bumped again, and she glanced at me a couple of times to see how I was reacting and I asked her if she knew about the jet stream and she shrugged the shoulder nearest me and I explained that strong upper atmospheric winds blew this direction—one hand in front of me—and here we were—my other hand passing diagonally over the first with little jarring motions—and she said like a car over railroad tracks, and I said exactly, she'd gotten it exactly right and I wanted to congratulate her on having experienced and survived her first turbulence in an airplane. She shrugged both shoulders and said if that was all it was, turning her attention back to her iPod, and I wondered, as she listened to music again, how Len would have tolerated the jostling around, given his terror of flying, and his oath that he would never do it again after his release from the Navy. Never, for any reason, no matter what, he would keep his two feet planted squarely on the ground, thank you, although maybe now, if we were going to the right place for the right reason he might relent. Home, say, and there was no other way to get there. Then he might come along. And once we'd touched down and taxied to our gate, we'd all get up at the same time to retrieve our luggage from the overhead bins, and my blue-haired, blue-lidded friend would gather with her group and I'd say goodbye and for her to have a great trip, and she'd smile again and leave, with me right behind, wheeling Len into the flightway, me saying there, that wasn't so bad, now was it? and him as usual saying nothing. Before we'd reach the end, he'd get up and walk in front of me, then beside me, growing shorter and younger as we went, until by the time we cleared the gate, he'd run off ahead of me with his gap-toothed grin, flap-eared cap and plaid jacket, pushing his bicycle for all he was worth and hopping on finally, pedaling hell-bent for somewhere until he'd vanish completely, consumed perhaps in that cosmic orgasm our father the old man thought was the be all and end all.

Act Three

Me

Beginning the End

This part of the story, the third of three, Connie and Len and now me, was supposed to start with me in bed, too, although not necessarily because of anything bad. I could have been just lying there, for instance, awake but not willing to get up, the mattress firm under my back, blankets warm over the top of me on a quiet Sunday morning with nothing planned. Or I might have been spent after good sex, my wife's naked body curled next to mine as she dozed. For whatever reason, I was to have been there, a nice tie-in with Connie and Len, balanced and symmetrical, Georgian, you might say, but not excessively so, since everyone who knows me would agree that nothing could be more antithetical to my personality.

And the lake that day was to have been as blue as Len's eyes, a pure blue you could at once see and see through, like the clear water and cloudless sky I would have glimpsed as I stood and took a step toward the bathroom, my own eye drawing my attention down the hallway, past the stools at the kitchen counter, through the window, across the park, beyond the breakwater, out and out and out to where lake and sky join, each becoming the other, indistinguishable. My wife says the water is blue because it reflects the sky, which is itself blue because light waves entering our atmosphere are refracted by water vapor and every other color is absorbed, so that in her theory when the sky's blue, the water's blue, when the sky's grey, the water's grey, simple as that. Except I don't know how you account for azure water when the sky never is or green ice on the lake, thick and chunky as Coke bottle glass or how, in space, the sun is not yellow but white and how, in space, light travels in a perfect straight line until it bumps into something and veers off and how, in that same space that same day, there could be a package on my kitchen counter with my address on it in Suz's handwriting and beside it a letter from Connie I would not yet have opened.

The parcel was to have been a cardboard box eighteen inches

square and a foot tall carefully wrapped in heavy brown paper, seams flattened and sealed with reinforced packing tape, and inside it, protected by pale green Styrofoam pellets, was to have been a black lacquered pot with a gold Grecian motif etched around its middle and repeated about two-thirds of the way to the top, where a matching lid was fixed in place by a smooth black waxy substance—all in all, a lovely vessel, one under other circumstances I would have been more than happy to display.

Taped to the small knob on top of the lid was to have been an unmarked envelope, its flap tucked inside its back, that I was to have taken off and opened to a blank card with a single row of white and blue flowers at the top and Suz's hurried message in black ink that said here, this was for me, since she had no idea what else to do with it, maybe I would, marking the first so to speak falling out between us.

The disagreement that was to have led to this scenario stemmed from a conversation Sonny and she and I had that didn't start but ended on the topic of death and the proper disposal of human remains, our opinions influenced, as you can imagine, by how deeply we believed in a judgment day and the resurrection of the body. Sonny held the most traditional position that Jesus will indeed return to judge the quick and the dead, who the Bible says will rise incorruptible on the day of his coming, so it was clear that dead people had to be buried if they were to be recognized and have any chance at eternal life. I was at the other end of the spectrum, saying if you're dead, you're dead and it would be a whole lot better for you and the rest of the world to be cremated and not take up the extra space. Suz was somewhere in between but leaning more toward Sonny than me because the thought of being burned terrified her more than being buried, although she said she could see my point, which I imagine, along with her not wanting Sonny to control what might become of their father, is how my position rather than Sonny's prevailed and I ended up with Len's ashes. Not to

175

mention, at least in Sonny's view, the sin of having denied their father, my brother, his one and only chance for immortality and participation in the joyous family reunion they expected on the other side, as though life were reflected in a two-way mirror that at some miraculous moment a person stepped through into an alternate eternal existence.

But I would know Len didn't belong here from the moment I lifted the urn and held it at arm's length toward the lake to the north and started describing to him like a tour guide how I loved the moods of the lake, the way the water was different every morning I awoke—tippled or troubled or smooth as a tabletop, how one day there would be small cupped-palm waves coming toward shore, like a Monet lily pond, and another they would mass far out, propelled by strong north winds, and curl finally in spectacular white sprays against the seawall that lined the shore all the way north and south as far as the eye could see, burst after wild and violent burst that cleared the walkway of anything but seaweed and sand and an occasional chunk of asphalt patching. And I would tell him how I loved to stroll along the seawall on less stormy days amongst more beautiful people than he could ever imagine and many not so beautiful either, everyone walking and running and biking and rollerblading and holding hands and kissing and cuddling and speaking all manner of languages I thought I recognized but didn't begin to understand, and how I loved the ducks and gulls and terns and the guys playing chess at North Avenue Beach, the black kid in a black snowsuit, work boots and two pairs of gloves, rapping to himself with all the right moves, the young Chinese couple stopping to play soccer with five- and six-year-old kids from a day camp, men and women, women and women, men and men, all ages and races and colors and features blending like flavors of ice cream on a hot summer day. And even if he couldn't love it because it wasn't Carter, Kansas, then at least maybe he could understand why I did and not be afraid. Not that there weren't things to scare you,

I would tell him, turning west now toward the skyline of Chicago, because this was the city of big shoulders, after all, mean and lean and hard-working, where the stench of slaughter-houses once fouled the air and carcasses the water, where the Mob used to and gangs still do roam freely, where ungodly drive-by killings go unchecked, where government corruption can seem a legitimate career, where money can still buy, legal or illegal, anything you want. But it was also where streets on the floors of artificial canyons thronged with people coming and going or standing to marvel at the scene around them, and if he looked he could see too the NBC building, the Wrigley Building, Tribune Tower, Trump Tower and behind them Sears Tower rising over everything, and to the north the Hancock building, Water Tower Place, the Gold Coast, Lake Shore Drive and cutting south to north through it the Magnificent Mile of Michigan Avenue. Who could not love that? I would ask. Who would not live here, given a choice? But I would already know the answer and what I was expected to do.

As soon as I could arrange it, I was to gather Len up and take him back to Carter, after alerting interested people there that I would meet whoever wanted to come at ten o'clock the morning of April 19 on the north campground pier at the Rod and Gun Club for an informal memorial honoring Len. Petey was to be there, if he hadn't drunk himself to death yet, and Connie, if she could muster the physical and emotional energy to have Sammo the rock drive her over—her letter would still be unopened, in case you were wondering—and of course Suz and Sonny would come and Jim and Sally, if they wanted, and, hell yes, Reverend Marty and the Doctors Hawkins and Khulhoff and Fran from The Main Street Grill and his eating and drinking buddies from the Carter Inn and definitely as many of the nurses from Twin Oaks Manor as could make it, especially the late-shift woman who had given him such special pleasure, and hell yes again, maybe even the elusive second love of his life, Grace, and by all means Josie, his one-and-only real love half-hidden by a tree at the back of the crowd, and somewhere beyond her the unseen but felt presence of Grandma Caulkins, Grandpa Doolan, Uncle Boyd, Aunt Louise, Aunt Kate and our mother and our father the old man and all the rest looking on from the Other Side. I was to step forth then, the urn tucked like a football in my right arm, onto the pier that jutted into the water of what wasn't even a proper lake, but a pond and not even a proper pond but one the railroad built to provide water for its steam engines and when it had no more use for the water, sold it to the Rod and Gun Club, which wasn't really a proper club, either, although there was a clubhouse where you could go and get in out of the rain and drink. But people loved it. It was theirs because they had made it so, as had Len, who, even after I had shown him a real and proper lake in Chicago, still preferred this one, his lake in his town with his people. And that was why I was there, I was to tell them, and why I wanted them with me as I returned Len to the place he loved best, at which point I was to cast the first of his ashes over the muddy water and ask anyone else who cared to to join me before we adjourned to the Carter Inn for a beer and a chicken-fried steak sandwich, just as Len would have wanted us to.

Readings

Gastroenterologists are modern-day shamans who read entrails like phrenologists read skulls or poker players faces, with a subset among them whose specialty it is to read shit—its color, texture, shape and sound—shitologists, you might call them, and I do, people who have spent their professional lives learning and teaching that the normal frequency for shitting is no fewer than three times per week and no more than three times per day— anything less indicating constipation, more diarrhea—that the shit should be soft and easily passed, slipping cleanly into the water like a graceful diver, no ker-plunk or violent splattering, and should have the texture and color of peanut butter, although the color might vary from darker to lighter brown and even green or red, depending on what you've eaten or the disease you might have, such as internal bleeding with black, tarry shit or colon cancer with blood-red shit or pancreatitis with loose green shit, any of which could signal imminent death or the green salad with beets you had yesterday at lunch. But always, always, the absence of shit is fatal, nothing going in, nothing coming out, as it was with Len the last few hours of his life, the hospice nurse saying he hadn't eliminated for some time before he reared up in bed, those blue-blue eyes fixed on something beyond the doorway of his room, his tongue in all its mass swelling up and out of his mouth in a gagged roar, and he slumped back down, eliminating nothing, not even breath, his skin changing visibly to a waxy pale yellow-slightly-green color, his hand growing cold in mine.

Beginning the End—Again

Len did die pretty much as I described, but I imagine not exactly, since all I have to go on is what I saw, what I felt, what I knew to be happening during that time, what I experienced and was able to recreate, which may have been slightly, or perhaps massively, different from Suz's or Sonny's observations were they to describe the same scene to you. But on the other hand, we would probably all agree that, in the aftermath, there was no cremation, no grandiose disposal of ashes by an ego-crazed brother and that there was not even a funeral, only a viewing one evening and a graveside service the next day, which was what Len wanted and what his children arranged.

My wife, who was on an extended business trip, made arrangements to fly to Kansas to join me, as did our sons, one from the east coast, the other from the west coast. I picked them all up at the airport in Wichita and the day of the viewing we drove to Carter. As soon as we got to the west edge of town, where there was a sign that said Carter next three exits, my younger son asked, never having been there, how big Carter was and I told him and he said so how did it get three exits, since most bigger places have only one. I said I had no idea, but if he found it that unusual, maybe he would like to stop and take a picture to show his friends, and he said yeah, he would, so I turned the car around and got everybody out and arranged them in front of the sign, the water tower and Co-op elevator looming in the background, the Carter Inn to one side, where Len and his buddies ate and drank when he still could, The Baitshop just to the east where he outfitted himself for fishing and tried to fend off Fat Louisa. I told them about those things and other things as well as we drove past, such as how when I was in high school the principal entertainment on a Saturday night was to cruise Main Street, not too fast and not too slow, left elbow cocked out the car window, right wrist draped over the steering wheel so you could raise your index finger in greeting if you saw an acquaintance coming toward you or give a quick toot of the horn if the approaching car was driven by a friend. And I told them how the route was always the same, starting where we were, at The Baitshop, and driving to where Main Street intersected with old Highway 50, turning there and going south toward downtown, all two blocks of it, wheeling a wide U-turn at the last corner before the Santa Fe tracks and starting back, over and over until the night was done and it was time to go home. On occasion, though, I told them, you might vary the course by going east instead of west, toward the cemetery road, a perfect quarter-mile stretch of brick pavement, where, if you were feeling especially wild, you could drum up a drag race or two. If no races were in the offing, you might stop instead at the Dari Delite at the top of Main Street and order a malt and sit on one fender of your car, your girlfriend on the other, if you were so lucky, and, like a prince and his princess waving to their people, watch the passing parade. I told them there was also a pool hall in those days that I frequented often enough I eventually bought my own cue and case to carry it in, you know, like a real hustler, which I wasn't, regardless what I thought at the time, although I was a pretty damn good player in my prime, if I did say so myself. Over there, on the other side of the street, a movie theater once occupied the building where the bowling alley was now and every Saturday afternoon I would go to see Gene Autry or Roy Rogers movies, with horror shows mixed in as I got older. And in that building, up those steps to the double doors, was where, people told me, I told them, the best beer joint in the county had previously been located—which was kind of odd, or even ironic, I said, when you thought it was kitty-cornered across from the old Santa Fe Railroad station where Russian Mennonite refugees had arrived to bring turkey red winter wheat to Kansas. We swung a U-ie then and headed back north, but only for a block before we turned left at the intersection of Main and First Streets—or turned west, as the locals would say, since everything in that part of the country is referred to in its relation to one of the cardinal points on a compass. The intersection was the smack center of town, through which or from which everyone passed to go anywhere, Corwell's Drugs on one corner, The Main Street Grill opposite it to the east, the bank to the north, the building that used to be the hotel before it burned down completing the square. So it was there that we turned and drove past the post office, a small café Grandma Caulkins once owned, a low red brick building that during World War Two housed captured German soldiers and later was the site of a series of small manufacturing plants, on farther still past the Co-op elevator and half block long steel Butler building where both Len and I had worked at one time or another, and finally to the park, its gate locked, where I'd played football and baseball and where the largest Fourth of July fireworks display in the state was held and where Dan Patch, the famous racehorse, had run in Sunday afternoon sulky races around the half mile circular dirt track. We turned north again, past Twin Oaks Manor, where I told them

Len had spent his last years. My older son said it looked decent enough and I said it was, basic but clean and comfortable, with fine people who cared so much for him that the day after he died someone went into his room and turned on the TV because he'd always had it on and the place seemed so empty and lonely without it. On up to Ninth Street and east toward the new high school and the vacant lot where the building I'd gone to classes had once stood and south past the house where my closest high school friend and one of the smartest people I'd ever known, Jack Naughton, had lived, on to the Christian Church our parents had sent Len and me to, east again, then north and east, coming finally to what was left of the Caulkins house or homestead or ranch, as our father the old man sarcastically referred to it the evenings he came back, which he fairly often did, I told them, from that best beer joint in the county.

For some reason at that point I stopped talking, which I'd been doing non-stop for almost a half hour, and absent the sound of my own voice, I became aware of the silence from my sons behind me, my wife beside me and the looks of bewilderment on their faces as they gazed at the house, the yard, the garage, everything on the verge of collapse, and my eyes teared and my ears burned and the only word I could muster was sorry, which lodged jagged as a crust of stale bread in my throat. And I was sorry, for this, for everything, since I had to be in some way to blame, if not totally, then partially, through a failure of concern or hope or will, of availability, perhaps even of love.

I put the car in gear and drove on.

Carter had a single funeral home, Moreland's, located a block west of Main Street and a block north of the Santa Fe railroad tracks in a rambling old house that had long ago been converted to its present use by adding a covered drive on the south side where first call vehicles unloaded bodies and hearses loaded coffins in relative privacy. A long single story box had been built off the back of the house between the drive and the sidewalk to accommodate the embalming and dressing rooms and a walk-in cooler, should more than one corpse arrive the same day.

The front entrance, likely the original for the house, was up a short curved concrete walk under a portico with trellises between its columns and the outside wall of the house on either side, but there were no leaves on the vines as yet since spring was still a month away. Even though we were early, the door was unlocked and we entered the foyer, a staircase to the second floor immediately to the left, a reception desk straight ahead, a lectern beside it with a registration book on top. Beyond the foyer, French doors opened into a fairly large room with rows of padded beige metal chairs arranged over faded rose Victorian carpeting so desiccated you could see the unevenness of the floor beneath it. Len's coffin was along the far wall, centered in front of a curtained archway, his body elevated enough to show the profile of his face and upper torso and the denim blue short-sleeved shirt Suz and Sonny had decided he would be dressed in. Neither they nor anyone else could recall ever having seen him in anything more formal, except the day he'd donned a suit for Sonny's wedding and swore from the minute he walked out his back door, red-faced and yanking at the collar of his shirt, that he was going to goddamn die if somebody didn't get that goddamn thing off him.

Which he did, of course, but not because of a suit, and we were there, as everyone else soon would be, to view the fact— see, witness, verify?—that he had. As we were the first to arrive and no one else seemed about to, I asked the old woman now sitting behind the reception desk, whose name I'm sure I should have known but had forgotten, if there was a restroom available for the public. She smiled as though I should have remembered that as well and pointed toward another foyer behind the curtained arch and told us it was inside and to the left, which meant you had to skinny around the end of Len's casket and duck into near total darkness, fumbling around for a light switch in a passage you didn't want to go down in the first place because you had no idea where it might end up and what you might find once you opened the door at the end, like, say, maybe, you know, a dead person, and you were actually relieved to find the musty-smelling, dark-paneled toilet in a space no larger than a broom closet that made you sweat the minute you stepped inside and felt the walls begin closing in upon you.

Other people had filtered in by the time we finished with the restroom—first, Suz and her husband, Morris, then Sonny and his wife and kids, Connie and Sammo and Connie's son, Ron, all of whom filed by the casket and said how good Len looked, Suz and Connie touching him, as though to make sure it was him, then moving on to the sprays of flowers, saying how pretty they were and reading the cards to note who they were and were not from, fanning out finally to chairs where they could either stay out of the way or receive townsfolk coming to pay their last respects.

Some who came by to greet me were gracious enough to remind me of their names, while others said things like they bet I didn't remember who they were, did I? No, they could see I didn't, and who would have thought that after all the time we'd spent together and all the things we'd done—it was Joe, goddamnit, Joe Johnson, a disappointed shake of his head and my feeble attempt to set things right by saying I knew that and if he'd given me a minute, because it wasn't like I'd left town yesterday, you know, and didn't have a couple of other things on my mind, but by then he'd have wandered off and another person would have taken his place.

Among the last to arrive was a group from Twin Oaks Manor, at least some of whom, judging by the smell, had dropped by the Carter Inn on their way over. They approached the casket like everyone else and said things about how natural Len appeared and it wouldn't surprise them if he sat right up and gave them a good talking to with that finger and those eyes and so on before they broke into smaller groups to talk with Suz and Sonny and Connie, who seemed to know some of them from her old nursing aide days.

One woman, though, in jeans and a denim jacket, long auburn hair hanging down her back—Annie, I believe I'd heard her called at Twin Oaks—lingered behind, clutching Len's hand and telling him in a raspy voice just loud enough for me to hear what a butthead he was to go on and die when she'd said he couldn't, like three nights ago when she'd come by to see him and all those other nights she'd stopped in before she'd gone home. But he'd done it anyway, hadn't he? gone and been a butthead, skipped out on her even after all the beer they said they were going to drink, the places they were going to go, the things they were going to do, by which time she was leaning over Len, hair dangling as she tried to keep it pulled back and her nose wiped at the same time. Suz came over to let Annie cry on her shoulder, and when she was able to straighten and talk without sobbing, she pulled a TV remote control from her bag and said, here, she'd brought this from home because she couldn't imagine him without it. Suz laughed and the two of them nestled it in the crook of Len's left arm, Suz saying that now all they needed was a can of beer and Annie grinned and said she just happened to have one or two in her truck, she'd be right back, and for the remainder of that day at least Len lay content with two of the things he most treasured in life. The next afternoon, at the graveside service, the remote control and beer were missing, out of respect for the sobriety of the occasion, Suz told me, but I like to imagine that they were still there, merely out of sight.

And Now the Letter

The lake that day was troubled, whitecaps riding azure-grey swells from the horizon, exploding one after another over the breakwater as a listless fog draped buildings, muffled footsteps, drove heads further between shoulders.

What bullshit, someone could say. Why all the gloom and doom? Why not write instead about how exciting it was when waves burst over the breakwater and how mysterious the fog was? Because I didn't want to, I would tell that someone. I was the one looking at the lake and I was the one choosing the words to describe it. But did I have to be so damned pathetic, that someone might ask, and fallacious on top of it, shamelessly manipulating my readers' emotions as I begged them at the same time to trust me, to believe that I was telling them the truth? Look out the window, I might say. There are waves, big ones, spilling over the breakwater. There's fog. In my view, the lake is troubled. To that someone, it's romantic. Which is more pathetic, I might ask, more fallacious, more manipulative, more true?

So let me begin again: the lake that day. . . What now? The letter, someone might say again, Connie's unopened letter on my granite counter? Wasn't it also a product of my imagination? Hadn't I created it along with the urn? I would say no, the letter was real enough. It had, in fact, arrived a week before I wrote about the ashes. God's truth? that someone might ask, and I might say in return, mine at least.

The lake that day was troubled as I sat at my kitchen counter to read the letter Connie had sent after Len's funeral. There were several sheets of brittle pale green paper frayed along the top edge where it had been torn from a stenographer's pad and folded multiple times to fit into a small white self-sealing envelope. I opened it crease by crease, smoothing the pages against the cool granite until it lay flat before me, Connie's penciled script more engraved than flowing.

Dear brother, it started, instead of with my name, and not dear brother and sister, because she had never thought of my wife as a sister, and not dear brother and wife in the manner of the nineteenth century, but dear brother to convey as honestly as she was able, I imagine, given her psychological and emotional state, that she recognized me not only as her sole remaining brother but her sole remaining family member. How was I? she went on, as she always did, followed, again as always, with fine, she hoped, but whether she actually did hope I was fine is open to question, at least to me, because I read it as an empty phrase, like asking how're ya doin when making eye contact with a stranger on the street, not out of interest in learning how the person really is doing but in order to say I see you, I acknowledge your existence and, for the moment, mean you no harm—a verbal handshake, if you will—which was how I took Connie's inquiry into my state of being. How was I, fine she hoped, they were fine, too, busy but fine, only tired, oh lord, were they tired. And I had to be as well, she couldn't see how I wouldn't be after all I'd been through and how hard I'd taken Len's death, no matter what I'd said at the time of the funeral. She knew, she'd seen it in my eyes and the look on my face. Not that she didn't miss him. She did, missed him like everything, I shouldn't take her wrong, they were so close, which she knew I realized (but didn't mind repeating for my benefit). They were more like twins than just a brother and sister, the same way we—she and I—used to be when we were younger. Surely I remembered the way she could fill in words for me and know what I was thinking and feeling almost before I did, the kind of thing she was certain we would have kept up if I'd not left the country and then kept moving farther and farther away even after I came back, as if I were trying to build an ever greater distance between the two of us. She didn't want to leave the impression that she thought I was mean or anything like that, not me or my wife, because she understood how it was getting our various degrees and having different jobs here and there and then our kids who for years took most of our energy and attention. But it was hard, she didn't want us to think it wasn't, with Len leaving to ride the waves and me to go to college, then graduate school, then for the two-year stint teaching overseas and her being alone at home all that time and moving to New Orleans, which she hated as our father the old man grew ever more abusive, verbally at first and finally physically, mainly to our mother. Or did I know about that? Had she ever mentioned it, like the night our father wanted our mother to go out drinking with him even though he was already three sheets to the wind and when she refused he dragged her to their bedroom and started slapping and punching her around and she, Connie, ran back there and jumped on him and threatened to kill him if he hit our mother again. Had I heard about that or another time when our mother got some man friend our father the old man was certain she was having an affair with to drive the two of them and as much of their stuff as they could back to Kansas because she could no longer stand living with the old bastard? And as soon as our father found out about the trip from the old woman who ran the trailer park where they lived, he drove off after them, found them near Texarkana and talked (bullied?) her into coming back—he'd straighten up, he promised, she'd see, he would, so help him God. That stuff and more, if I wanted to know about it, which was why she left home when she did. Had I ever wondered about that, or did I just assume she was stupid and unmotivated and so horny she couldn't wait to hop Bax Billingsly's bones?—a question she would like a straightforward answer to, she wrote, because she'd always wondered, had always thought I thought, we thought, she was failing us, not living up to our expectations of going to college and making something of herself, becoming a teacher, maybe, or a nurse, or hell, why not a doctor or a lawyer or a business owner, someone important, as she'd always wanted, opening a boutique that sold designer clothes or books on needlework and knitting or dried flower arrangements or ceramics, that sort of thing, or getting a degree so she could work with sick and neglected animals or kids nobody else wanted. Had we ever realized that those were the things she'd wanted, too, but had never had a ghost of a chance of achieving? And I wasn't to say nonsense or bullshit or any of my other pet phrases and start off on how I didn't have advantages either but had to work and scratch for everything I'd gotten from life, that it was a matter of will—willpower—and not luck. Luck had nothing to do with it, goddamnit. Especially that nonsense everybody went on about Caulkins luck, as in bad luck, perpetual bad luck that never once had turned good. But she didn't care what I thought, she said, there was such a thing as Caulkins luck and she'd suffered from it her whole life, just like Len had (did he ever tell me about the Caulkins curse—how all the men died by age seventy—Grandpa at sixty-one, our father at sixty-seven, Uncle Boyd at sixty-nine and now Len at sixty-whatever, but sure as hell not seventy. And what about me, she wondered, or her, if the curse applied to women as well, and it surely must considering her current condition, how could she have had much worse luck than that?). That was neither here nor there now, she supposed, since what was done was done and we were who we were and where we were and needed to move on, since god only knew how much longer she had to live—or any of us, for that matter—and there were so many things to do and especially say that she didn't even know where to begin and would therefore most likely not get most of them done, except this letter. She'd finally written it, such as it was, and was glad for it. She hoped I was, too, sorry she couldn't write more, love (whatever that meant), Connie, Sammo and kids, although none at the time were living with her.

About Me

Male of an age older than I think of myself but still handsome to some people, so I've been told, reasonably tall, in decent shape although with more weight than I should carry, and hair everywhere but on my crown, a condition my stylist says she is slowly but surely overcoming, since, according to her, I now have twice the hair on my head I did when I started seeing her, a claim I neither accept nor reject, as the illusion seems to make her happy and believe ever more strongly that she indeed does have magic fingers.

I dress for comfort more than style yet have a reasonable if not perfect eye for complimentary colors and patterns—no plaids with stripes, for example, although I realize that makes me even farther out of the current fashion loop—and tend on work and leisure days toward blue or black jeans and a solid color non-white t-shirt, an unbuttoned, untucked long-sleeve flannel shirt over it, with cuffs rolled twice and only twice to mid-forearm. While this attire may seem overly casual, it has been said that I do stand up well to a sport coat or a suit and tie or the tuxedo I recently bought for more formal occasions, even though I had resisted the idea for years, being, as I had always considered myself, of the people and not someone who attends charitable black-tie events, mixed drink and frozen smile in place to anchor myself against tides of have we met looks and introductions, coming perilously close in that situation to, as our father the old man once warned, forgetting how to talk to my own.

On a typical day, I might eat toast for breakfast or toast with a couple of slices of cheese or granola with soy milk and a banana sliced on top, with leftovers for lunch—plain pasta, parmesan sprinkled over it, chicken or pork tenderloin in a sandwich—or lettuce salad, tortilla soup or a turkey wrap from a local deli, and for dinner an actual sit-down meal with my wife, if she's in town and available, cooked from fresh ingredients bought that afternoon at a nearby grocery—mushroom ragout over brown rice, for example, or turkey burgers and oven fries, Cajun pork chops with mashed potatoes and green beans or Greek salad and crusty bread or lamb curry with raita or—one of my favorites—spaghetti smothered in sauce made from fresh tomatoes and basil, accompanied by an artichoke heart/pine nut/sliced olive salad drizzled with my own vinaigrette dressing. If we're going out before a concert or the theater, we might stop for Mexican, Italian, French, Chinese, Middle Eastern or Thai food. If we're staying in for a movie, we might opt for a good pinot noir with

walnut bread, sharp cheddar cheese and strawberry preserves—
none of which is meant to imply that we would turn down the
home-cooked meat/bread/potatoes kind of meal we grew up
with, god no, not on your life, or a hot beef sandwich smothered
in gravy at a truckstop.

I have a wife, two sons, one daughter-in-law, no grand-
children, a sister, one mother-in-law but no parents or grand-
parents, a dead brother, somewhere between twelve and
fourteen cousins, depending on who has survived and how you
count them, five nieces, four nephews, four brothers-in-law (ex's
not included), three sisters-in-law (without Josie, whom I've
known so long it's hard not to count her but won't for the sake of
accuracy) and myriad second- and great- this and thats far too
complicated to figure out. My wife's family on her mother's side
harkens back to fourteenth century English and Irish Quaker
stock and her father's family, Anabaptist pacifists, immigrated
from Germany in the eighteenth century to escape forced
military conscription and settled in central Pennsylvania, while
my mother's people came directly from Ireland in the late
eighteenth century, traveling west from Delaware over the next
hundred years, settling finally in Missouri and Kansas. My
father's family, as told in Ezra's Story, has largely unknown
origins, which I imagine to be the most quintessential American
account of them all.

I am not, as you may have already concluded, a member of
any religious group, nor do I adhere to a formal set of beliefs but
have come to realize recently how much of my thinking,
imagining, world-viewing is informed by religious and Western
philosophical metaphors—Platonic ideals and Aristotelian
empiricism, for example, an end of time, experiences framed in
dualities, the involvement of godheads in human affairs, primal
symbols of windearthfirewater as the basis for life and the
perpetuation of life. I do not believe in the Apostle's Creed, do
not recite the Lord's Prayer, do not partake of Holy Communion,

do not believe in a traditional Judeo/Christian/Greek god figure and tend toward a socially activist/humanist approach to life in which the meek not only should but deserve to inherit the earth.

Although I no longer smoke, I drink and eat too much, exercise daily, and have regular fulfilling sex. I read two newspapers a day, several magazines a week and a wide range of books, mainly novels, that pile up with regularity on most surfaces of the house. I have controlled hypertension and high cholesterol and my feet are stiff when I walk to the bathroom in the morning. I have season tickets to three theaters and regularly attend musical concerts and art shows, including permanent and temporary exhibits at museums. I have traveled to twenty-two foreign countries and every state but North and South Dakota, Idaho, Montana, Alaska and Oregon. I do most of the shopping and cooking for our household, with the exception of holidays and large parties. I love to watch basketball, football and baseball. I play tennis with more passion than skill and golf out of social necessity. I am claustrophobic, mildly paranoid and have an utter fear of dying alone, which of course makes no sense—fears never do—given that there is no other way to die, as I realized when Len reared up and roared out his final breath and saw no one even though Suz and Sonny and I were there right beside him—Connie wasn't, remember, because she was running behind again.

The Sound of the Second Shoe Dropping

Okay, okay, I should have known, and probably did when I'm honest with myself, that Connie was exactly where the statisticians predicted she'd be, smack in the middle of the curve: she'd survived lung cancer symptom-free between two and three years against overwhelming odds—most doctors thought she would already be dead—and regardless what I did to ignore the possibility of a recurrence, Sammo ruined it with that mid-Saturday call. He told me he and Connie had been out for breakfast and after they'd eaten, it looked like she was raising her arm over her head to stretch or something and it dropped back onto the table, splat, like a dead fish. Sammo said she finally dragged it with her left hand and cocked it in front of her on the table so it would look even slightly normal, and he asked if anything else was wrong, thinking she might be having a stroke, and with tears in her voice she said no, well, maybe, and he said what and she said her head ached a little and her eyes were kind of blurry. He said he got her up and into the car and rushed her as fast as he could to the emergency room, where they did a CAT scan, during which they found a mass about the size of a fifty-cent piece on the back of her brain, just sitting there, her doctor said, weeping. Weeping? she asked and he said, yes, weeping fluid. But that same weeping, leaking, seeping, whatever they wanted to call it might very well be to her benefit, the doctor said, because that was more characteristic of an abscess—you know, a collection of fluid and pus that walls itself off, sort of like a boil or a cyst. It can still swell and cause some of the same symptoms a tumor does—headache, muscle weakness, nausea, vision problems—and therefore needed to be attended to. For a case like this, he would usually prescribe IV antibiotics instead of surgery because the growth wasn't malignant. But because of her history and just to be doubly sure, he wanted her to go ahead and have a biopsy and for that he was going to transfer her to a Wichita hospital to be under the care of a neurosurgeon.

The next afternoon Sammo called again to report that they had already seen Dr. Bloom, a quiet, kind and serious young man who explained things thoroughly and listened well and also began calling the growth a tumor. When Connie asked why he was using that word rather than abscess, he said because what she had was a tumor and not an abscess—she could trust him on that—and besides oncologists in general and her doctor, Dr. Sims, in particular, tended to be more optimistic than not. That didn't mean of course Dr. Sims had done or said anything wrong.

To the contrary, in fact, getting her into his, Dr. Bloom's, care immediately was what should have been done, and as soon as they had performed a couple of tests to be sure she could stand up to the operation, they were going to get her right into surgery and take that tumor out before she knew what was happening, any questions? She said she thought there was to be a biopsy first, and Dr. Bloom said that whatever was in there would have to come out anyway, so they might as well go ahead and remove it now and biopsy it afterward, didn't she agree? She said she guessed so since he was the doctor, and he said that wasn't exactly the attitude he'd wanted to see. She asked what would happen if she said no, she didn't want surgery. He thought a minute and said it would be no then, and she smiled as much as she could, Sammo said, and told him in that case he could go on with it, she was ready.

So let's say he took her in and peeled back her scalp and cut a hole in her skull, removed the growth and put her back together and declared that the operation had gone better than he'd ever expected. Let's say he even went so far as to admit his error about what he was cocksure he was going to find, because Dr. Sims, the optimist, had indeed been right on this occasion—it had been a seeping/weeping/leaking abscess that looked for all the world like a jellyfish out of water when he laid it in the specimen bowl and announced to his staff how nice it felt every once in a while to be wrong. And let's say that was that and she had no complications and no further symptoms and went home in two days, as Dr. Bloom had said might be possible, and that we all took a couple of deep breaths and sat back and relaxed—sort of, let's say.

Men and Toilets

That morning I turned on the lamp near my desk as I always do and the bulb hissed—I swear it did—then crackled with a brilliant flash, followed by a lazy blue tongue of flame and a singed metallic odor wafting up from it. I tried to turn the switch knob again, thinking—what? that it had all been a mistake and the light would now come on as usual?—and found the switch wouldn't budge, forward or backward, and I said cocksuck or something similar and unscrewed the two-hundred-watt bulb I had substituted for the three-way one I was supposed to use to keep this very thing from happening and went to find a new, correct bulb. When I screwed it in, nothing happened. No sparks, no fire, nothing, and I said fuckshit or to that effect, unplugged the lamp and took it to our bedroom where I left it beside the armoire in place of the lamp that had been there, which I now carried back to the study. The problem was that the original lamp, an antique brass swing-arm Victorian with a single socket inside a cone-shaped milk-glass shade, rim dimpled as a pie crust, was a near twin of one on the other side of the French doors into the study, both being the perfect height for paintings that hung above them. Although the lamp I'd brought from the bedroom was also a swing-arm, it had a shiny brass finish, two sockets with dangling chains and a pleated linen shade that made it too tall for the picture above it and too bulky for the space it was in. It would be okay there for a few days, maybe, but would never work as a permanent replacement. I spent the next two hours browsing lamp websites to determine if anything resembling the Victorian was available for a reasonable price and found that regardless what I could or was willing to pay, nothing came close, being (for the most part) too tall or the wrong finish or too ugly, and I decided the only thing left was to repair the broken lamp.

Even though the closest I'd come to rewiring anything was to replace an electrical outlet or two, I assumed fixing the lamp couldn't be that difficult, since I had tools, a reasonable sense of how things worked, and the lamp would be unplugged. But ah, you're saying, that was my first mistake. Otherwise, professional lamp repairers wouldn't be in business, would they? Besides I should have known better, shouldn't I, given the number of things I'd screwed up in my life? As anyone knows who has ever tried to repair a lamp, or anything else for that matter, things like these are never as simple and straightforward as they seem. After an hour and a half and numerous references to the idiocy of the engineer who had designed the lamp, I finally got the old socket out—piece by bloody piece, much the way a dentist might extract a rotten tooth—made a list of what I thought I would need to install a new one and headed to my nearby Ace-is-the-place hardware store.

As I walked home with a three-way socket, electrical tape, light bulbs and extra keys to our door—I was of the opinion that you could never have too many keys—I thought about what we should have for dinner, sized up progress that had been made on a new high-rise condominium building in our neighborhood and of course reviewed the task ahead of me—the myriad sleeves, nuts, set screws, wires and such that had to be reassembled in the correct order for the lamp to work and before I could step back, glowing with the satisfaction that I'd done the job right.

Which for the most part I did, except for not remembering the exact reverse order in which everything fit together and having to take the lamp apart and start over. Twice. But after another two hours, voilà!—if you could ignore the switch knob being a bit more difficult to turn than it should have been and exposed wires somewhere inside creating the potential for electrical shock. I carried the repaired lamp back to my study and the temporary replacement lamp back to its place by the armoire. I plugged in the repaired lamp and screwed a new three-way bulb into the new socket, as I should have in the beginning, and turned the switch, my pulse quickening as fifty, a hundred, a hundred fifty watts of light came on. I ran it through its wattage again and again, as though I needed to convince myself it worked, and when my wife came home, I showed her, beaming next to the lamp like a proud father. I told her what I'd done and that she should try it, which she did—fifty, a hundred, a hundred fifty watts—with no visible reaction, meaning she hadn't been shocked—and she said how nice, what a good job I'd done and started to leave. I asked her if that was all, just nice, and she looked at me and said yeah, nice, why? I ran the bulb through its paces three or four more times, and she wanted to know what it was with men and toilets, that they didn't seem to be able to leave them alone once they'd fixed them—flush, flush, flush and flush again. I shrugged and walked away.

That night, as we were going to sleep, she rolled next to me and said in a quiet voice that she was sorry, she understood now, and that it was more than nice to have the lamp working again—a lot more.

When All May Not Be as It Seems

Everything might have been okay if it were only a picture of Grandpa Doolan, a what'd I tell you look on his face as he hoisted the winner's half of a turkey wishbone—you know, the part with the arch and that thin thumbnail turned sideways brace at the top that connects the whole thing together? And there I am, too, a ten-year-old version of him—same build, same shape of face and head, pouches of flesh already pooling under my eyes—gripping the slender loser's bit between my thumb and index finger like a featherless quill. A wrecked turkey carcass lists in front of us, tags of skin lapped like torn sails over the rib cage, wads of stuffing dribbled along the spine, as various aunts and uncles, cousins, Grandma Caulkins, Len, (Connie somewhere out of camera range), our mother, all gaze on at Grandpa Doolan and me completing a ritual that stretches back at least to Roman times, the oldest and youngest male vying for the right to make the wish of his choice, in good sport, of course, in a spirit of togetherness and continuity. But for our father, who sits Cassius-like in the lower left-hand corner of the picture, neck and head straining forward, brows gathered in thunderheads aimed directly at Grandpa Doolan. Why? you might ask. What has brought on this reaction from a grown man that is akin to a child on a playground who imagines his up until then best friend has thrown him over for someone more interesting or engaging or fun?

The truth is, anything could have set him off, especially if it had to do with Grandpa Doolan, who our father the old man considered far too full of himself, always having the right answer or knowing the best way to do anything. He made fish bait, for instance, from flour and molasses that in its last stages he rolled between his palms into a clayish dark glob called doughball that he would break a chunk from and fashion around a fishhook until it hung there like an extra-large sinker. Our father invariably asked at that point why the hell anyone would ever use such a disgusting concoction to try to catch a fish, and before the day was over Grandpa Doolan had invariably reeled in what somebody in the group would call the biggest carp he'd ever seen, forcing our father the old man to say yeah, a lot of good it did, since nobody in their right mind could or would eat that shit. Grandpa Doolan dutifully took the fish home then, cleaned it and cut it into steaks which he steamed smothered in sliced onions in a pressure cooker to soften the bones and brought it back across the alley for us to have for dinner—a dish our mother would politely accept and our father refuse to eat. Grandpa Doolan was also, according to our father, a pack rat who salvaged everything from lumber he cut into standard lengths and stacked in the shed behind his house, to nails he painstakingly straightened and sorted by size into glass jars on his workbench. He also scavenged screws and small bits of metal, stones he thought interesting in shape or color, tools people threw in the trash that he retrieved and repaired. He sharpened his neighbors' knives and scissors and lawn mower blades. He fixed faucets and squeaky doors and got rid of mice. He weeded flower beds and pruned bushes and trees. He sat on people's porches and told stories. And everything he did, he did well—down to the way he dressed, whether for work or to go out, clean-shaven in full-length creased pants, a long-sleeved shirt, cuffs and collar buttoned, his hair parted and combed back, hat squarely on his head, gloves at the ready in his left hand, all of which our father the old man said was just a way for the old fart to get more attention.

Like in the picture, the way he was holding the wishbone with what our father would have called that damnable smirk on his face, taunting him, he would have said, goading him to leap out of his chair and make a fool of himself again, as he had the day Grandpa Doolan brought him an armful of tomatoes—which anyone else might have thought an act of kindness and generosity. But not our father, for whom the gift was as offensive as a slap in the face. Maybe even worse, since our mother immediately laid two slices of Wonder Bread on a plate, slathered one with softened butter and carved the largest, reddest, firmest blemish-free tomato in the batch, still warm from the sun, into thick slabs which she salted and placed with loving care on the buttered bread, covered it with the plain slice and brought the sandwich to lips she had just licked, opened them and closed her eyes, toes curling as she took her first bite, mmmmmmmm. Grandpa Doolan smiled and said something about how he couldn't ask for more thanks than that and left but hadn't gotten more than halfway to the alley before our father the old man gathered up the remainder of the tomatoes and ran outside with them, yelling that he could take his goddamn, good-for-nothing pieces of shit with him and lobbed the tomatoes, like a kid pitching stones, so they would splatter the ground around Grandpa Doolan's feet. But he didn't stop or say a word, even when the last tomato hit his hat and knocked it from his head. He bent down, retrieved the hat, dusted off the brim and, without looking back, continued home.

The tomato war—somebody said that's what it was, all right,

a war sure as hell, only they weren't shooting at each other—had started as a good-natured a rivalry as possible between our father and Grandpa Doolan who had both been raising Big Boys for years. But for some reason our father—always the adventurer, remember, with a pig farm and all those get-rich-quick schemes—one spring decided to try a new hybrid instead and Grandpa Doolan asked what the hell he wanted to go and do that for and our father told him the name said it all—**Better** Boy. Grandpa Doolan nodded and allowed as how time would tell, he guessed, whether that turned out to be true or not, and our father the old man asked if he was ready to back up that cocksureness with something more than talk. Grandpa Doolan wondered what he had in mind and our father suggested a steak dinner with all the trimmings for the one who grew the best tomatoes, and Grandpa Doolan said that depended on what he meant by best and who would make that judgment. Our father the old man suggested that I be the judge and Grandpa Doolan said shit, I didn't know green from red when it came to tomatoes. Our father asked if Grandma Caulkins would be acceptable and Grandpa thought a minute and agreed but then went on to suggest that if they were going to bet on the outcome anyway, why not make it for something more worthwhile than meat he'd have to grind up to eat, since he had no teeth. Our father asked what he had in mind and Grandpa Doolan said how about money, knowing, I imagine, that would immediately get our father the old man's attention, both of them being veteran poker players. Our father took the bait like one of Grandpa's carps going after doughball and asked how much he had in mind. Grandpa Doolan suggested five dollars, which our father laughed at, even though at that time five dollars could buy close to a tank full of gas. He asked what was wrong, didn't Grandpa have any confidence in his Big Boys? Grandpa said ten then and our father laughed again and started to walk away. They agreed on twenty-five dollars and the definition of better: the most red, ripe tomatoes per plant, by count of the judge would be awarded four points, and the heaviest five tomatoes of the gardener's own choosing to be placed together on a scale, the total weight recorded by the judge, with the winner receiving, again, four points. The grower accumulating the most points would win, a final two points, if necessary, to be awarded for taste, although both Grandpa Doolan and our father the old man agreed that quantity and size were far more important markers of success than taste, which fell, as you might imagine, into that indeterminate, wishy-washy world of women's concerns.

The battle was joined, Big Boy versus Better Boy, in early March when Grandpa Doolan hand-planted Burpee hybrid seeds in a blend of potting soil and fertilizer, one to each square of a plastic plant tray he brooded over daily beneath a window on the sun porch off his kitchen. Our father would have nothing to do with that, saying greenhouses knew better than he how to grow seedlings. Besides, he said the bigger and healthier the plants you started with, the bigger and healthier they would grow, right? So the first week in May both he and Grandpa Doolan transplanted twelve seedlings of their choice to plots of land they had meticulously groomed and fertilized, Grandpa Doolan's a fifteen by thirty foot space between his shed and his neighbor's fence, earth raked to the consistency of coffee grounds, our father's in a similar area north of our house. Grandpa Doolan slipped an empty toilet paper roll over the base of each seedling as he planted it to protect it from cutworms, our father preferring to sprinkle the ground around the young plant with egg shells which would slice the belly of the worm as it crawled over them — which he felt was exactly what any goddamn worm out to eat his tomatoes deserved. After planting was complete, each man dressed his plot with mulch and watered — Grandpa Doolan with a hand-held Right as Rain nozzle attached to his hose, our father with a soaker system he threaded between his rows of plants.

Then they waited—our father smoking and sipping beer in the lawn chair by the apple tree in the back yard that Len would one day occupy, Grandpa Doolan as straight-backed as a general surveying his troops, hands folded on top of the rake handle in front of him. When the plants were tall and bushy enough they each constructed cages to support dangling branches. Our father made cones of wire mesh fencing with four-inch square openings he could reach through to inspect the plants, while Grandpa Doolan, wanting nothing to do with metal he thought could burn the delicate plant skin, made derrick-like lath constructions out of wood he had salvaged from a neighbor's home remodeling project. They each fertilized again when the first blossoms on the plants set fruit. They weeded, watered when necessary, and, of course, they worried—about blight and spider mites and stink bugs, about whether to sucker or not, about whether it was too wet or too dry, too hot or too cool, about when to pick or not pick the ripening fruit to force the best production.

One night our father and I came across Grandpa Doolan inspecting his tomato plants with a flashlight and our father asked if he'd found any snipes yet, and Grandpa Doolan said no since it really wasn't snipes he was after but snipers and our father should be sure to keep an eye out and his head down. Our father asked if that was supposed to be some kind of threat and Grandpa Doolan said he'd said what he'd said.

Not long after that, footprints appeared in our father's tomato plot, which he showed to our mother and me, as if presenting evidence to a jury. There was one set of tracks, going the length of the garden, straight forward, end to end. They were harder to see in the mulch, our father's finger outlining one of them, but there they were sure as hell, he said, and big—size twelve at least, he guessed, although he admitted footprints tended to look larger than the shoes that made them. And these had heavy treads, he said, the kind you'd see on serious mud-hoppers or hiking boots, pretty unusual for around those parts. But that didn't mean anything, he said, since the old fart—thumbing toward Grandpa Doolan's house—could have picked them up alongside the street or on somebody's porch, for that matter. He'd bet anything if you went into that shed of his, you'd find them right there under his workbench. Proving what? our mother wanted to know. That the old man had been in his garden our father said, and he had no right to be because a bet was a bet, fair and square. What the hell did she think would happen if he'd done something like that? and she told him he'd better not even think about it, and he said yeah, well he'd see about that and stomped into the garage, where he kept a whiskey stash near his tool cabinet.

At first, our father began watching his garden from the back door, pulling the curtain aside to take a peek whenever he went to the kitchen, then started opening the door and sticking his head out after announcing that the house was too damn hot, he needed some air. And one night he flipped totally, gathered a cooler of beer, a pack of cigarettes and a light blanket in case he got cold and planted himself in the lawn chair until the sun came up the next morning. He kept up the vigil week after week when the weather was decent, and none of us had the courage to say anything. The nights he worked, he assigned Len or our mother or me—Connie was too young—to sit there in his place and watch that nothing, meaning Grandpa Doolan, got into his tomato patch. We did it, of course, since no one wanted to stir his wrath—that is, until the car he was in had turned the corner on its way to Wichita.

Still, the spots came, brown leathery splotches at the blossom-end of half-ripe tomatoes that spread until the fruit rotted and dropped to the ground. Too much nitrogen, too much water, too much plant growth too quickly, people said, except for our father, who knew the problem had nothing to do with what he'd done or not done and everything to do with his competitor, whose own crop couldn't have been healthier or more abundant.

And just how could that be? our father wanted to know. How could one tomato patch—his—be lying in ruins while that old windbag's was thriving to the point that, even this early on, he was bragging about having so many tomatoes people were already locking their doors and closing their curtains when they saw him coming with another armful? Why was it that any time our father raised the subject the old weasel got that shit-eating grin on his face and said he had to go home? Why, if he wasn't feeling so guilty about what he'd done and knew he deserved to be punished, did he install motion-sensor lights on the corner of his shed overlooking his garden?

Most people said you didn't need to look any farther than our father the old man to know who did it. Think about how bitter he was at losing his own crop, they said, or how angry he got at Grandpa Doolan, warranted or not, when he found those boots with a tread matching the garden footprints in his own garage, obviously planted there, he said, by the only person he knew who could stoop so low and then try to blame it on somebody else. And what about the fact that the night after Grandpa Doolan came to our house to offer his condolences to our father, the old man rubbed his face with charcoal, dressed in his darkest clothes and asked where Len had put the BB gun? Our father denied none of what was being said about him and even went so far as to agree that if he were in his accusers' shoes, he'd probably think and say the same thing—that he'd gotten drunk that night and dressed up like they said he had and filled a couple of plastic two-liter Dr. Pepper bottles with gasoline from the five-gallon can in his garage and crawled, BB gun cradled in his arms like a commando, across his back yard, the alley and Grandpa Doolan's yard, shot out the floodlights by the shed, doused the tomato patch with gasoline and set it on fire, because it all seemed to make sense.

But none of it happened, he said. He didn't do it, no matter how good the story was or how much **proof** there was. He plain didn't do it, and if they didn't believe him, they could ask the old skunk himself, who, as our father was quick to point out, had remained strangely silent during the whole discussion. Grandpa Doolan allowed as how he didn't have much to add to what had already been said, because that night when he looked out his back door after the fire started, he definitely saw the shadows of two figures against the flames—men he would guess, about the same size and all—but he didn't get a good look at either of them. The police, such as they were, confirmed that they'd seen at least two sets of footprints on the ground, but they couldn't be sure whose they were because of all the tramping around the firefighters did. All of which proved nothing again, Grandpa Doolan said, and it really didn't make any difference since the bet was off, seeing as how neither he nor our father had a good tomato between them and that it might be for the best anyway just to let bygones be bygones, what did our father say to that?

It was a resolution that satisfied no one, as you can imagine. Was our father the old man lying or telling the truth, and if he didn't set the fire, who did? Could it have been Grandpa Doolan? Had he made up the story about seeing two people by the shed in order to divert attention from himself—which would make sense, given how eager he seemed to say forget it, no harm done. But if that were the case, why would he have done it, unless to make himself look even better at our father's expense? Or what if neither of them had done it? Who did then and why, and did any of it in the end, as Grandpa Doolan said, make any difference?

Gamma Knives and The Great Beyond

We were sitting at a round oak table littered with newspapers, stacks of bills and amber medicine bottles that had been jammed against the wall at the end of the living room just inside the front door, a cramped space that served as entryway, dining area and office. Connie, in a ragged charcoal grey t-shirt and blue and white checked pant-length pajama bottoms, slouched weary and wan in a chair to my left. A shirtless Sammo the rock, opposite her by the door, drummed the fingers of his right hand between a pack of cigarettes and a dirty but empty ashtray in front of him. I had arrived a few minutes earlier, having driven my rental car from the motel where I had stayed in Wichita following my flight in late the evening before and she asked, still watching Sammo, how my trip had been and I said fine and she said flying must get to be old hat as much as I did it. I said I supposed so but that I had nothing on my wife who flew somewhere at least a couple of times a month. She said she could believe it since it seemed to her that either I or the two of us together were always going somewhere or getting back from somewhere, but she was glad we were in a position we could do it because we certainly deserved to as hard as we worked. And by the way, she wanted to thank us for sending her pictures of our trip to Italy. It looked so beautiful. She had always dreamed of going there, not that she ever would, though, because even if Sammo, as hard as he worked, worked the same hard from now till he dropped, they could never afford to go off and do something like that. I said I wouldn't be so sure since you just never knew what might happen. Her head quivered, like she'd had a sudden chill, and she looked away from me to the window in the storm door and said what a nice day it was supposed to be.

I asked her if she would like to go out for a walk and she said that would be great but she really didn't think she had the energy for it, that it wore her out even to go to the street to collect their mail from the box. I told her I was sorry to hear that and she said she hoped I wasn't too disappointed. I said of course I wasn't, why would I be? She smiled a rough little smile and exchanged a glance with Sammo, who stopped drumming his fingers and picked up the pack of cigarettes, put it back down as she said she was worried, was all, that I'd get bored just sitting around doing nothing and not want to come back to see her. I told her not to be silly and she said she wasn't being since she knew damn good and well how it was to be in that house in that chair all day and do nothing but stew and fret and talk to bill collectors on the phone who refused to take no for an answer, a comment, I'm ashamed to say, that made me instinctively touch the hip pocket of my jeans where I keep my billfold, the way I do after jostling through a crowd of people in the city to make sure it hasn't been picked.

She wanted to know what was wrong and I said nothing, why? and she said the look on my face. I told her there wasn't anything I could do about that, ugly was ugly, and she didn't laugh, didn't even smile and said she wasn't talking about those kinds of looks but the others that let you know what people were thinking even if they didn't say a word. I said okay, fine, but I still didn't know what she was referring to, and she said there, just then, I'd done it again, and I said what? I didn't have the slightest idea what she was talking about. She said the hell I didn't, she knew me better than anybody, with the possible exception of my wife. I told her that remained to be seen, and she said she did and that she could see that something was wrong and I needed to tell her what it was.

Sammo was sitting back now, looking at me, his hand silent, and Connie was still looking at me and started in about how hard she knew all of this had been for me, first Len and now her, but it was okay, she was there, I could talk to her, get it off my chest because it wasn't healthy to keep things bottled up. The next we knew I'd be down with something, too, and be as bad off as everybody else, so I needed to come on, she said, and let it go, let it out. I said again I had nothing to let go of, and she shrugged and looked back out the window and said fine, I could have it my way, she was just trying to help. I told her I appreciated her concern but I really was okay and didn't need her or anyone else to interpret for me how I felt, thank you very much.

You'd have thought I'd smacked her or called Sammo a stinking pig fucker the way everyone got so quiet before Connie finally said she guessed we'd probably better talk about something else, and I said yeah maybe so. She said it was probably all her fault anyway, all in her mind, her imagination, and might have something to do with, you know, touching her head in the area of the horseshoe-shaped scar where the tumor had first been removed. The doctors had told her those things could cause personality changes—mood swings and such, she said, all manner of shit—so maybe it wasn't her talking after all. Maybe it was another Connie in there—wouldn't that be something, though, more than one of her? I'd sure like that, wouldn't I, but like they always say, two heads are better than one. And she started laughing, an eerie, scary laugh that wasn't her at all but more forced and mechanical, her face never changing, and then she stopped as quickly as she had begun and said six weeks. It had been six weeks from the time Dr. Bloom had opened her skull and discovered, despite our hopes to the contrary, the tumor he'd been convinced was there all along. Six weeks from the day he'd cut it out and it had grown back in the same place, larger than ever, even though he'd been sure he'd gotten it all, absolutely sure, he'd told them, over and over, like a mantra, up until the very morning he'd passed her case on to yet another doctor, Samuel Friedlich, a neuroradiologist, so he could, along with an even more specialized neurosurgeon, Dr. Nickle, administer treatment in the form of gamma knife surgery, which, she said ended up having nothing to do with knives. If not knives, what then, I asked, and she said beams. Beams? Yeah, beams. As in beam me up, Scotty? I asked, and she said not exactly, although it did kind of feel that way—the room, the machine, the whole works. Even the light, which wasn't exactly dim, she said, but soft, indirect, and the place didn't have a stick of furniture other than the gamma knife itself, a big metal cube— off-white with grey accent stripes and a yellow bed or cot, whatever they called it, to lie on. In the middle at one end was a dark space where two technicians dressed head to toe in blue surgical scrubs told her her head would go—sort of like an MRI or a CAT scan, they said, no mess, no pain, and she'd be in and out and ready to go home in a couple of hours.

Was I still with her? she asked, did I need for her to slow down so I could take notes? I said no, I was getting a pretty clear picture of what had happened, and she said, good, because she wanted what I wrote—I was still going to do that, wasn't I?—to be accurate and not a bunch of made-up shit, and I said I would never do that—and she said yeah, right, and went on then to tell how the technicians fitted her with the metal frame that would stabilize her head while it was in the machine. Not much to it, according to them, a little numbing agent there and there, she said, touching her scalp where they had slipped the frame over her head and tightened the bolts through her skin and against her skull. She might feel a little pinch, they told her, and she did, she said, more than a pinch, but it was okay, tolerable, except that she had to sit around a couple of hours wearing that contraption while the doctor did everything he had to to be ready for the procedure. When he was ready, they laid her out just so on the bed/cot thingy, put a metal helmet on her head frame and wheeled her into position in the chamber. They asked if she was comfortable—did they really expect her to say no?— and left her there alone, telling her she could still talk to them via an intercom system built into the helmet, if she had to, if it was an emergency. After a few minutes, a voice told her they were going to start and she should just relax and go to some quiet place in her mind, which she did. I asked where that was and she said she'd always been able to dream up a quiet little lake surrounded by pine trees, probably up north, in Canada maybe, where she sat on the porch of a log cabin and watched the sun set over the water, and sooner than she'd ever imagined possible— they told her later it had been about fifty minutes—they came back in, disconnected her and asked how she was doing. She said fine and they said wonderful and covered the four points on her head with adhesive patches, put her in a wheelchair and took her out to where Sammo was waiting. By dinnertime that evening she was home.

So that's where the screws went in? I asked, pointing to the white, ghostly indentations on the side of her head, and she said the pins, yeah, just like Frankenstein, and she leaned toward me and turned her head so they were more accessible and said I could touch them if I wanted to. I said that was okay and she said go ahead, they didn't hurt any more and I said no, really, and she pulled her thinning hair back and leaned even closer so it was nearly impossible not to put a fingertip on one of those pale puckers. And I did, god help me, jesus christ, I did and Sammo laughed and said I should see the look on my face and I said what's all this with how I look? and Sammo asked if I knew what he'd told the doctor—you know, Dr.Whatshisname?—Friedlich, Connie said, and he said yeah, that was it. He told Dr. Friedlich the last time they'd seen him that those marks were where they'd cut off Connie's horns, and the doctor had laughed so hard he'd almost wet himself, Sammo said, and I said I could imagine so, since I doubted he—the doctor—was used to any kind of humor from his patients, let alone that kind, and Sammo said, no, he didn't think so. Connie said the only thing was it made her sound like an old cow or something, and I said that might not be so bad because in some cultures goddesses were depicted as cows— Hathor in ancient Egypt, for instance, or Brigit in Celtic Ireland, who became St. Brigit when the Catholic Church took over. She could do worse, I said, and she cocked her head at Sammo and said so there, and he shrugged, saying she could be whatever she wanted to, he didn't care, and he glanced at me, hurt, I imagine, that I had taken over his joke, like he probably thought I tried to take over everything when I was around. Then he asked if I knew what a smartass was and I said no and he said somebody who can sit on an ice cream cone and tell you what flavor it is, and he got up and said he was going out to smoke a cigarette, the screen door banging shut behind him.

Connie told me I shouldn't be upset, and I said I wasn't, and she said he really hadn't meant anything, he was just worried about her and all that silly stuff was just his way of relieving the tension he felt. I said there really wasn't a problem—his story about the horns was funny, his smartass joke was funny. I enjoyed a joke as much as anybody else. She said she could appreciate that since being able to laugh was one of the things that kept her going and I said that was pretty much true for everybody, and she said yeah, a good laugh and the Good Lord, and I didn't say anything.

She went to the bathroom and when she came back she asked if I'd ever heard of Susan Gower. I said no, and she said a friend had given her a couple of Gower's books and a CD to listen to and even though she didn't buy lock stock and barrel everything Gower said, she thought the woman had some good ideas about death and the hereafter. Such as? I asked, and Connie said such as the idea that everyone goes to Heaven, regardless, and everyone becomes an angel. Everybody? I asked, and she said yes, that according to Gower (she called her Suzy, as if they were close personal friends) no one was so bad they were beyond the power of God's grace, and I said even our father the old man and Uncle Boyd, and she said everyone. Hitler and Stalin and Idi Amin? Everybody. Then what made people care whether they did anything good in life, I wanted to know, if there was no punishment for committing acts of evil, or what we call evil because we haven't developed a non-religious word to describe it? She said something about the other side or odor side—I couldn't hear for certain—where people stumbled around in a gloomy, dark place, feeling all pissy and ready to do mean things once they got out, but that wasn't where normal people went—people like us. And anyway that wasn't what she wanted to talk about, meaning she didn't want any more questions or sarcastic remarks from me. This was her time, and she wanted to instruct me, direct me, charge me, change me, and I was to keep my mouth shut.

When you die, she was saying, Suzy believes you're met in the Great Beyond by a member of your own family who takes you in and gets you set up—gets you your angel credentials, you might say, your wings. Wouldn't it be wonderful to see Mom or Dad or Len again, or Grandma Caulkins or Grandpa Doolan—even Uncle Boyd? Who would I like to see? she wanted to know, and I said nobody really and she said come on, who? I meant it, I said, nobody, and she said that wasn't true. I said there she was again, telling me what I thought and felt, and she said it was pretty damn clear somebody needed to. I asked her what she was afraid of, why she needed any of them, when for the most part they'd caused her as much misery as anything, and she said that wasn't true and I said bullshit and she said I needed to learn to forget and forgive, and I said wings my ass and the angelic face she'd been mustering flew off as she told me if that was the way I felt, I could go fuck myself.

Later, she laid her hand over mine and said she was sorry she'd overreacted, and I told her not to worry about it. Pray for me, she said, and I said sure, and she said she meant it—that was about all she had left, putting herself in God's hands, at His mercy—and I said I meant it, too, I would do the best I could.

The Dark Arts

She wasn't hungry any more. She no longer begged everybody who passed within hearing for something to eat, and now when I took her and Sammo and whoever else was around out to eat at one of those sprawling buffets where the breakfast bar eventually merges with lunch and then dinner, where you can stay as long as you want and eat to your heart's content for a single price, she wasn't much interested, going through the motions of piling her plate full and saying after she sat down she didn't know what she was thinking, there was no way in hell she could eat all that, and boxing it up to take home for Sammo to have later. She was, as they used to say, wasting away before our eyes—the unremitting fatigue, the grey wash of her skin, the whiffs of dry rot on her breath—and all we could do was watch and wait and say the things we were supposed to—hang in there, keep your spirits up, be strong, don't let the bastards win, we love you—and wait still more. But waiting wears on you, and eventually even Sammo the rock told me how tired he was of it. I asked what exactly he meant by *it* and he said the whole damn mess—the it in her head that didn't vanish or get larger but just stayed, no matter how many chemicals they pumped into her or how many gamma knives they used, the it that she said felt like a million cockroaches skittering around in her head—something she wouldn't even wish on Mason, as big a sonofabitch as he was— the it that made her so goddamn cranky sunny days were too bright because they hurt her eyes and breezes weren't pleasant because they kicked up dust that made her allergies worse, the it that made her say things like he could go right on and fucking fuck himself if all he was going to say to her was how thankful she should be instead of being down all the time. I told him that was her sickness talking, and he said yeah, he knew, but just because she was sick didn't mean everybody else had to be, too.

The truth is— What? I imagine you're asking or are about to ask. What truth am I, the smartass, presuming to present? The fact, then—is that better?—the reality, the truth is she is going to die, that's what, sooner than later, and we all, her included— All? I hear you saying again, how can I be so arrogant as to think I'm speaking for all concerned, when I hardly know what I think and mean myself? Okay, maybe not all, maybe only Sammo and I or Sammo and I and a couple of others, but I'm sure more than one person—me—thinks the way I do, that if she is going to die, we would like for her to get it over with. I know that sounds harsh— and let me finish before you ask any more of your supposedly incisive yet still rhetorical questions, designed, it seems, to divert me from the topic at hand rather than help me clarify it. My point is, she wants me to finish the story she asked me to write, and damnit, every story has an ending, a conclusion, and the only logical (real or fictional) ending for her is death. I simply want her story resolved so I can move on to something else, as crass and selfish as that may appear, although I doubt it's any more so than Sammo's wishing to be released from the day to day drudgery of it. A person can witness only so much misery and hopelessness—like Len in his final minutes, one raspy breath after another, even when there weren't supposed to be any—until I said to myself stop it stop it stop it, and he did, and I hated myself.

Much as I did the day I got back from a walk along the lake shore, winter waves just shy of ice lapping the seawall, washing over it here and there with the beginnings of a soon to be permanent glaze, and found a message from Sammo on my answering machine about Connie, saying I should call him as soon as possible.

A Little Levity, Please

Some time ago, although exactly when no one seems to remember for certain, a famous magician, The Great Carnini, was invited to perform on a grand stage in a large city, where he was to attempt a feat no one had ever dared undertake before— hypnotizing an entire theater audience. The Great Carnini's show was advertised for weeks in advance, and the night of the performance the theater was indeed filled with the city's wealthiest and most influential people, many of whom had commented publicly that what the magician had proposed was impossible, since not everyone was equally susceptible to hypnosis. The continuing debate flowed, together with the crowd, into the great hall that evening, subsiding only when the curtains parted and the tuxedoed Great Carnini made his dramatic entrance on stage, followed by two pretty women in diaphanous gowns who assisted him in a number of routine yet entertaining tricks. One of the women was sawed in half, the other levitated above the stage while a ring was passed back and forth to show that no invisible wires were supporting her. Rabbits appeared, doves flew, silk streamers filled the air, and everyone seemed duly amused but still waiting for the grand finale, which was announced by a silencing of music, the disappearance of the pretty women and the descent of a black curtain behind The Great Carnini. He said in a steady, soothing voice that what they, the audience, were about to see was unique in the world of magic, and it was only after years of training with the finest hypnotist in the world that he, The Great Carnini, was ready to try it.

The magician lifted the fine gold chain looping across his abdomen, withdrew a watch attached to it from his vest pocket and dangled it between himself and his audience. He said he was holding before them a timepiece made of gold and the finest jewels that had been passed to him from his father, whose own father had given it to him, and so on for many generations. It was with this watch that he was going to guide them—the audience—into a hypnotic trance, from which they would awake only upon his command—the snap of his finger three times, thus—and would remember nothing of the incident. Were they ready?

The Great Carnini held the watch aloft and began swinging it slowly side to side like a pendulum as he told everyone in a low, measured voice to relax and concentrate on the watch, to think only of the watch as their eyelids grew heavier and heavier and heavier. They should look at the watch, watch the heirloom watch and feel their eyes—

And just as he achieved one of the greatest feats in the history of magic, that beautiful, ancient watch suddenly slipped from The Great Carnini's grasp and fell, smashing into pieces on the stage floor.

He said shit.

It took two weeks to clean up the theater.

So. . .

Connie died on a Sunday—which, if she were aware of it, must have suited her just fine, being on the Lord's day and all—and was buried the next Wednesday under cool, damp skies in a cemetery in the town where she'd lived for twenty years so she'd be close to friends and in a place Sammo could get to more easily. She'd told me earlier that was what she preferred, rather than being near Len in Carter or our mother and our father, Grandpa and Grandma Caulkins and Uncle Boyd in southeast Kansas where nobody had a reason to go other than to visit graves, and she knew she wouldn't be able to count on me to do that. She'd heard what I'd said to our father the old man when he had tried to guilt me into saying I'd take over the duty of making the yearly Memorial Day trek to lay wreathes and flowers on family graves. I'd told him I wanted nothing to do with it. I said the dead are dead, and I honor them to the extent that I do in my memories of them. So I imagine she had that conversation in mind when she made her decision about where to be buried.

In the same way I feel more comfortable if there are the equal numbers of glasses on each side of the dishwasher rack or if pictures on the wall hang straight, things would have felt more balanced if I'd been with Connie when she died, as I had been with Len, holding her hand as I had his, even if she wouldn't have been any more aware of my presence than he was. It's difficult to think that she may well have died alone—no one has said one way or the other for whatever reason—which I realize sounds silly, since we all die alone, don't we? We each experience our own death in our own unique way—ours and ours alone. But still, I find disturbing at best the thought of no one being with her in her final moment of life—Sammo on his way to the hospital from work, me in Chicago because I'd been out to see her only a week before, her own children scattered here and there and unreachable at that time of night. Perhaps a nurse was around, perhaps not—she had been resting comfortably, according to the chart, when someone had stopped in only minutes before. We were told she suffered a hemorrhage, a sudden, urgent release of blood that, unlike in Len's case, would have rendered her unconscious almost immediately and soon thereafter, dead. Or that's what we imagine, that's what we hope, have to think, believe.

The funeral was small—Sammo and his folks, Jim and Sally, Janice, Suz and Sonny, Bo and Ron and Shelley, and even Mason the sonofabitch because Sammo said he could come. And me and my wife and sons. Plus some friends of Connie's and Sammo's. But not a whole lot, and that was okay. A couple of hymns and scriptures and the preacher talking about Connie like he knew her. I wrote her obituary and gave him a copy and he read it verbatim. And that was okay, too. He did his thing at the graveside—ashes to ashes, dust to dust—and I kept trying to imagine her crossing over to The Great Beyond and being taken under the wings of our mother and our father, Uncle Boyd, Aunt Kate and Aunt Louise, bless her heart, and Grandma and Grandpa Caulkins and Grandpa Doolan. And, of course, Len.

And that was it. No more Betty Boops, no more Mr. Blue Eyes, nobody. But me.

On our way home, I decided what I was going to do, after I talked it over with my wife and sons, since it mainly affected them now—the reason we'd set up the eight-hundred number to begin with was so they could call home for free while they were at college, but now they didn't really need it with cell phones and their own land lines and e-mail and so on. And Connie had been the one who'd used the number most often anyway, when she was sick and wanted somebody to talk to, but now that wouldn't be happening, and if I needed to get in touch with Sammo, I could call him. So the minute I got into our house, I went straight to the phone before I lost my nerve and dialed the eight-hundred company and cancelled the number, and that was that.

Oh, Just One More Thing

Four months after Connie died I got a call from Sammo's mother Sally. She said the rock had fractured, split, fallen apart. My words, not hers, and I'm serious here, I'm not making this up. She said one night Sammo didn't show up for work, and somebody from the plant called her to see what was going on—he must have given them her name for emergencies—and she said she didn't know anything was but she'd try to find out. So she woke up Jim and they went to Sammo's place about midnight. All the lights were off and his car was still in the driveway. They knocked and knocked, she said, and all they heard was the dog. By then they were pretty worried and Jim said they should probably call somebody and she asked just who that might be in the middle of the night and he said the police. He had a cell phone Sammo had made him carry because of his heart and he used it to call 911. He told them everything he knew and it wasn't more than ten minutes later, she said, that the whole place was full of police and an ambulance and a fire truck. The whole neighborhood was up by then, the front yard full of people. Firemen had to smash in the back door, and even then, she said, the dog wouldn't let them in, so she and Jim had to go and try to quiet him down.

They found Sammo on his bed, thrashing around and talking out of his head—complete nonsense nobody could make heads or tails of, she said—and there were pills all over the place. They got him on a stretcher and into the ambulance, and she and Jim tried to clean up and fix the back door as best they could. Oh, and they did find a note on the table that was in Sammo's handwriting. It didn't say a whole lot, she told me, other than he couldn't take it any more.

And he didn't have to. He died before daybreak in the hospital where Connie had been.

A Final Word on Chicken Fried Steak and the Weather

I know what you're thinking: that can't be the end, right? Endings should be more satisfying than that. Or maybe satisfying isn't the right word? Maybe less gloomy would be better, as in endings should be less gloomy than that. The way it is, it's like watching Shakespeare, you're thinking, one of the tragedies where everybody dies for some basically stupid reason. The hero or heroine has a flaw, something they can't overcome. In fact, even if they try to, the situation only gets worse, not better. No good old American optimism there. No pull yourself together, damnit, and get on with it. In Shakespeare it's all death and destruction — and blood, lots and lots of blood and long-winded death speeches. At least Len just roared. Didn't say a word. Neither did Connie, I imagine, at her actual moment of death — or crossing over, as she would have called it. If you remember, she did all her talking, created all the chaos she could, beforehand and died, as they say, peacefully — as far as we know, as far as anyone knows, peace being a relative term. But she died, nonetheless, just like Len and Sammo and our mother and our father and Grandpa Doolan and Grandma Caulkins. Uncle Boyd, Aunt Kate, Aunt Louise, and all the rest. Dead. The whole stage littered with them. And was it all because of a tragic flaw, I wonder, some collective fault I may even share?

A friend — a good friend whose word I trust — told me if a story ends with a funeral, it's a tragedy. If it ends with a wedding, it's a comedy. Hmm, I say, a comedy, I've never written anything close to a comedy, but what the hell, if it'll make the story more satisfying and less gloomy, why don't we just go ahead then and have ourselves a wedding? Not even Connie could argue with that.

Fool that I am.

First, she'd tell me I couldn't have Suz's and Morris's daughter get married, and I'd say why not, and she'd say because they don't have one. The hell they don't, I'd counter, maybe leaping on a table for dramatic effect, and she'd ask what was wrong with me, had I gone crazy or something, and I'd say no, just the opposite. For the first time everything made sense, and she'd tell me it couldn't because the daughter I was talking about wasn't real and didn't even have a name. Liz, I'd say, her name is Liz and she's getting married, goddamnit, because I say she is.

Connie would slump against the wall then to pout, and I'd lower myself cross-legged to the tabletop to wait for her next objection, which would be to question where I thought I got off deciding to have a wedding on my own—we were in this together, weren't we? So why the hell did I want to go and ruin a perfectly good story? I'd say what did she mean ruin, and she would say it was pretty clear to her, making up a bunch of shit like a wedding and people and such, what was wrong with the way it was before? It wasn't finished, I'd tell her, which should have been perfectly obvious, if she'd taken even a minute to think about it. What made me so mean? she would start in for the I don't know whath time, sniffling whatever ghosts sniffle. Why did I have to be such a sonofabitch to a dead person? But never mind her, she would go on, she could take whatever I dished out. Always had, always would. It was just that— What? I would want to know. Well, if I was going to use anybody's kids in my made up wedding, why couldn't it be *hers*? But she guessed she knew the answer to that before she even asked, because I always had thought better of Len's family than hers, hadn't I? No matter what she did or tried to do. It was true, I shouldn't try to deny it. Otherwise, why would I go to all the trouble to completely make somebody up to put in my story, when there were perfectly good— Now what? she would say, looking at the finger I'd be holding up to stop her, and I would say right there, she'd just said it: it was *my* story and I could do whatever the hell I wanted to with it and in it. This was all about Liz getting married in *my* story and nothing else. Was that finally clear?

At that point she would hang her head with a humph and mumble if that was the way I was going to be as she retreated back into a far corner with all the other shadowy figures, for the moment at least allowing me to get on with my plans.

Which include, I've decided, giving you and anybody else who wants one an invitation to Liz's wedding. So here it is. You're invited.

So let's imagine first that Liz decides to have her wedding in June, with an outdoor ceremony, let's say, at a small park not far from Wichita that has a little lake and several groves of trees that cast shadows as soothing in the summer heat as a glass of tepid water drawn from a sclerotic lime-lined pipe. And it turns out to be hotter than she thinks possible, literally a hundred degrees in the shade, dust as fine as flour sifting into the air from the brittle grass we pass over. No one wears a tie, save the preacher and the groom, a lanky, boyish-looking young man named, what? Mike, let's say, Mike with the crooked but winsome smile whom Liz loves with all her heart, or at least seems to the way she eats him with her eyes and holds fast to his arm. People stand in small groups, depending on who is related to or friends with whom, but no one touches and we all draw slow, deliberate breaths.

Josie is alone, her post-Len husband noticeably absent, as he always is, due to personal reasons everyone seems to understand but never mention. She is directed by Mike's mother to a weathered picnic table that has been turned to face the site of the ceremony and sits, hands relentlessly rubbing each other atop a crossed black-panted leg as though trying to rid herself of a pain that won't go away. I am alone as well, because of my wife's more legitimate, long-term scheduling conflicts, and would be happy to sit with Josie, as we represent what is left of an elder Caulkins generation, but I'm not invited to. So I stand slightly to the left of the others, a small silver camera dangling from my wrist. Anyone taking a picture of me now might wonder why I seem so isolated. Do people not know me? Are they angry with me for some reason I'm not aware of? Do I smell bad? But it will all become clear when it's explained that I'm Liz's grandpa's brother, and people will nod and say oh, yeah, him.

The ceremony is short and elegantly simple. No music, no wedding party but Liz, Mike and the preacher. Vows, rings, a brief homily, a kiss. Then pictures. Dozens and dozens of pictures, same scene—the elm tree the ceremony is held under to the left, a backdrop glade dead-center and a shaded gazebo on the right—with constantly changing rows of people—his family, her family, his friends, her friends—those not in the pictures either taking their own pictures of the pictures or standing silently by watching and wanting in the worst way to retreat to the air-conditioned shelter house where the reception is to be held.

The building tops a sunbaked rise a quarter of a mile from the wedding site. It is a red, rectangular structure crouching in a deep pool of shade thrown down by a weeping willow in front and a mixture of cottonwoods, sycamores and elms scattered around it. People drop onto picnic table benches on the open but roofed porch, some to have a smoke before going inside and others simply to rest. A small stand snugs the wall beside the wooden double doors that open to the interior. On it are a guestbook with a half page of signatures, to which I add mine, and next to it small white place cards propped on stands, with the names of Morris's mother, grandfather and grandmother, our mother, our father and Len inscribed on them in flowing script, a simple message behind them saying that they are missed. A lovely reminder but one that I imagine causes stirring in a shadowy corner inside the building, Connie no doubt throwing a hissy-fit because her name isn't there.

I open the door and am immediately drenched with cool air. I take several deep breaths as my eyes adjust to the natural light filtering through windows along each wall and flanking the fireplace at the far end. I spot the sign for the restroom and step in. By the time I come out, people have gathered according to clan—Morris's people, Mike's and Mike's parents' people, Suz's and Liz's people, including Sonny and his family, along with

Josie, hunched around a table at the front to the right of the fireplace. Josie motions for me to come sit with them. I do, a couple of empty chairs between me and them, and they carry on talking about people and places and events I have no idea about. Which serves me right, Connie says. Just what he's always been afraid of, our father the old man says. Eventually, in order to have something to do, I start taking pictures with my silver Canon. I shoot Sonny and his family and Josie. I shoot the three rows of tables covered with crinkly white paper and artificial red roses arranged the length of the room. I shoot Mike's people, Morris's people, Liz and Mike, Suz and Morris. I shoot the card table for the bride and groom at the end of the middle row in front of the fireplace. To the right of it, I shoot the wedding cake and mint and nut dishes adorning the single folding table that angles diagonally across the corner. At the other end of the room near the entrance, I shoot the drink table, the food table, the hot and sweaty servers behind them. I shoot the fieldstones around the fireplace. I shoot the floor and the ceiling and wind in the trees outside the windows. I try to shoot the shadowy figures in the corner who are watching us, Connie frowning, scowling, still pissed at me for having this event without her.

I run out of things to shoot by the time food is served.

I don't know whose idea the menu was, but let's say it was Suz's. Who else would have thought of chicken fried steak, and not only that, but of having it alone in all its glory at the start of the buffet, so that everyone can have it to his or her liking, with mashed potatoes and white gravy, if they prefer, or fries instead, with or without mustard, catsup and mayo, lettuce and tomato, pickle chips, sweet or dill. With or without whole corn or peas or green beans and bacon. And who else would have thought to put together a plate with Len's favorite, and some might argue, the only meal he ever ate—a chicken fried steak on a white bun, no dressing, no lettuce or tomato, a pile of crisp curly fries and a pleated white paper cup of catsup on the side and set it in a separate place of honor at the end of the food line?

I imagine it's my fault for thinking about her in the first place, for wondering whether Connie might like a plate set out for her, too, if her appetite is back now. And the others as well, for that matter, although they wouldn't have as much of an emotional stake in the whole recognition thing. Anyway, as soon as the thought enters my mind I begin hearing a sound that starts off like the whine of tires on the interstate highway a mile or so away, or closer in, a loose belt on the air conditioning unit outside the kitchen. Once you hear it, of course, it won't go away. At first it seems mildly humorous but soon becomes irritating, until it has reached the volume of a coyote's howl coming out of the dark corner. From what I can tell, though, I'm the only one who hears it, like an advertising jingle or a single line from a song that gets stuck in your head. The only way to get rid of it is to ignore it, do something else that makes you forget it. I go to the bathroom again, get a glass of tea that sets my teeth on edge, twitch my head a couple of times to try to dislodge it. Everyone else seems fine, chatting and working their way along the buffet line. I fall in behind some distant relative of Morris's who talks non-stop in a too-loud voice, which you think might cover the sound, but it only makes it worse, and in my growing dis-ease I grossly overfill my plate to the point that people stare at me as I make my way back to the table.

As soon as I sit down, though, an idea comes to me that is so simple, so perfect the sound dims in its presence. I'm going to give a speech. It's the right place and the right time now that nearly everyone is seated and has begun to eat. It will be a short speech, more of an iced tea toast to the bride and groom. I go over in my mind what I want to say, including a joke or two I came across a while back.

Like:

Things NOT to say on your wedding night:

—It's okay, we all look funny with our clothes off.

—You woke me up for that?

—What do you mean you're allergic to whipped cream?

—You know, you're almost as good as my ex.

—Do you think the ceiling needs painting?

—Did I tell you Aunt Lillian died in this bed?

OR

—As the banana said to the vibrator:

What are *you* shaking for, she's going to eat me.

Of course I don't say anything, the sound immediately drilling itself back through my brain, nor do I do anything but eat— every damned bite—and go back for a refill. Two more heaping plates, in fact, one with mashed potatoes and gravy, the other with curly fries and gravy. One for me and one, I decide finally, for Connie. I eat mine first, even though I'm not hungry in the least. I eat until I can hardly stand the thought of another bite. I eat until it's gone, just as I was taught. If you take it, you eat it. Otherwise the starving children of the world might suffer even more from your wastefulness.

Connie's plate remains, the mountain of curly fries covering the chicken fried steak soggy and cool by now under the gravy. But the same rule applies, and since she can't in reality eat it herself, I dig in, bite after red-faced sweaty bite, for her and our mother and our father and all the shadow people. Wedding cake, too, when the time comes, and as I sit back finally, hand on my hard and painful belly, I realize the howl is gone, replaced now by a ringing roar that blots out all but the scrape of my shoes on the cement floor as I rush outside, across the porch, and fall on my hands and knees under the weeping willow and vomit. Again and again until I collapse into throat-clearing gags.

I take a handkerchief from my pocket and wipe my mouth and face and the back of my neck and feel almost chilled from the cool breeze blowing on the backside of a front that has passed through. I turn to see if the few people who were on the porch have noticed either me or the breeze, but no one is there. I refold my handkerchief and go back inside.

The room is empty. No Liz, no Mike, no Morris or Suz. No relatives of anyone's. No tables and chairs, no food. Nothing.

I call Connie's name. No answer. It's okay, I tell her. It's over.

Mom? Dad? Len?

I try to remember but can't.

The only car in the parking lot is mine. I get in and start it and look back one more time at the dark windows of the shelter house.

A crisp white column of dust rises between me and the scene in the rearview mirror, the car fishtailing, gravel popping in the wheel wells, as I drive faster than I imagine I should down the lane toward the main road.

At Roundfire we publish great stories. We lean towards the spiritual and thought-provoking. But whether it's literary or popular, a gentle tale or a pulsating thriller, the connecting theme in all Roundfire fiction titles is that once you pick them up you won't want to put them down.